This book broke my heart and challenged me in so many ways ... the rawest representation of how easy it is for a teenager to become stuck in a spiral and slip through the threads of society without anyone realising before it's too late.

Ashling Brown, Netgalley

'When an author is able to make you stop reading because it is uncomfortable, you know they have done something right ... Needs to be read by many people far and wide, of any age, because anger and hate can grow from a feeling of not being seen. I applaud the author.'

Robyn Spacey, The Book Club Blog

A really compelling but difficult read ... the phrase emotional rollercoaster never felt so apt. With themes of grief, loss, mental health, racism and pressure as well as thought-provoking social commentary, it's one that should have a place in every secondary school library.

Rachel Bellis, Netgalley

'This book left me emotionally raw ... ultimately I think it is a must read about racism and extremism told

Vicky Bishop

Luke Palmer is a poet, author and secondary school teacher. He lives in Wiltshire with his young family. Grow is his first novel.

For H
like sparks & shining dragons

grOw

Luke Palmer

Firefly

First published in 2021
by Firefly Press
25 Gabalfa Road, Llandaff North, Cardiff, CF14 2JJ
www.fireflypress.co.uk

A CIP catalogue record of this book is available from
the British Library.

3 5 7 9 8 6 4 2

print ISBN 978-1-913102-39-5

There won't be any explosions in this book.

Sorry if that's going to be a problem. And, while we're at it, there won't be any chasing around at night, or encounters with the undead, or werewolves, or vampires or anything of that kind either.

Sorry.

A few years ago, I loved those kinds of books. I'd imagine myself in a world where all the adults were dead, or gone, or both. I think I'd have been OK. Maybe not the leader of one of the rebel gangs that stalked through the abandoned streets, shouting orders that various underlings followed with glee. It wouldn't have been me that was surrounded by hard-faced kids in ragged clothes. But I'd definitely be surviving, a sharpened stick in one hand, straddling a bike kitted out like a tank, ready to dash back to my stash of pilfered tins in the belly of an old barge down on the canal. I used to love imagining myself in those situations.

But I grew out of them.

I don't know why I liked them, really. It's pretty grim stuff, imagining your parents are dead. And enjoying it. This book won't be like those books.

It will be real.

It won't be about the future, or the past, or a world

where the superpowers have gone crazy and bombed everyone back to the stone age.

You don't need all that to create terror.

ONE

Mum burns the toast, again. The blare of the fire alarm cuts through my dream and has me on my feet in seconds, waving a pillow at the flashing plastic disc on the landing outside my room. It takes a few more painful moments to clear the sensor.

'Sorry, love. Would you like some?' Mum's head appears around the banister. There are big red circles under her eyes. The fire alarm's light carries on flashing for a while after the sound stops and it feels like there's a place in my ears where it's still echoing.

'Please,' I croak, suddenly aware of myself standing in a pair of grotty boxer shorts. I've passed the age when it's OK for your mum to see you in your pants.

I have a quick shower and put my uniform on, lug my backpack downstairs and sit at the table. Mum smiles and pushes a plate towards me, and a mug of tea. Despite having burned the last round – hers – the toast is cold. The tea's not much warmer. I wonder how long she's been up, waiting for me.

She leans back against the counter, her dressing gown coming apart a bit at her neck. I stare at my plate, pick up crumbs that have spilled over the edge with the end of my finger. Neither of us speak. A few times she looks like she might be about to say something, ask me about what I'll be doing today, how my friends are getting on, whether I've done all my homework. But she doesn't.

It didn't used to be like this. Mornings used to be full of noise and energy and lost keys and the cats needing feeding and making sure I had my lunch and have I got my bus card and where did I leave that folder and when'll you be home this evening.

But not anymore.

After a few minutes Mum turns away, starts opening and closing cupboards and making scribbled notes on a pad we keep stuck to the front of the fridge. It's Thursday, the day of the big shop, which means she'll be late home.

I finish eating and go back upstairs to clean my teeth. The fire alarm still blinks at me on the landing. I keep the tap running, rinsing my mouth a few times to get the gritty, burnt crumbs out. They get stuck and turn into doughy sludge.

On my way out of the house, Mum stops me in the hallway and puts her hand on my cheek – just holds it there and looks at me. She's been doing this a lot recently. I think it's because my eyes are the same level as hers now. I smile. She does too. And then I walk through the door.

It is one of those frosty, late-autumn mornings where it hurts a bit to breathe. I push my hands deep

4

into the pockets of my coat and pull the collar right up over my chin, the zip between my teeth. The zip has a sharp, metallic taste. Like blood. You can tell it will be a sunny day later; the cloud, or mist, or whatever it is, seems to stop not far overhead, and there are definitely some blue bits on the other side of it.

It was on a day like this, a Monday morning in October just over two years ago, that I heard Mum shout my name as I walked down the street. I had run back to her as fast as I could, shrugging my bag off my shoulders as I went. There was something in her voice that sounded like I had to, as if Mum were hidden inside her own body and was shouting at me to get her out. When I got to her, she looked at me as if she wasn't looking at me. She had the phone clenched to her chest.

After a while, she was able to tell me.

There had been an explosion. In London.

Dad was dead.

TWO

So I lied about the explosions.

Sorry.

The Sunday evening before that phone call – before our lives were taken away from us, skinned alive, cut in half, tossed into the corner and stamped on – we'd all been sitting at the kitchen table. Dad was about to leave to catch the train into London. He worked in our town, on a leafy, high-tech business park doing something I never asked about. I regret that now – among other things. But he went into the capital regularly to meet clients or try to pick up new ones for whatever it was he did. This particular Sunday had been bright and unseasonably warm, and Dad kept finding reasons not to leave. He'd spent most of the day in the garden.

'Sunny again tomorrow, Josh. What do you say we both ditch work? We've got gutters that need clearing, leaves to sweep, and the last of those plants could do with a—'

Mum interrupted our fantasy while still tapping away on her laptop, reminded me that I had a science test the next day, reminded Dad he'd been preparing for this meeting all last week.

'But you don't mind skipping that, Josh?'

'Not at all, Dad. The house is a much more urgent priority, wouldn't you say?'

'That's exactly what I say, Josh. But your mother...'

Mum gave us both one of her looks.

'Ergh. London!' Dad's head clunked as it hit the table. One of the cats pawed at his leg.

I smiled, thumbed my phone, copied the address of a website, hit send. Dad looked down as his pocket buzzed, grinned at the screen, gave me a covert thumbs up.

Then he'd grabbed his panier bag, put his bike helmet on, and left.

Later that night, I'd received a picture message of his finger poised above a 'book now' button on his laptop screen – the website of a holiday company that I'd sent him the link to earlier.

I don't know if he'd *really* booked that holiday or not. One of the things that got lost in the time afterwards. What I do know is, on that last Sunday evening, I'd gone to sleep in a state of happiness I didn't realise I'd had.

Until afterwards. Until it was gone.

Dad had been on his way to that meeting when his train exploded.

Or rather, it had *been* exploded.

A young guy with a backpack had got on at Dad's station, stood in the middle of the carriage, swaying with the other commuters for a few minutes. Then his backpack blew up.

They said that Dad was near the centre of the blast and would have been killed instantly.

We were supposed to see this as a kind of bonus, I think.

Some weren't killed so instantly. One woman took a week to die.

THREE

There was a service at Westminster Abbey for all the victims' families. Some important people talked about *sacrifices* and how they *won't be forgotten*. We sat right at the front, just behind the important people who kept getting up to make speeches.

All the way through I couldn't stop thinking about Greek theatre. Mrs Dinet, our drama teacher, had told us that if one of the characters in ancient Greek theatre died, they wouldn't perform it on stage. The death would take place off stage and someone would describe it to the audience. Then, to prove that it was true, they'd part some curtains at the back of the stage, or bring in some kind of trolley on wheels, and reveal the body. Sometimes they'd use animal blood or intestines to make the death look realistic. Especially if it was a violent one.

All the way through that service I wondered whether they were going to open a curtain or roll out a trolley. I couldn't decide whether I wanted them to or not.

How do you show someone who's had a bomb rip through them?

The papers were all saying how it could have been worse. There was only one bomb, but they'd planned another one. The other bomber was left paralysed after his bomb didn't go off properly and the detonation blast took a chunk out of his spine. His trial was very public. And quick. This was supposed to show our efficient justice system and our intolerance of acts of terror against our way of life.

A few weeks later, the train line re-opened. This was supposed to be an act of defiance against the people who killed my dad.

There were a lot of things that were *supposed to be*.

If you ask me, Dad being killed wasn't one of them.

There were thirty-nine families in that service. Thirty-nine things that weren't supposed to be.

Thirty-nine trolleys.

All this was just over two years ago. About the time when I stopped reading books about the end of the world, and all the adults dying.

FOUR

I get to school just as the first bell goes. I am neither the first nor the last into my lesson. Things are easier that way, I've noticed. You can flow in with the others and don't have to say anything when the teacher says 'Good Morning'. They all do this nowadays, stand in the doorway and say 'good morning', or 'how are you?' or 'ready to get going?' one foot inside the door, one inside the classroom. Mostly, after they've done this, they go back to the front of the room and talk to us like they always have done; like we're all the same. This is fine with me. When they do their politeness thing, trying to treat us like people, there are only a few of them that I actually believe. Most of them sound totally fake.

I'm not sure about Mr Walters, whose Biology class is the first lesson today.

After a whole morning, nearly two hours of cellular differences between plants and animals, he calls me over as I'm about to leave.

'Josh, a quick word, please?' It sounds like a question, but it isn't. That's another thing they all do.

A few other pupils look at me as they walk past. I stand by his desk, watching the side of his face as he

11

scrolls through something on his computer. His rimless glasses reflect a blue-green light from the screen.

'Ah, here it is. Last week's test. Josh, I was very impressed with your result.'

He waits for a reaction. I nod.

'Almost full marks. Almost.' He winks a bit at this. 'Now some of that paper I took from the A-Level syllabus. Not much, but enough to push a few of you. Sort the wheat from the chaff as it were. And you, Josh, are definitely wheat.'

I smile a bit.

'I just wanted to say how well you're doing, Josh. Are we challenging you enough in these lessons? I know it can seem a bit slow sometimes. I've got to make sure everyone's on board.'

I shake my head. 'It's fine.'

'You're sure? Good. You will let me know if we're not pushing you enough though?'

I'm never sure what teachers expect when they ask this. I smile again.

'Good. It sounds to me like you're doing brilliantly everywhere, Josh. Hard to imagine it's been…' He slows down, looks at me closely.

I feel myself getting hot, a high-pitched ringing starts in my ears.

'Never mind. Sorry, Josh.' He pauses for a few seconds, then says it. 'He'd have been proud of you, you know.'

And I leave, quickly, my ears ringing.

Mr Walters is the only one who ever mentions Dad. The first time he did it was a few months after it happened. I was in a revision class after school, catching up on the work I'd missed. Mr Walters was reading a news website. He didn't realise the projector was still on, beaming everything he was reading up onto the whiteboard. He was looking at pictures of the bombing, and people in orange jump suits, and people sitting in front of black flags. He kept tutting and sighing, rearranging himself in his chair. It must have been during the trial. Mum and I had been trying hard to avoid the coverage as much as we could, but the news had been pretty full of those kinds of pictures for ages. Even before the London attack, there were bombs in other countries and reports of 'constant threat'.

Dad used to say it was ridiculous fearmongering.

Mr Walters had looked over and seen my eyes on the screen, then realised. 'I'm sorry, Josh. I forgot you were here,' he'd said, picking up his remote control.

Click. And it was gone. Just like that.

FIVE

The house is empty when I get home. I drop my keys on the shelf by the door and kick off my school shoes.

Sometimes I still expect the cats to greet me, but they were shipped off to live with someone else a couple of months after the explosion. Someone from the Cat's Protection League came round while I was at school. Mum told me when I got home. To be fair, they were getting pretty mangy, and one or both of us kept forgetting to feed them or let them out. The empty spaces on the kitchen floor where the bowls used to be still trigger an ache somewhere deep in my gut – a kind of guilt that we didn't do right by them. Mum says that she could smell the difference after the first few days.

I turn the radio on in the kitchen so the house doesn't sound so empty, then go and get changed upstairs. Mum has a thing about being in school uniform in the evenings. She says it's good to come home and 'peel off the day'. She still holds me to some standards at least. This done, and with my homework spread out on the kitchen table, I fall into the rhythm of quadratic equations, and lose track of time.

The cats were all Dad's idea. He and Mum got a pair of kittens a few years after they got married. They called them Salt and Pepper, which is about as generic as you can get. Dad always used to joke this was on purpose, that it was part of 'what you're supposed to do'.

It's not as if the cats ever got called by their real names anyway. Dad always called them Bowie and Robert Smith after a couple of musicians that he'd liked back in the 1980s. He'd play me their music sometimes – old records, big black discs that shimmered in the light like oil – insisting that I listened for the moment before the needle touched the vinyl. He said you could hear something in that moment, something like suspense. A magic moment, where waiting and what you were waiting for happened at the same time.

Mum called them Ratchet and Mother, because – she said – they made her feel trapped and tied to the house 'like a skeleton in the basement'. I don't know what she meant.

The cats didn't seem to care what you called them. They never responded to any names.

The radio DJs' change-over at 7 o'clock wakes me up. They howl with laughter at something that one of them has said and I come to with a jolt. I'm sat in the only pool of light in the house, having fallen asleep mid-question, my hand scrawling a smooth arc across the page. I scrabble the books together, stuffing them back in my backpack. In my bleary rush I knock over my mug, the last dregs of tea spilling onto a couple of letters from this morning. Almost instantaneously, I hear Mum's keys in the lock, the rustle of shopping bags coming through the door. I grab some kitchen towel and mop up.

Mum enters with a loud sigh of accomplishment. She's always more cheerful after she's done the shopping, wearing the achievement like a badge as she unpacks food into cupboards and drawers, arranges the fridge with the older stuff at the front.

'Hello, love,' she says, beaming at me and the shopping all at once. 'Good day?'

I wonder (but don't ask) why she still goes shopping every week. We must throw away most of the stuff she buys. We've got at least six tins of kidney beans in the cupboard, probably a dozen of chopped tomatoes. I found a bag of peppers at the bottom of the fridge a few weeks ago, unopened. The contents were almost completely liquid – you could only tell what they used to be from the picture on the packaging. And there are potatoes in the vegetable cupboard that have sprouted long, white tendrils, reaching towards the light like tiny hands and arms.

'Fine,' I reply, taking my bag into the hallway. 'Nothing to report.'

She ruffles my hair as I pass her, and maybe thinks about doing the thing with her hand on my cheek again, then doesn't. 'There's another two bags in the boot,' comes her voice from the kitchen, warm, homely, comforting. But I know this, and I'm already halfway down the driveway. Every week it's the same number of bags, the same things in each one. And, when Mum's having a good week, the same schedule of meals each night.

Just the same as when Dad was alive.

But hey, it is what it is.

SIX

It is what it is.

It was a line in a TV series that Mum and I watched together a while back. We'd started watching it after the accident, during the time when I didn't go to school, Mum didn't go to work and we would shut the curtains and not move all day. I call it the The Drowned Time.

We'd kept watching that show, episode by episode, through the time when the phone calls and the visits from journalists had become almost unbearable; through the time when the phone calls and visits were from people checking that I was being looked after properly. It was a long-running show, loads of series, and we were thankful for it.

Whenever the characters in this TV series were talking about the situation being really bad – which it often was – they'd look at each other and say, *'It is what it is'*. It became our mantra for a while. We'd kept watching after we re-surfaced from The Drowned Time. And we still watch it now, when we need it. We've started again from the beginning, episode after episode. The mantra still makes us smile.

'It is what it is' sums things up nicely. It's definitely not good, but it's not bad enough to make you stop and

want to lie down and never get up again. At least not anymore it isn't. It's a situation that you have to deal with, even though you'd rather not, and everyone accepts that it's crap and does the best they can.

It is what it is.

This evening, after chips and chicken Kiev – 'brown dinner', Mum calls it (we always have brown dinner on big-shop day) we're watching one of Mum's property shows on catch-up.

'I don't get this, Mum. So, there's a couple looking to move house who need to look at houses, and they get shown some houses by some people who are really good at looking at houses. Why can't they do it for themselves?'

'I don't know, smartarse. It is what it is!' Her mood hasn't gone down again since we unpacked the shopping. 'It's my escapism.'

'You should just go and have a nose around next door every now and again. Wait until they're out. I'll call you if they come home.'

She hits me with a cushion. We're both smiling. One of the professional house-lookers is talking to the couple about 'outdoor space'. 'Isn't that all there is outdoors? Space?' Mum says.

The couple are standing in a green square at the back of the house they're looking at. It's astroturf, like I used to train on every Wednesday evening with the football team up at the school. Mum scoffs, 'I don't understand why people are doing this nowadays. What's wrong with grass? Why are people too busy to mow lawns or deal with mud or give worms somewhere to live?'

'It is what it is,' I say.

She smiles.

Evenings like this are rare now. I've got homework to finish – English Lit revision as well as the Maths from earlier. But these are tests I'm willing to fail.

As if reading my mind, Mum asks, 'Homework?'

'No, finished it all.'

'Liar. Off with you.' She digs her feet in sideways, under my leg, and pushes. I make to complain. 'Hey, it is what it is,' she says.

I throw a cushion at her on my way out.

Later, she puts her head around my door to say goodnight. 'Thanks for your help this evening, Josh. With the shopping. We'll watch something you want to watch tomorrow night, OK?'

I nod, knowing that tomorrow night Mum probably won't be like this, if she's here at all. And even if she was here and we did find something to watch that she agrees to, she'd probably fall asleep before it's halfway through.

So I'll go and watch things upstairs, on my own, on my laptop, the house around me so quiet I'll think it has eaten itself.

But hey, it is what it is.

All the students do it too – *the look*. Even the new Year Sevens. Word soon gets around I guess.

But no one has ever actually mentioned Dad yet.

Except Mr Walters.

A few weeks after that first time, when I'd caught up with the rest of the class again and didn't need any extra sessions after school, Mr Walters had asked me if 'He' was good at science at school. Somehow, I'd heard him pronounce that capital 'H'. I'd stared back, blankly. Mr Walter's carried on – did I get my abilities from my mother's side of the family as well as His? I'd shrugged and said I didn't know. Then went straight home in the middle of the day and cried.

I told Mum about it.

The next day, I'd got a note telling me to go to Miss Amber's office at the end of school. Mum was there with Mrs Clarke, Miss Amber and Mr Walters. I froze when I saw them through the little, grilled window in the door, wanting to melt into a puddle and be mopped up before they saw me. I was too late.

But when Mrs Clarke opened the door to me, she seemed to be laughing. So did Miss Amber, and Mr Walters. And Mum.

'Hi, love.' Mum's voice sounded puffed up, full of air, the way it did just before she started to cry.

Mrs Clarke showed me to a comfy seat between her and Mum. Mr Walters sat opposite, on Miss Amber's office chair. Miss Amber stood leaning on the windowsill.

It wasn't a very big office. Mum took something out of her bag and held it on her lap.

'Josh, I'd like to apologise,' began Mr Walters. 'I'm sorry that I keep mentioning your father. I know that you don't like it, that it makes you uncomfortable. And I wanted to let you know that I didn't want to upset you in any way, or bring up any bad memories.' He sat leaning forward with his clasped hands between his knees, looking concerned.

'Mr Walters was at school with your dad,' Mum said next, definitely on the verge of tears now. She passed me what she was holding – a rolled-up piece of paper. I unrolled it. It was an old picture of Dad's class at school. I remember him showing it to me once, years ago. We had laughed at the haircuts.

Mr Walters leaned over, pointing to a boy in the top row with short, dark hair and big-rimmed glasses. 'That's me,' he said. 'I was in your dad's year, but we weren't in the same classes. We weren't close, and we didn't keep in touch after school. When I heard about … what happened…' He trailed off.

'I think Mr Walters is also upset about your father, Josh.' Mrs Clarke took over. 'If you would like to change Biology class, then Mr Walters will not be at all put out, and nor will we. But he wanted to tell you himself that he has his reasons for thinking about your dad.'

'You look just like him,' said Mr Walters, weakly. This was true. In the last few months, I'd often looked

24

at our photographs side by side on Mum's bedside table as I'd tried to wake her with a cup of tea before leaving for school.

'It's fine.' I managed a hoarse whisper. 'It's OK.'

Mum had actually started crying now, quietly, smiling at Mr Walters.

Mrs Clarke clapped her hands once. 'Good, that's settled then. Josh, Mrs Milton, thank you both for popping in. And at such short notice. I can't imagine what a difficult…' and it went on like this for a few minutes. I sat hunched in my coat, trying to smile, following the conversation that moved very slowly around the room like a car about to run out of petrol. Mr Walters was asking where we were living now, he said that he'd regretted not meeting up with Dad for a pint and a catch-up. It was so silly, he said, the two of them still living in the town they grew up in, and not in touch with each other.

'And now…' he'd faltered. 'And now…'

All I could think about was how many pupils would be outside to watch me leaving the school with my mum, whose face was blotched and red, and who wouldn't let go of my hand.

As we were standing to leave, Mr Walters had placed a hand gently on Mum's elbow, then turned to me. 'I'm truly sorry, Josh. I promise you that it won't happen again.'

But it does.

EIGHT

I might not speak much, but I listen well. And I pick things up. All day there's been a buzz around school about a party at Jamie's house this evening.

Jamie and I used to be good friends, from the football team and before, but I haven't spoken to him for a while. The excuse I used to Mum about dropping out of football was the same one I told Jamie: I wanted to 'focus on my school work'. It worked better with Mum than with him.

I was never the best or most important player in the team, nor was I the worst, so I don't think the team have hugely missed me. I used to enjoy playing though. I was what you'd call 'solid'. A dependable, mid-field player who would scrap for the ball and then, normally, do something half decent with it. Not going on a run, beating three players and slotting the ball into the other team's net, but giving it to someone who could, or sending the ball out wide, into a space I'd noticed was empty but was sure our wingback could get to. Dad used to say that there weren't many players that could spot those passes, and that I made them more often than the rest of the team put together. I wasn't sure about this. Dad said I should get used to being under-appreciated.

For a while I'd tried to keep playing. Mum still came along, but she didn't shout anything anymore. I got the impression she wasn't really watching. I realised then how much football had been a part of her life too. Watching her standing on the touchline there in the rain, staring out into the middle distance, it felt like I was drowning. The worst bit was knowing she was just trying to keep something alive for me, and that every second was killing her. When I said I was going to stop, she tried her best not to look relieved.

Jamie and I didn't fall out, just stopped talking, and we still nod at each other in the corridors. Jamie knew that people had started treating me differently, even though he never did. We're still in a lot of classes together, and the teachers' habits of keeping us apart lower down the school (when we used to talk a lot) have been carried over to this year as well. Even though I don't really speak to anyone, not anymore.

I'm sitting just behind Jamie in our English class, the test I'd revised for last night about to start, when he turns around.

'You coming?'

'What?'

'Friday. Are you going to come? You're invited.'

'To your house?'

'You remember where it is, right?' Jamie smiles.

I smile back. 'Maybe.'

And that's it. Moment over. He goes back to his

work, chatting to Louisa sitting next to him. He says something that sounds like 'I tried'. She looks concerned.

I think about it. Mum won't be home this evening; Fridays are when she goes to see her parents. She's stopped insisting that I come with her ever since we've started GCSEs, so I'll be on my own. And will be until Sunday morning, probably. So Mum wouldn't have to know about this. Not that she'd have a problem at all, I just know she'd make a big fuss and say things like 'it's good that you're getting out again' or 'will there be girls there' or, even worse, 'fine, I'll just sit in on my own'.

I throw my pencil at Jamie's shoulder. It glances off, clatters across the desk in front of him. He turns around.

'What time?'

'Er ... after half eight?'

'Josh. Stop talking,' hisses Mrs Burgoyne from the front, and I'm not sure if she or Jamie is more surprised.

NINE

Since Mum hasn't changed the shopping list for a while, we've got a good supply of beer in the garage, all stacked up. Dad was the only one who drank it. There are bottles at the back that are probably off by now. I grab two four-packs from the top and replace them with a few packs of cokes a little further down so that the tower of beer stays the same height. I doubt Mum would mind if she knew I was taking them, but it saves time this way, and I don't want to phone her at my grandparents' house. It's never a short conversation.

Nanna and Grandad have been really good for Mum, and are happy that I'm mostly 'keeping out of it' as they say. After it happened, they were coming over a lot, so much that I started calling the spare room their room. But they have lives like the rest of us, so before too long their visits got less frequent. Now Mum goes there instead whenever she feels like she needs a rest. Which is every weekend. And sometimes during the week.

She's never mentioned moving house, but I've seen her browser history and I know she'd like it if we went to live near them. I think she's just waiting until I finish school. Or this part of it, at least.

I sling a pizza in the oven while I go upstairs for a shower, stuffing it down before I leave the house, the beers clinking in a carrier bag.

For some reason, as I walk the short and familiar route to Jamie's, I'm nervous. There's a knot in my stomach like I used to get before kick-offs. It's half excitement and half dead-weight, and it pulls me down and makes me want to turn around, go home and just curl up on the sofa all evening watching chat shows and online videos.

I make a list in my head of people who are likely to be there, and it's mostly people I know – or knew – quite well. There's not been much change in the social groups at school for years now, and everyone pretty much still hangs around with the people they've always hung around with. Even so, having to have the same 'how are you' conversation a dozen times this evening isn't filling me with much joy. Maybe they'll just leave me alone like they always do.

That's another thing that's changed. I used to be pretty popular: lots of friends, active social media, all that. Then I stopped watching and it all just fell away: the online stuff first, then the real-life friends not long after.

I guess it's like this: when I came back to school after the first month, it was like there was a cloud of silence around me. At first it was pretty big. You could hear it spread out from me, like a wave. I'd walk into a room and people everywhere – even on the other side of the lunch hall – would notice me and go quieter. Then the cloud got smaller, until it was just a thin, wispy covering that only covered me, not anyone else. It was like a barrier that seemed to stop people looking my way. In fact, when I walk into a room now, people's voices get louder. If anything, their backs turn further away. They get even more closed.

Maybe it won't be too busy. Maybe it'll be just me and my clinking bottles.

But the noise from Jamie's house breaks on me like a tide as soon as I turn the corner into his road. I can see, even at this distance, people standing in his front garden, a few sitting on the wall that his dad always used to get angry at us for sitting on. It's a huge party – much bigger than I thought it would be. The weight in my stomach gets heavier, but I push against it. People look up as I get closer, the bottles noisy against my leg, and a few raise their chins by way of saying hello. I nod back and slip in through the open front door, trying to find Jamie as soon as possible.

He's in the kitchen with Louisa and a few others. He looks up as I come in.

'Josh! Wow!' He almost spills his drink as he jumps down from the counter he's sitting on – it was Jamie's mum who used to tell us not to sit up there. Quite a lot of childhood is learning where you can't sit. To my surprise, Jamie throws his arms around me in an awkward hug that I'm too slow to return properly, knocking him on the knee with my carrier bag. The people Jamie was talking to – Louisa, Harry and Kyle – all look as surprised as I do.

Jamie takes the bag, lifts out a bottle and gives me a knowing smile. Of course it's the same, dodgy euro-brand beer we used to steal from Dad years ago.

'Did you leave the coke in the stack?'

'Of course.' And I laugh, the weight lessening slightly.

Jamie puts his soft drink down, cracks the top of one of my bottles and passes it to me, then opens another for himself. We tap bottles. I look around and notice there isn't much alcohol here except what I've brought. I begin to think that maybe I've made a mistake, misjudged the party. The weight comes back again.

I don't remember the first time I had beer. Probably when I was really young, like eight or nine. But the first time I got drunk started out a bit like this. It was Jamie and me in my kitchen. My parents had gone out for the day and left us to our own devices. We were in the garage looking for the coke, or something more drinkable than water, and when we saw the stack of beer we had the same thought at the same time. We did the coke-switch trick, thinking ourselves criminal masterminds, and must have only had two bottles each. It was enough though, and when Mum and Dad came home, I'd fallen asleep in the lounge under a pile of DVDs, and Jamie was passed out in the toilet, his head underneath the bowl. I'd expected Dad to find it more amusing, but Mum drove Jamie home while I cleaned up the mess Jamie had left – he'd missed the toilet. Dad watched sternly from the doorway and made sure I didn't miss anything. I could smell the antiseptic for days and it made my head spin.

'It's good to see you,' says Jamie. He seems to have forgotten the group behind him as we wander outside, where it's a bit quieter.

I smile, and the first beer goes down easily as we talk. About school, football, how his dad used to coach us until he left Jamie's mum and moved away, about holidays, about everything. Before I know it, we've been talking for nearly an hour. Which means *I've* been talking for nearly half an hour.

I go inside for more beers and spend ages looking for a bottle opener so by the time I'm outside again he's gone. I walk back in, sipping at one of my two bottles, and sidle through to the sitting room, trying not to look out of place amongst the crowd, music and smiling. The party has now moved inside, the walls heaving with a condensed mass of people.

Molly, a girl in our year, is kneeling down and fiddling with her iPhone. 'Josh! Shit, how are you? What do you want to listen to, stranger? I'm on Jamie's mum's speakers. They're awesome.'

I tell her the name of an old-ish song. It's the first one that pops into my head, and I cringe as I say it. Music hasn't been a big priority this last few years.

'Classic!' Molly shouts over the racket. There's a second's silence, then the song comes on. She jumps up and gives me a hug, then dances off to the middle of the room. I look around. I nod to a few familiar faces, then realise that Molly's shouting at me.

She wants me to dance.

I smile and turn around, the weight building back up in my stomach. I try to get back to the kitchen but barrelling through the door at that moment are Will, Mike and Ben – all from the football team. The song was played a lot on a tour we went on together about four years ago, when we'd all just met at the start of secondary school. Ben grabs me around the waist, and I just about manage to keep my mouthful of beer inside my lips as I'm lifted up and planted firmly in the middle of the lounge. Will and Mike are on either side of me, jumping up and down to the music, singing along. Ben puts an arm across my shoulders, and soon we're a big circle, singing and laughing and jumping up and down to the music.

There are scenes like this in a few of the naff movies I watch with my mum. Normally it's the end of the film, or nearly, and all the characters are back together and at some kind of wedding or celebration or birthday that – at some point – they didn't think they were going to get to. They all look at each other, raise their glasses and don't speak. I didn't think these things happened in real life. l thought that the glow you got in your stomach from just watching was as good as it got.

But tonight, I'm singing and laughing and jumping too.

TEN

I don't know where a lot of the night has gone. It's almost eleven o'clock and I'm sitting on Jamie's sofa talking to someone. The music is still on but it's quieter, or it seems quieter, and I'm shouting. Maybe that's why the music seems quieter.

I'm shouting at someone and they're laughing at me. Or with me. And it's Dana.

It's Dana Leigh from school, the one from school who looks at me and I usually don't look at because she scares me a bit and is always being called to Mrs Clarke's office. Dana who stopped wearing her school jumper a year ago and who now wears a jacket instead, and ankle boots. Dana who's wearing an expensive bracelet on her wrist that I keep grabbing and saying 'wow'. Dana who's rumoured to have a boyfriend who's left school already and picks her up some lunchtimes in his car. She's got a full face of make-up on, even more than Mum used to wear when she wore make-up to work. Her eyelashes are huge. And I'm shouting at her and she's laughing. And I'm shouting and doing an impression of Mr White, the Maths teacher, and she's laughing. And I'm laughing, and we've both got beers – not the ones I brought, there must have been more after all – and we're laughing and she puts her hand on my arm because she says she might fall over because she's laughing, even though we're sitting down she says she might fall over. And I laugh. And then all I can hear is me laughing because the music's stopped.

And when I realise the music has stopped, I stop laughing.

In the doorway there's a man. And I mean a man – not a teenager or even someone a bit older but a man. There's a layer of short stubble all around his head – his buzz-cut skull the same as his unshaven chin. He's wearing a white shirt, buttoned to the neck, black jeans, military boots. He's standing there with his hand on the top of the doorframe, leaning in. He's standing there and he's looking at me. And he's not happy.

'Comfortable?' he says. I feel Dana's grip on my arm tighten as the man walks into the room. Everything around him seems to shrink back as he passes.

'Carl, I…'

'Shut up. Go and get in the car.'

'Carl, leave him. It's OK. We were just talking.' She lets go of my arm.

'I said shut up, you little slut. Think I don't know where you went? Easy enough to find a kids' party.'

I stand up, a little unsteady. 'Hey, I don't think you should—'

And then I sit down again, quickly and without meaning to, my ears ringing, my face warm and getting warmer, a ball of fire centred on my left cheek where the man has punched me.

'Carl, he's just a kid from school. Don't. He…'

The man stares her down. 'Go and get in the car,' he hisses.

Dana goes. I try to stand up again, suddenly more sober, but another fist lashes at me. It catches me on the other side of my head and I'm back on the sofa, head pressed against the cool, soft surface of a cushion. I think I'm groaning.

'Don't let me catch you talkin' to her again. Right?'

And then he goes.

ELEVEN

The walk home is taking longer than it should. It's hard to walk straight and I can't see too well. A girl, I think it was Louisa, found a bag of peas in the freezer and pressed them against my cheek where a mouth of warm blood had started to form around the cut from Carl's fist. I still have the bag with me, though all the peas must have fallen out by now because it's empty. It doesn't do much to stop the blood which is now running down my face, along my chin and onto the front of my shirt.

I can feel a lump coming up on my right temple where his second fist caught me. It's just under the hairline. When I touch it, it feels like a bag of nails has fallen open inside my skull.

The party broke up soon after Carl left. Jamie insisted I stay, but I insisted I go. I'm not sure that was the best idea.

I fall over, the pavement coming up suddenly before I can get out of its way. I lie unmoving for a few seconds, enjoying the world being still, then my phone vibrates in my pocket. It's a text from Jamie telling me to let him know when I'm home safely. The clock on the phone says half past midnight. I don't know what time I left. I text back – *I'm fine. Nearly there.*

Getting to my feet, I look for an idea of where I am. There are no streetlights, and the road is uneven, with lumps of black tarmac around raised iron manhole covers and drains. There are dim outlines of houses a little way back from the road. They look odd, empty. Behind them is a beaded line of street lamps, softly orange. Did I come from over there, or am I going that way? Slowly it dawns on me that I must have wandered into the new estate they're building up the hill. I'm not far from home at all – maybe a mile – but a lot further away than I should be. I just need to get back to the main road, so I set off to find a way through between the shells of houses.

It's not easy going. The ground, although it hasn't rained for a while, has been churned into jagged teeth by the heavy machinery, and I fall twice more in the first hundred metres or so, each time finding a shallow puddle at the bottom of a long tyre-track. I aim to get closer to the houses to my right, thinking there won't have been as much traffic around there, but pretty soon I'm cut off by metal fencing. I use this like a handrail, hanging from it by my fingertips as I tread carefully over the ruined earth, or letting it take all of my weight as I lean in to it, avoiding a huge puddle right along the fence line.

When I get to the houses, they're terrifying. The smell of concrete dust makes them seem more like ancient caves, and all of the windows are just empty spaces. Through the upstairs openings, you can see the sky. They look like skulls lined up, peering down at me. For a second I get the idea that Dad is in one of them, watching me. I wretch, and a tide of hot vomit springs suddenly up my throat and onto the clay soil at my feet.

I have to get away from here. I see a narrow gap between two terrace blocks and head towards it. It's a tight squeeze. When I get to the end of this makeshift alley, the ground starts to level out and I can move more easily. But it's not long before I get to another fence. This one is a wooden hoarding and it must be the edge of the developer's land. There's mud splattered about halfway up it, as if – like me – it is trying to escape. It's too tall to climb, and I rest against it for a while, leaning my forehead against the rough, warm boards.

Then, low down on the fence, I see that the edge of one of the wooden boards has slightly come away from the fencepost. I prise my fingers into the gap and lean backwards, hearing a damp 'pop' as another couple of nails pull loose. I can feel something happening to the ends of my fingers, but they're so numb it doesn't register properly. When there's enough room to squeeze through, I drop to my chest and heave myself underneath. A fresh pain starts up in my leg as I scramble though.

Out from under the fence, I try to stand, managing a couple of steps forwards before the earth comes up to meet me again.

TWELVE

I wake up. Or at least my right eye wakes up. My left seems glued down, pushed hard into clammy, wet mud.

Grimacing, I gather my hands from wherever they have fallen at the ends of my cold arms, put them under my chest and push myself clear of the ground.

I'm freezing. The cold starts at my shoulder blades, nibbling away, then takes great chunks of my legs and finally swallows my feet.

I roll over. And last night comes back in one violent tumble.

My trainers are ruined, caked in yellow-brown clay. There's a rip, about a foot long, down one leg of my trousers. The top of the tear is red with blood. I must have caught myself on a nail when I squeezed under the fence. I probe it with a gentle finger. It's swollen and ugly, but the bleeding has stopped.

My shirt is in strips, blood-stained, covered in mud and stinking like the first time I got drunk with Jamie. I check my cheek, just beneath the eye that won't open. That too has stopped bleeding, but that may be because of the mud that has crusted over it.

I stretch my limbs to check that everything's still there. Nothing feels broken. Just sore. And cold.

My phone says 5:48. The light feels strange: ash grey and milky, but clean. There's a smell that is the same: clean. And there's a song playing in my head.

It's not in my head. The rise and fall of notes are coming from nearby. I turn slowly towards it. On the top of the wooden fence that I crawled under last night there is a blackbird. It's looking at me.

'Morning,' I croak.

The blackbird turns its head, flies off. I watch it as it comes to rest on a stone wall about five metres in front on me. Patches of moss, cascades of green leaves and purple flowers cover most of the wall's significant height. I realise there are walls on three sides of me and, with the wooden hoarding at my back, I'd say I was lying in a pretty even-sided square.

The blackbird trills on, and above its head a scurry of wings brings two more birds into view. I don't know what these birds are, but when they move they look like pale blue streaks. One of them arches its flight to land in the branches of a small tree in the corner of the square. When it lands, I see its chest is yellow against the bush's purple spears of flowers.

I force myself upright, every joint in my body complaining.

I realise that it's not mud I've been lying on, but grass – bushy tufts of dew-wet grass. I rip chunks of it off in my fists and rub them gently against the sides of my face. They come away streaked with brown, yellow and red.

I take my shoes off and beat them on the ground, scour their edges against the grass, trying to get rid of the worst of their clay jackets. This is working. I look for anything else I can use.

The moss on the wall comes away in great, sodden handfuls. Up close, it looks like it's made from intricate ropes of tiny, furry stars. Before I question what I'm doing, I jam a fistful against the pain in my leg. At first, the cold water that flows from it is like another nail entering my flesh, but that soon subsides and the sharp pain of the cut lessens and is replaced by a warm throb. I do the same to my cheek and almost sigh in pleasure as a spigot of water runs into the corner of my mouth. My tongue, like my cheek, begins to numb and warm. I start to feel clean.

Well, cleaner.

After about a dozen handfuls of the moss, I notice a low wooden door in one corner of the square. It complains against its ancient lock and hinges as I try to force it. I lean against it with all my force and hear something start to splinter. With a dry cough, the lock finally gives way and the door springs open. I almost fall through, finding myself in a narrow, dark hollow under dense bushes growing against the backside of the stone wall. The occasional sound of a passing car tells me the road is to my left, and I part crawl, part walk beneath the thick canopy in that direction, keeping my shoulder against the wall. I have to push through about a metre of weed and nettle before I emerge, bleary eyed and filthy, onto the pavement. Realising where I am, I set off as fast as I can for home. I don't look at the drivers' faces in the few cars that pass me, but I can feel their shocked looks fuelling my embarrassment.

When I get through the door, I go straight upstairs, put all my clothes in a bin bag, and run a hot bath.

THIRTEEN

I spend most of Saturday on the sofa, a bag of frozen peas over my swelling cheek. Mum calls in the afternoon. I let her go through to voicemail and almost smile when I listen to her message. She says she is staying away an extra night, and that there is plenty of food in the freezer. I don't know why she still says 'an extra night', and I tell her unresponsive message that there aren't any peas left. I almost smile at that too.

But it hurts to smile.

If Dad had a Monday meeting in London, he'd often go in on Sunday and 'make a weekend of it'; meet up with old friends, then get to his hotel in time for an early night. We'd spend the Sunday evenings watching a film together, or whatever sport was on, our phones clamped to our ears, the tiniest delay in the sound from each other's TVs like an almost-echo. We wouldn't speak for ages at a time, but I'd hear him shuffling on his bed, or coughing, or just breathing, and it would be like he was next to me. I'm thinking of those evenings now, a bag of peas on my face.

But it hurts to smile.

Alongside the selection of bad TV I flick through, my aching mind wanders in and out of a few other things – Mum, school – but keeps coming back to last night. The party. How I was. *Who* I was. It felt like no time had passed at all since I was that relaxed with Jamie. I remember just ... *glowing*. That's the right word – glowing. The beers helped, I think. They don't help now though, as I interrupt myself to get another glass of water to try to squash my headache.

But it wasn't just that. I'd felt somehow whole again. Delicate, maybe, but definitely whole. And that song. The dancing, arms wrapped around a group of people. Dana.

What had I said to her? I can't remember big chunks of it. I follow the swirling patterns on the lounge ceiling as I try to recall, but like them my thoughts just go round and round and round.

And it hurts to smile.

I camp out in the lounge until pretty late before hauling myself off to bed, and I sleep deep into Sunday. I've just showered when Mum gets home, opening windows and complaining about the smell of 'cooped-up boy' as I come down the stairs.

I let her cradle my head as she asks about the cuts on my face, feeling like a little kid again. It's so comfortable on her lap. I tell her I was texting Jamie, fell up the stairs and hit the banister. She jokes that we can't have two of us coming apart at the seams. Mentioning Jamie was a good idea. She says she's glad I'm talking to people again, and I let her dab some anti-germ cream on the cut and the worst of the bruising. I notice she's crying a little as she does this.

My eye is still half-closed when I wake up for school the next morning. Again, Mum's hand holds my face before I leave.

The Biology test isn't going very well. It's stuff I know, but my concentration is waning, and my cheek pulses, hot and urgent. Quite a few people have noticed it. It's hard not to, to be honest. Jamie sought me out before the first bell and asked me if I was OK. And Louisa said she'd seen my trail of peas when she'd walked home on Saturday morning. Her smile widened when she realised how embarrassed this was making me.

I'm not sure what people want to ask me about more, the fact that I got drunk, or being punched by Dana's boyfriend. Will says he used to be in the army, that I should count myself lucky to still have a head on my shoulders at all. Someone punches him on the arm, as if he's made a distasteful joke.

Mr Walters has seen me too. He's watching me from the front of the room, and I know he's picked up on the gossip in the corridor and on our way in.

I want to crawl under one of the big wooden benches.

As he collects up the test papers at the end of the

lesson, he looks at me for a long time, as if he's about to say something. I keep my head down and shuffle things around in my bag. After what seems like ages, he moves on.

The rest of the day goes by slowly, but every time someone stops me in the corridor, or whispers across a desk about Friday night, it slows down even more. People run up behind me and clap me on the back, or half spin me around to ask what it felt like to get punched, whether I'm going to get him back.

Mike tells me he knows a guy – a friend of his older brother – that Dana's boyfriend put in hospital just before last Christmas. 'He wasn't there, my brother, but he said his mates were all back from their first term at uni, in the pub, the Green Man, you know? And one of them said something about British military intervention, or something like that. He wasn't even *talking* to Dana's boyfriend. and wasn't anywhere *near* him, but apparently the guy crossed the pub and nearly took the back of his head off with a pint glass. He's a *psycho*, Josh. Watch yourself, yeah?'

I find myself wincing as each person comes towards me, and before the afternoon's lessons, I wait in the toilets for the corridors to go quiet before walking to English.

There's a squealing in my ears all through the lesson and again I can't concentrate. When Mrs Burgoyne asks me a question, I don't hear her. The first I know of it is when the class start laughing. I think someone made a comment. Mrs Burgoyne is looking down at me. It's definitely not *the look*. I have some trouble in placing it, despite having one eye half-closed. It's a look I've not seen in a long time. It's got a smile in it.

I shrug off the last few questioners at the end of school and walk home alone. No one seems keen to follow or walk with me; everyone probably thinks I'm just going back to normal after having a holiday from my solitude on Friday night. I walk the same road that I emerged onto in those gritty, early hours of Saturday morning and I pause, staring at the patch in the hedge that I vaguely recall pushing through.

Apart from a broken stinging nettle flopping out across the pavement like a trip-wire, you'd never know anyone had been through it.

FOURTEEN

The noise in the corridors and the noise in my head both quieten down as the week goes on. People seem to forget about what happened, or perhaps because I won't talk about it they forget a bit quicker. Pretty soon, it's Thursday.

I failed the Biology test. It wasn't an important one, but since we started this year, all the teachers keep saying that *everything is important*, and that we *can't afford to fall asleep at the wheel*, and that we must *keep our eyes on the prize*. Mr Walters is no different.

Despite our conversation a few weeks ago, when he said I was doing fine – better than fine – he pulls me to one side on my way out of his lesson.

'Josh, I think it would be a good idea for you to come to the catch-up session after school today.'

Everyone knows the catch-up session isn't really there for catching-up. The only people that go are four or five boys who miss a lesson every week because they get alternative provision because they can't cope with school, which means that every Wednesday, they get taken in the school minibus to team building sessions, which are normally in the woods and involve lighting fires and cooking toast, or courses which teach them how to build walls. They're not the kind of kids I want to spend time with.

'I really think it would help, Josh. There's a couple of things on the test that you missed. Real howlers. Are you OK at the moment?'

I nod.

'I've already spoken to your mum and she's fine with you staying. So I'll see you after school, in here, OK?'

I nod again, and force a weak smile, 'Thanks, Sir.'

'Hey, that bruise has really come up. It'll stay pretty colourful for a few days but should start healing soon. Fell up the stairs, your mum said?'

The noise comes back into my ears again; a high-pitched whine, like a little electric motor that's running too fast.

'Your mum told me on the phone. Looks like you did a real number on yourself.' He leans a tiny bit closer, then adds, 'I hope you punched it back.'

Another weak smile. There's a taste in my mouth that's a bit like blood and my cheek flushes warm again.

'Don't worry. Your secret's safe with me.' Mr Walters taps the side of his nose.

After the bell for the end of the day, I walk back to Mr Walters' classroom.

There's always a strange atmosphere in a school after everyone has gone home. The corridors seem surprised that they're not full anymore. They're like arms that have forgotten how to be arms. I used to think it was the school relaxing after a long day, but walking through the science block this afternoon I get the feeling the corridor is watching me, almost willing me to be noisier, quicker, more boisterous, to make up for the fact I'm one person, not one hundred. It feels like it misses being full.

I breathe in as I step through Mr Walters' door. Four faces look up as I enter. Hard faces. Closed faces. The conversation, that I'd heard from outside stops.

'Josh, hi. Grab a stool there.' Mr Walters sits with his feet up on the desk, pointing to a bench in the last but one row. A newspaper is open across his stretched out legs. 'I'll be with you in a minute.'

'What do you think they should do to him, Sir?' asks one of the closed faces. It's a boy I haven't been in a class with for years. I see him around school sometimes, wandering the site during lessons.

'Well, Brendon,' answers Mr Walters. 'Some would say we should extend the freedoms and privileges of our country to him because he's here. And that he's human and so deserving of proper treatment, regardless of his thoughts or actions.'

On the front of the newspaper, from behind which Mr Walters is talking, is a middle-eastern man. He's shouting at the camera whilst being bundled into the back of a van by police officers.

Mr Walters continues, 'Some people, on the other hand, are not so sure. There is an argument that leniency here may come back to bite us on the arse.'

There is always a small ripple of laughter when a teacher swears; in this classroom it's a gruff ripple, more like a deep rumbling.

I know what they're talking about. I caught a bit of the news on Saturday afternoon and they were talking about a deportation – there have a been a few recently, high profile ones. The middle-eastern man is a radical cleric, whose mosque – up north somewhere – has been accused of promoting terrorism.

Mr Walters continues, 'The new government, Brendon, voted in with quite a majority, take the second view. They say that if certain people are preaching against the country in which they are living, they should look for another place to live.'

'Too right, Sir, he's a—'

'Brendon, before you say something I'll have to report,' Mr Walters' eyes flash over to me for a second, 'I wonder if you would extend that logic to anyone born in this country. Should people be asked to leave if they propose violence against the state or towards the people in it?'

'Even white people, Sir?' The voice comes from another of the closed faces. A tall boy with a thin, pointed face and almost a full beard. His wide-set eyes are rimmed with pink. He brings to mind one of those dogs you're not allowed to own anymore because they keep mauling people. I've never met him before.

'Yes, though we know it's wrong to differentiate on the basis of colour, don't we, Vince? Now, enough politics for one day. Do you boys have your workbooks?'

A flat chorus of yeses.

'Time to get on then. I need to sort Josh out.'

Four heads turn again to stare at me. I try not to, but I meet Vince's eye. Almost automatically, I nod slightly in greeting.

'What's that poof doing here?'

I've never heard Mr Walters shout before. From the fact that all five of us jump a few inches in our seats, neither have the others. His voice goes off like a gun shot. The words seem to lash into Vince, physically. The effect is definite. Vince seems to shrink. It doesn't last long and it doesn't have to.

'Josh, Vinny has something to say to you.' Mr Walters returns to his usual calm, soft tones.

Vince bristles at the childish nickname, but keeps his mouth shut.

'Vince?'

'I'm sorry, Josh.' Vince's voice is barely above a growl.

Mr Walters raises his eyebrows at me.

"S OK,' I mumble.

'There you are, Vince, a nice, polite boy come to join our group. Perhaps it'll rub off on you. Now, Josh.

Page twenty-six in this one, just give it a read and try the quiz on the next page. Should be OK for starters.'

I look at the textbook he holds out to me. The front cover says 'A Level'.

'Should be appropriate for your intellect, I think?' Mr Walters winks.

I open the book and make a start.

About half an hour later, as I'm working through the textbook, Mr Walters gets up from his desk, picking up his coffee mug.

'I'll be five minutes, ladies. No funny business.'

As soon as the door shuts, Vince is at my desk, leaning hard against it, his clenched teeth not far from mine. There's a definite smell of tobacco on his breath, and under his close-cropped hairline, I see a vein throbbing.

'Prick. I will cut you if you look at me again. Understand?'

I nod.

'Vin, leave it. Just 'cause Walters battered you, don't take it out on the new kid.'

Vince wheels round. The boy he's looking at was in my geography class for just one term, years ago, but I don't see him much now. His name is Alan. We used to sit on the same table. He would always complain that my coloured pencils were blunt and had broken leads, and once blamed me because I'd throw them across the table to him when he wanted to borrow them. He said I should take more care of my things. I was never sure if he was joking or not.

'Fuck you.' Vince grumbles back towards his seat, but not before knocking my textbook onto the floor.

I move to pick it up.

'Sit still!' Vince shouts, his pointing finger like a dart, inches from my nose. Brendon laughs. 'Leave it there.'

Vince struts back to his seat as Alan comes over, bends down and picks up the textbook, dusting it off with a sleeve.

'Thanks,' I murmur.

Alan gives me the briefly raised chin of recognition. 'What are you in for?' He plants his elbows on the desk, leans on his hands.

'Messed up a test.'

'What a ball ache. You should be more like us. They don't let us take tests anymore, right, lads?'

A murmur of agreement.

'Thing is, Josh, they think we're junk anyway. What's the point of ruining the school's place in the league tables for kids like us?'

Vince is carving something into the bench with a compass. He hears Alan's comment and digs even harder.

'Mustn't grumble though, eh? I'm gonna join the army anyway. You seen this?' He gets his phone out of his pocket and turns it in my direction. The screen is full of greasy flesh colours and jerking movement.

I look away.

'Not your kind of thing? Best looked at in private I guess. How about this?'

The next video starts shakily. It shows a street at night. Across the road, behind a row of parked cars, two men are running, the camera tracking their hooded heads. They come up quickly behind a third head, this one with a white or yellow cloth wrapped around it. It takes a second to realise it's a turban, but by this time the head has disappeared beneath the roofs of the cars.

'Hang on, I'll turn the sound up.'

Behind the background noise of nearby traffic, and the breathing of the person filming, there's a muffled thud, thud. It sounds like stamping. Then there's a loud noise, halfway between a moan and a scream. The two heads, who have been standing where the turbaned man fell, come out from between the parked cars, running towards the camera, shouting 'Go, Go.' The camera goes shaky again, following the back of one of the hooded men, and then the clip ends.

There's a few seconds of silence. I think I know what I've just seen, but I'm not sure.

'Good, right? The prick didn't know we were coming. No chance we'll get done. And no CCTV on that road – my brother told me.'

Then it clicks. Alan's face looks a lot like Carl's, the

man who hit me. Alan's hair's a bit longer, his jaw rounder, but the resemblance is unmistakable now.

'That's my brother, running off in front of me,' he says, playing me the last half of the clip again. 'He used to be in the army. Knows just how to do a raid like that. He says if I work on my fitness I could be invable as an infantryman.'

'In*valuable*. Prick,' says the fourth head. I don't know him. He doesn't introduce himself.

'Invaluable, yeah, whatever. He was a great soldier, my brother. Too good. They wouldn't let him stay. He was too dangerous. You can't have soldiers who can think for themselves, can you?'

'Right, yeah.' I don't know what else to say.

'But I'm not clever like him. So I'll be alright. But this is good, right?' Alan's eyes are lit up with excitement. His finger hovers over the play button again.

'Yeah.'

'Al!' An urgent voice from the stool nearest the door.

Alan is still sauntering back to his place as Mr Walters re-enters. He looks quizzically at Alan, then at me. I quickly open the textbook again, to a page I can't even pronounce the title of, and start reading.

Mr Walters sits back at his desk. In the brief moment that I look up, he raises his mug at me.

FIFTEEN

I spend a long time packing my bag after Mr Walters tells us we can go. I'm the last one in the room, and as I come out into the corridor, I listen for the other boys' voices. I'm not keen on walking the way they're walking.

Outside the school buildings, I see them heading down the main drive and towards town, so I turn the other way and head for the side gate that opens out onto the housing estate and the park. It'll more than double my walk home, but I'm OK with that.

As I'm crossing the road before the park, I hear someone calling my name behind me. I ignore it and speed up, but the shouting gets nearer and nearer until it's at my shoulder.

'Josh. Why didn't you stop?' It's Dana. She sounds out of breath.

'Sorry, I didn't hear you.' I look over her shoulder, up and down the street. I'm flushing with nervousness again.

She seems to know why I'm uncomfortable, 'Don't worry. Carl's nowhere near here. He's got a job this afternoon out of town.'

I relax, but only slightly.

'Can I walk home with you? Just had an hour with Amber.'

'What for?'

'Told Mrs Beasley to shove her ingredients up her arse in Cookery. And Amber never misses a chance to tell me about how crap I'm doing. "Your choices have consequences, you know." I could do with someone who makes me laugh. What were you in for?'

'Biology. Walters.'

She looks slightly startled. 'Aren't you, like, really clever though?'

I shrug my shoulders.

Dana smiles. 'Don't worry. I won't tell.' Her smile fades quickly. 'Was Alan in there with you?'

'Yeah. And a few others.'

For a second, a cloud crosses her face. But then she loops her arm through mine and starts to march me up the road, past the park. I'm going even further in the wrong direction.

We walk on up the hill for a few minutes in silence, the sound of construction machinery getting louder as we approach the edge of town and the new estate.

'I'm sorry about Friday. Carl can be horrible sometimes. But he's alright really.'

My cheek goes warm. I'm not sure what to say. So I say just that. 'I don't know what to say.'

'He shouldn't have hit you.'

'Yeah, well.'

'He just gets jealous. It's because he loves me, he

says.' Dana was starting to smile again, and there was more of a spring in her step.

I'm stuck for words again. I can't really remember the me that she was laughing with just under a week ago.

'Can you imagine that, Josh? Loving someone so much that you want to hurt other people for them? He says that he'd kill people if they threatened me. Could you kill someone?'

She stops walking. I almost fall over.

'Oh my god – I'm so sorry. I didn't…'

'What? Oh. Don't worry. It's fine.'

'No, but, with your … dad. And everything. I'm … I shouldn't…' She trails off.

We start walking again, her arm through mine, along the road that borders the park. The noises from children playing are drifting on the evening air. In a few minutes, it will be starting to get dark. Dana keeps looking across at me, as if I've got something on my face – besides the bruise, of course.

'Does it hurt?'

'No, it's fine now.'

'He really caught you proper, didn't he?'

'Can we talk about something else, please?'

We walk in silence for a few minutes. She's still looking across at me every ten paces or so.

'If all you're going to do is admire your boyfriend's handywork, I think I'd rather—'

'It's not that.'

'What then?'

'I'm trying to work you out. It's what I do. I'm good at working people out.'

'Really?'

I can't help but think about her poor choice in boyfriends.

'I'm wondering if you really mean it or not?'

'Mean what?'

'That everything's OK?'

I know I'm starting to blush. 'What do you mean?'

'Don't take this the wrong way, right?' She places her other hand on my chest as she says this, 'but your dad died, what, two years ago now?'

I breathe in hard against my tightening ribs.

'And you seem, around school, to act like it's all OK. All the teachers think you're brilliant, apparently, but you don't talk to anyone. Ever. I get that. I understand it as a coping strategy, I really do, but...'

'But what?' If I don't say something at this point I'll pass out. Speak. Breathe.

'No, I get it. When my dad left I didn't talk to anyone for months. But you're still *here*, Josh. In the world. Friday night, you were really funny. Talking about all the stuff you used to do together, what he used to say. What was it you were saying about 'listen for the moment just before the song starts'? '*Try to hear the moment of expectation*'! That's it! Had me in stitches

63

about four songs in a row! You remember that? We were listening so *hard* for it, and every time, 'nothing'. Remember?' Dana's impression of my voice, saying those words, is like pins in my gut. 'And you were so good at looking angry when the song started again. Remember you made that girl – Molly, was it? – start the same song about three times in a row. You were *so* funny! Don't you remember that?'

I don't remember. Not a single word or note. I'd been talking about Dad. At the party. And laughing. A wave of nausea hits me like a wall. It's like Saturday morning all over again.

Dana continues, 'I wondered whether that was the *real* you and this,' she indicates me with a general sweep of her arm, 'this is some kind of show? A sort of performance?'

When I speak, it's louder than I mean it to be. 'So your dad was killed too, was he? Blown up? Is that what you're saying? That you coped with it and I should act more like you?'

'No! No no no! My dad's not dead, for one thing. Mum thinks he might as well be, but he isn't. What I meant was … you were so happy talking about him I was almost convinced that … I'm not explaining myself very well, am I? Hey, let me show you something.'

She grabs my hand and starts off again at a rapid pace. We walk – almost running – to the end of the road, then turn along the front of the building site, then onto the main road where she stops in front of a hedge. One nettle dangles across the path like some kind of arrow.

'In here,' she says, and pulls me through the undergrowth. As we stumble through the greenery, I begin to feel oddly light, being led back to this place. How would she know?

Seconds later, we emerge from under the hedge, through the old wooden door which someone has put back in its place, and into the walled, square patch of garden.

We stand for a few moments, Dana still holding on to my hand, breathing heavily, looking at me.

'What do you think?'

SIXTEEN

We're sitting on the grass, Dana's knees are tucked under her skirt and she's running her hands along the long, thin leaves of the bush with purple flowers on. A few are beginning to turn black. We've been talking for a while now.

'I've been coming here for years. It used to be my grandad's land, all this. Remember that old cottage that used to be here, by the main road, before they started building?'

They'd bulldozed the land so long before the building work had started that I can't remember clearly, but there's a hazy image in my mind. 'With the yellow walls? Had a strange kind of pattern on the roof?'

'Yeah, that's it. That was my great grandad's house, apparently. He used to be the gardener for some big manor that's long gone, and they let him have that cottage to live in. Until they condemned it.'

'And no one else knows about it? About this?'

'My dad does. But he hasn't come here for years. Not since he went away. But I think he might have come back the other week. Or over the weekend maybe.'

A few yellow and blue birds flit up and land on the wall, behind which the sky is growing darker, more delicate.

Dana continues, 'I came here after school on Monday and the door had been kicked in. The lock was all broken, so I've fixed it. Took me ages. But at least now I *know* that I've got the only way in.' She holds up a key. I hadn't noticed her unlocking the door.

Dana mistakes my guilty look for one of disbelief, 'What? So because I'm not good in school I can't fix a lock?'

'No, it's not that, it's just—'

'Just that I'm not clever enough to join your little gang because I don't get on with books?' As I watch, a wall goes up behind her eyes, not as big but just as old and solid as the ones around the garden. Her garden.

'Not at all. I'd have no idea how to fix a lock. And I don't really have a little gang.'

'I had to do the door first, bought some wood filler and replaced the bits that had been broken off.' She hands me the key. 'Go and have a look, if you don't believe me.' She says it like it's a challenge.

'Alright.' I get up and go to look at the lock I'd broken. There is a hard, yellow substance where the wood used to be, rounded slightly at the edges and fitted snugly into the old wood. If not for the difference in colour, it would look like part of the door. I tap it with my fingernail. Rock solid. In the space that Dana has cut out somehow, the new lock nestles perfectly, half the mechanism buried in the wood with a gleaming, gold-coloured block that slides out from the side of the door when I turn the key. The action is smooth and satisfying somehow. A few years ago, when there had been a number of reported thefts from sheds in the area, we'd had our old shed lock replaced by a professional. It hadn't been as good a job as this.

'What tools did you use?' I ask.

Dana grins. If it was a challenge, she knows she's won. 'I've stolen a bunch from school over the years. I've pretty much got a full set now, though I have to haul them around in a plastic bag, which keeps ripping. I haven't got around to nicking a tool box yet.'

'Or making one,' I offer. 'You're really good.'

'Maybe.' The wall in Dana's eyes is coming down again. 'I just want this place to be private, you know? Special. Like this.' She walks back to the big bush with the thin leaves and purple flowers. 'This is a buddleia.'

'A bud-what?'

'A buddleia. Butterflies love them. It's nearly finished for the year now – there's only a few flowers left because autumn's been so warm. Most of them have turned black, look. But you should have seen it over the summer. You couldn't see them for butterflies.'

As if to illustrate her point, a large, black-winged butterfly with red and white tips lands on the bush above her head, stays there for a bit, then flies off again and over the wall. We watch it go.

'And this moss. It's sphagnum.' She almost runs to the wall which I'd ripped handfuls off of only last week.

'Ss-fag…' Languages have never been my strength.

'It's an astringent. You should know *that* word, Biology kid. They used it for putting on soldiers' wounds in the war.'

I remember again the warm, numb feeling that had replaced the pain in my leg.

'And in the spring, you wait, there's a whole bunch of crocuses that'll shoot up in the middle of the grass all over the place, pink, white and purple, with little yellow tongues in middle. They're waiting, underground, for the cold to pass. Then they'll pop up. Boing!' She jumps over to me.

I watch Dana go from place to place around the small, square plot, pointing at places in the ground where things will rise, or where they used to be. She shows me where birds nest in the higher branches of the buddleia and on the tops of the walls. She finishes the tour at another large bush. It has dense glossy leaves and small red stems are pushing out of the ends of the green ones. I'm not sure, but Dana seems to stiffen slightly as she pulls back a few leaves and sticks her head into the gap.

'Look in here.'

It takes a few seconds to get used to the gloom. It's getting dark anyway, and inside the bush there's not much light to see by. But I can just make out the outline of a circle, about a metre across. It's made of bricks – crumbling now. A little, circular wall about a foot high.

'That's a well,' Dana says. 'My dad reckoned it might link up to all the caves that run under this hill – you know, the old mines?'

I nod. The leaves rustle.

'He tried to send me down there once, my dad. Tied a rope around my waist when I was about seven, six maybe, and starts lowering me down, telling me to be brave. I was screaming so loud he pulled me out, said I'd bring the social services round. That was just before he left.'

We stand a few moments longer, our heads in the bush, staring at the bricked circle that swims and twitches in the fading twilight.

'I should go,' I say eventually.

'Yeah, home to get to. Mum worrying about you. I get it.'

'Something like that,' I reply.

'Listen, before you go…' The wall comes back behind Dana's eyes, bigger than before, harder, as if she's building something that will never be knocked down. 'If you tell anyone about this place, or about me showing it to you, I'll tell Carl you were with me, OK? That you hurt me. And he loves me. You get it? He. Loves. Me.'

As I leave, Dana is still standing in the middle of the grass, the key clenched tightly in her fist.

SEVENTEEN

I have to pick films carefully with Mum. Anything too dangerous or adventurous and she won't watch it, and will get angry if she knows I'm watching it on my own. And anything where people die is also risky, particularly if they're the henchmen of some evil villain, and not really people, just things that the hero has to clear out of his way as they stop him doing his job of heroing. That's why I watch so many films in my room. Films, online videos, stuff that Mum needs protecting from.

This evening, I've chosen a comedy. It's about a couple of policemen who are partnered together when they shouldn't be, and they have to bust a drugs ring. There's a couple of car chases early on, so it's pretty close to her tolerance levels. I'm not surprised when she gets up and goes to bed half an hour in.

So I do too.

In my room, I turn on my laptop and carry on watching the film. It's not very good, but I don't feel like sleeping.

An email alert pops up in the bottom corner of my screen. It's from my school account, which I haven't used in years. There was a big IT initiative when I started at school, and we were all told to sync our mailboxes at home. But after the first year, it all kind of fell away. It was a bit useful when teachers were emailing me work after Dad died, I suppose. Though I ignored most of them.

The sender's address is one I don't recognise – a list of letters and numbers. It looks like spam, but then I see the email subject. *That video you liked.*

I open it, and there's a link to a private website with a bunch of videos. The first one is the one that Alan showed me this afternoon. In a mid-film daze, I watch again as the grey, hooded head of Dana's boyfriend chases down the turbaned head of a stranger, and I listen again to the muffled sounds of his crying. The video ends this time with a close up of Carl's face, turning to look straight into the camera a few seconds after the group have all run down the street. Well, it's his mouth at least. The top half of his face is part covered by his hood, and the rest is in shadow. If you didn't know who it was, it'd be impossible to tell. But his jaw seems rigid with anger. It's as if it's in his bones. I feel I should turn it off, now, delete the email and go to sleep. But I can also see something like satisfaction in his half-smile, his gritted-teeth, angry grin.

I've been looking at it for a few minutes when Mum knocks on my half-open door. I jump a little, the headphones slipping from my ears.

'How'd it finish?'

'What?'

'The film, love. How did it finish? Any good?'

'No.' I breathe a little easier. 'Not really. As you'd expect, I guess.'

'It is what it is,' Mum says, pulling the door closed. 'Good night.'

EIGHTEEN

The next day, Jamie catches me after English and asks if I want to come and watch the old team play tomorrow morning. It's a home game, district cup, first round. I say that I might.

Eating lunch in the canteen, I sit in one of the window seats. There's a big bench that goes all the way around the edge of the dining hall, so you can sit right against the glass and look out. It's another one of those bright, clear, cold days. Autumn is well and truly here, so we had to do the inevitable lesson on poetry this morning with Mrs Burgoyne. I thought she'd forgotten this year, and I wouldn't mind if it wasn't the same poem every time, about mists and fruit getting ripe and vines and stuff. This time though, I found myself thinking of Dana's garden, and that butterfly, and the circle of bricks under the bush.

She'd asked me, at the end of the poem, what I thought of it.

I stumbled at first, then came up with 'It's like something's coming.' I'd continued, noting the confusion on her face. 'Something's on the way,' I'd said, trying not to sound too loud or too sure of myself. Trying to give her the response that I think she wanted, but with my thoughts in it too. 'Even if what's on the way – winter – is bad, it's still good to have something to look forward to.'

She'd said that it was a very interesting interpretation.

As I eat, I'm suddenly aware of someone behind me. I wait for them to move on, but they don't. I turn around to see Vince, looming like a tree. He leans in quickly, and stamps. I flinch. He seems happy with my reaction and stalks off.

As he goes, I see Dana and Alan on the other side of the canteen, looking at me. Alan raises a thumb. He gestures with it when I seem reluctant to raise one back. Dana tries to bat his arm down, looking embarrassed. I offer a single wave, a flash of a smile, then go back to looking out of the window.

Jamie finds me again on the way home, steering around the knots of younger kids that seem to fill the pavement.

'You'll never guess what,' he says.

'What?' I ask.

'Amber got me to come to her office this afternoon. Middle of double-chem, so I'm fine with that.'

'What for?'

'I figured it might be something to do with you, you know, last weekend? There's been rumours, I guess.' He looks at me, slightly guilty.

The bruise, as Mr Walters said, is still glowing. I hope it means that Jamie can't see me blush.

'Anyway, it wasn't,' Jamie continues. 'I get to her office and there's this kid there I've never seen before. Amad, Ackmed, something like that. Syrian kid, Miss Amber said. And he's there with his mum. Or she looks like his mum. Turns out this kid is starting here on Monday, and Amber wants me to be his buddy.'

I look at Jamie. I can't work out whether he feels proud to be asked, or put out. Jamie's the kind of guy who always gets asked to do things like this. He's bright, well liked and good with people.

'That's alright though, right?' I answer.

'Yeah, I guess I can be his "buddy"…' There's something Jamie's not saying. I feel like he's asking my permission.

'So what's the problem.'

He sighs a bit before he answers. 'You know Alan Almes, right?'

I nod. 'Sort of. Haven't spoken to him for years though.'

'Sure. Well, there's people saying that his brother,' Jamie looks at me sideways at this point. 'His brother and him have been doing pretty nasty stuff. Like, anti-Muslim stuff.'

I think I can tell where this is heading. The word he wants to say. To me.

'It's not that I think like that. Not at all. You know that, right? I'm not a racist.'

I nod, unsure if I want him to continue or not.

'It's just all over the place at the moment, isn't it? That's what you're supposed to think. About "*them*" or whatever. I just don't want people thinking I'm hanging out with a ... *terrorist*.'

And there it is.

NINETEEN

We don't get many Muslims here. We don't get much of anything here except more of the same, but of the things that we do get, Muslims are quite far down the list. There are two kids in our year whose parents are Polish, and one whose dad is Romanian. Maybe there's a handful of non-white kids in the whole school. That's about it for diversity.

I once heard someone say that if you've never been to England before, just seen the films and read the books, this town is what England must look like in your head. I'm not sure about that; the estates are a bit grim, and you have to really hunt if you want to see anything old, like those wooden beams crisscrossing old-fashioned houses. The real ones, I mean, not the ones they paint on the posher estates. There's a stone archway and crest above the entrance to the shopping centre. Not much else. On the high street there's a few shops amongst the coffee chains. Beyond that, there's the estates. Then it's mostly just fields. Occasionally, some traveller families set up just off the bypass and everyone talks about it for weeks, reminds you to double-lock your doors, sheds, cars, wallets. They say things like 'Give 'em an inch…' and everyone knows what they mean, whether they agree or not.

There's a lady who used to do the washing and ironing for Mum. She'd put the ironing board up in front of the TV and watch the news in our living room. She revelled in telling the TV what she thought. 'Foreigners' this and 'immigrants' that. Her husband lost his job at a local factory that was closing down. They made light-fittings, or something like that. Whatever it was she was, angry about his job being 'taken' and seemed to be blaming 'them'. She'd always ask if there were any of 'them' at my school. She'd heard lots of stories about 'them', what 'they' got up to, what 'they' ate. 'We're as English as the hills around here,' she used to say to anyone else in the house, then make some comment about the white horses carved into the hillsides. So, I guess people around here are very 'English'. And there's a heap of assumptions thrown in with that word that you can almost hear dripping from the sides of some of their mouths. English means Natural. It means Normal. It means Native. Whatever that is.

So the word 'terrorist' doesn't really fit in here, even though it's been used a lot lately – on the news, online, in the classrooms – and I still don't know how I feel about it. Every time I hear it, I think of Dad. *Victim of terrorists*, killed by an *Act of Terror*. And that makes me angry. Why does someone have the right to take away a person's life for living in a different way from them?

But that's just the point, I think. They don't have the right. That's what makes them terrorists.

Maybe people are just too scared of each other, or of people and things they don't know. Dad worked in London a lot, and me and mum used to go to meet him sometimes. Quite often actually. We'd do the standard tourist stuff – go to the theatre, do the London Eye, have dinner in Chinatown maybe. Or a few times we went to exhibitions, grabbed some food from a street market, or somewhere like that. I'm not saying I saw a lot of the world, but I think I saw a bit more of it than people do who never leave here. The woman that did the ironing never knew why we bothered. 'You'll never get me in one of them foreign places,' she used to say. I think she meant London as well.

I'm not sure what I'm saying, but I get this hot feeling in my stomach when people throw that word around. *Terrorist.* It's all over the newspapers. That's why Mum won't have any in the house. It's why I have to get all my news (when I want it) on my laptop, normally after she's gone to bed.

A while back, about six months after the explosion, Mum was asked to appear on some TV show and talk about what was being done about Muslim communities as a result of all of the attacks that kept happening. I think she was supposed to say how terrible it was that people were turning violent, and that we had to stay peaceful and not let *our* anger spill out and treat *them* as some of *them* treated *us*. She never did it, of course, and she only told me about it after she'd said no, spitting out the 'them's and the 'us'es. I do remember hearing her swearing down the phone a few times to mysterious callers though – that must have been it. I wouldn't have liked to be the person that asked her.

And then I think of the video that I watched – that I chose to watch – last night. And how I almost watched it a third time. And I think of that half-grin, half-snarl at the end. And my stomach gets hot again.

Of course, I say none of this to Jamie, who's still looking at me and waiting for a response to the word he's used.

I'd like to say, 'he's not a terrorist'. But I don't. I just feel my cheeks burning even more under my bruise.

I'd like to ask Jamie if he's asking my permission to look after a kid with brown skin because my dad was murdered by a person with maybe a slightly different shade of brown skin, which somehow makes me an expert on the matter.

I'd like to show Jamie that video and ask him if he thinks *that's* OK, and whether he'd just stand by and watch that kind of thing happen, which is what it feels I've done by watching it. I'd like to ask him if *that's* OK.

I'd like to ask him what that smile on Dana's boyfriend's face at the end of that video is all about and I'd like to ask him whether, if I spend more time with her, her boyfriend might smile like that after doing to me what he did to the man in the turban, the man who might not even have been Muslim – not that it mattered to Dana's boyfriend, I guess – and whether he'd stand by and watch *that* happen as well.

I'd like to do all of these things. But I don't. I just keep walking.

'See you tomorrow?' Jamie calls after me as I leave him at the top of his road.

TWENTY

Saturday, and I'm hunched on the side lines at the recreation ground. The weather's turned; it's drizzling, and even though there's only been a few hours of it, it feels like it won't stop until March.

Jamie and a few of the other guys – Will and Mike – nod hello as they jog out of the changing rooms and onto the pitch. Being here again brings a few memories back. Sights, sounds, smells. I don't think the smell in those changing rooms will ever leave me – a mixture of damp socks, deodorant and that sharp, hospital smell you get from deep-heat spray. On days like today, when it's cold and damp, a cloud of smell wafts over the field every time the door opens.

Ben was always last out of the changing room, and still is. He's got a strange ritual about touching all the benches in a certain order before he steps outside, and the rest of the team just leave him to get on with it. As he sidles past, heading for the goal which he'll guard for the first half, he says that I'm like a bus. 'Don't see you for ages, then twice in two weeks!'

'Yep, a really crap, slow bus.' I smile. And I start to admit to myself that I've missed this.

It's not much of a game, the ball skidding around

on the surface and neither team able to get it under control. There's a goal apiece at the end of the first thirty minutes, both of them scrappy and more by accident than design.

At half time, it seems that Mike's mum still brings quartered oranges for everyone. I watch her in the centre circle, handing them out, collecting the skins in another bag. Will's dad, the manager since Jamie's dad left, is giving his usual talk. At one point, everyone turns my way and they wave. I wave back, a little confused.

Standing on the left wing and ready to start the second half, a kid called George tells me they've been told to play up because I'm watching and I might want my spot on the team back.

I grin, 'Maybe.'

They end up losing three – one.

'Some mascot you turned out to be,' Ben half-jokes on his way back to the changing room. He's covered in mud and doesn't look happy.

'Good to see you again Josh,' says Will's dad as he passes, not so muddy but just as deflated. 'You're welcome to bring your boots any time, you know. You can see we're lacking in the middle of the park.' He gestures over his shoulder at the field of their recent defeat. 'The lads'd like to have you back, I think. Those passes you used to make are sorely missed, wouldn't you say?'

I smile, 'Yeah, maybe,' and watch his departing back, shoulders stooped, as he trudges off.

I walk home, and consider going past Dana's garden, but the rain is starting to trickle down inside the hood of my coat, and the thought of pushing through wet nettles doesn't appeal to me too much. Besides which, I don't have a key, and Dana would probably kill me herself if she found out I'd broken her new lock, never mind asking Carl to do it for her.

Mum seems oddly buoyant when I come through the back door. It's a rare occasion she comes home from her parents' this early on a Saturday and I'm surprised to see her.

'Josh,' she half-whispers, conspiratorially. 'There's a girl in the living room.'

'What?'

'In. There.' She points over her shoulder with her thumb, as if I don't know where the living room is. 'She's waiting for you. Gosh, you're soaking.'

It must be someone posh. Mum only says things like 'gosh' and makes a fuss of me when she has people to impress. She peels my coat off and more or less pushes me through the door of the sitting room, thrusting two scalding hot mugs of tea into my hands as she does so, spilling some on the carpet. 'Give her one of these,' she hisses. And then, in her 'gosh' voice, 'I'll leave you two alone for a while.'

Dana stands up as I spin into the room.

TWENTY ONE

'Hi.' She sounds sheepish, out of place.

'Hi.' So do I.

We stand and look at each other for a little bit, then I hand her a cup of tea and we sit down. At her feet, her school bag yawns, zip open. There are a few dog-eared exercise books and a cracked biro on the coffee table.

'I told your mum we had a revision date,' Dana offers.

'Oh.'

We go back to silence. I run a thumb across the scrolled paper of her books.

'I actually am a little bit behind.'

'So, do you want to…'

'Only if you…'

'Yeah, OK. Sure.'

At the window, the rain persists. We watch it for a while.

'My mum had some friends over. She told me I had to get out.'

'So you came here?'

'Yeah, is that OK?'

I'm not sure, yet. It can't have been her first choice. We sip our tea. I've got a strange feeling that the wet world outside and all the small channels of water are about to unhook themselves from whatever it is that they're hooked to, and the whole lot will slowly slip away, leaving just this room and its window looking out on nothingness.

'Oi!' I'm shaken from my daydream.

'Sorry. Shall we… er?'

'Your room? Sure. Why not?'

I can think of one good reason. A big reason. With hard fists.

Dana seems to know what I'm thinking. 'I do just want to revise though. Right?' Her eyes narrow at me. Suddenly I want to go and stand out in the rain and flow away with the great unhooking of everything. Then she smiles a bit, throwing the pen and her books back into her bag.

'Come on then. Where is it?'

We do about an hour's worth of revision. Sciences, mostly. Then Mum calls up the stairs. We come down to beans on toast – not burnt. Mum really is making an effort – and more tea.

'So you two know each other from school?'

'Yeah, a bit. And Josh is really good, and I'm really behind and not that good, so I asked if he could help.'

'You didn't say that, Josh. I wish you'd have let me

know Dana was coming today. I almost wasn't here – found Dana dripping under our tiny porch. It looked like she'd been there for hours.'

'Sorry, Mum.'

'No, it's fine, love. I'll wait until you're done to run the hoover round. Now, who's for flapjack? Nanna did a batch yesterday, Josh. Said they were for you, to make sure you stay big and strong. He loves his nanna's flapjack, Dana.'

I can feel Dana grinning, Mum grinning back.

'Look at him, Dana, if it weren't for that big bruise, he'd be as red as a tomato all over!'

Back upstairs again, I can tell that Dana's lost interest in working. She starts to flick her pen against my desk while I sit on the bed and talk about osmosis through a semi-permeable membrane.

'What's a perm-able what?'

'Semi-permeable. It means it lets some things through. Really small things.'

'I'm bored. Can we do something else?'

I lean over her to pluck a Chemistry textbook from the shelf over the desk, and she jabs a playful hand into my armpit. Three books tumble off the shelf, one hitting her on the head, another upending the dregs of cold tea.

'Jesus, careful.' She picks up her notes, shakes off the tea.

I step back towards the bed. 'Sorry.'

'I didn't mean more work.'

'So … what then?'

'Just … talk and stuff.'

I sit down again. 'About what?'

'I don't know. Stuff.' She's intently concentrating on the loosening end of tape that's holding her biro together.

'OK.'

The rain has stopped, but there's a slow and steady drip from the gutter above my window. I count drips; one, two, three.

I get to twelve before she speaks.

'Do you want me to go?'

'No.'

'God's sake, Josh, why don't you just—'

'Why did you come here?' The question surprises me as much as her.

'I … I don't know. I don't really have many friends at school that I can drop in on.'

'So the guy that your boyfriend beat up last week is an obvious first choice?' I'm angry. I hadn't realised.

It's Dana's turn to watch the window. The grey light catches in the small pools that are forming at the corners of her eyes.

'I'm sorry,' I say. 'It's not a problem.'

'Yeah,' she sniffs, wiping her eyes with a sleeve. 'It is. I feel really bad about last weekend, and I guess I thought that if I came over then we could…' There's a long pause before she continues, and she wipes her eyes again. 'I don't know. I guess I thought you'd like me again like you did last week if I came over.'

'You're not the one who hit me. Why wouldn't I like you?'

'Because you don't really know me.'

'Maybe. But on Thursday…'

'I'm sorry about what I said on Thursday. At the end. When you were going.'

'It's fine,' I say. But again I'm not quite sure.

'I've never shown anyone that place before. I guess I was scared I got it wrong. I think I showed you because, last week, it felt like you would understand it. That you'd like it. Because of what happened to your dad and everything and how you don't seem…'

I wonder, in the pause that follows, about all the things I don't seem.

'You don't seem … too … *affected*. Like, I'm sure you are and everything, but you seem to have it together, you know? Like you're *coping* with it. Like you know how to act. Last week at that party.' She spoke now as if something had unhooked the words from inside her, and they were all flowing out like the stream of fallen rain. 'You were laughing, and it felt, somehow, like you actually *meant* it. I mean, I've been trying to laugh like that for ages. Years. And I can't. I can't seem to mean it. And Carl, he doesn't get it. I don't think he really wants to get it. He just wants …what he wants.' Dana hugs herself tightly at this point and shivers a little, as if unwanted imaginary hands have come to rest on her shoulders, in the small of her back. 'But you. I can't figure you out. It's not like being near him. I can't go there at the moment because… I just can't, not at the moment. Sometimes… Sometimes, Carl doesn't get it. He doesn't understand that I don't want to be near him.'

'Oh. OK.'

Dana looks directly at me. 'Can I tell you something, Josh? For some reason I feel I can trust you. Maybe it's because you never speak to anyone.'

I offer a weak smile.

'It's not just "sometimes" when Carl doesn't get it.' Her eyes bore into me. Through me, almost. There's no wall in her eyes at all now. They're dark, deep and crystal clear. 'Do you understand what I'm saying?'

I nod. There's a grown-up part of me that wants to understand what Dana's talking about. But it's not big enough, regardless of how it seems to her.

'It's like I told you about my dad lowering me down that hole in the ground. It's like it was exciting at first, with Carl. He was so protective, and I really needed that. I think. I felt all grown up, you know? And it was fun, too, I guess. And then it wasn't. Then it *really* wasn't.' Dana goes back to picking at the flap of tape on the biro. 'It was like being in that well when I was seven. It was my seventh birthday – did I tell you that? Dad took me for a special big girl's picnic in the garden. "It'll be our secret," he said. I was so happy at first, just me and him. And then he got the rope out of his bag and said we were going to play an adventure game. It was exciting at first, and I trusted him. But then something switched. He lowered me inside and I started asking him to stop, to take me back up. And he stopped listening to me. I couldn't get out, not on my own, no matter how much I screamed.' Dana has gotten through the tape and is cracking needles of plastic from the broken end of the pen. 'Carl's a bit like that. And you know those times in your dreams when you're screaming but no noise will come out? And you're scared you've lost your voice completely but then you realise it's not that, it's that you're falling down a well or something, and falling so fast that your mouth is packed full of air and you can't…'

She stops. Stops like her words have hit the bottom of that well and are lying there, heavy and broken.

I want to get off the bed and go to her and stop the tears on her cheeks. I know I should do it, but the words are lying on me as well. Heavy on top of the anger and confusion of *coping with it*. Fallen on the dead ground of *knowing how to act*. I feel completely useless in my anger, unable to see past it.

And even if I wasn't angry, what does Dana expect me to *do* about it? She saw what happened when Carl caught me just talking to her. She had a front-row seat. I don't know why she's telling me this.

I don't even move as she gets up and leaves. I just listen as she bangs down the stairs, listen to Mum's surprised call of 'goodbye' after her, listen as her footsteps in the long puddle of the outside world quickly unhook and fade away.

At the window, the gutter is still dripping. I count: one, two, three…

TWENTY TWO

Mum doesn't ask about Dana for the rest of the weekend. I'm so thankful I could hug her. But I don't.

On Monday, I quietly avoid everyone. I go back to being in the middle of the class as we pass through the halls and doorways, sit in the middle of the lesson, hiding in plain sight. Hands go up all around me, conversations radiate outwards from my calm and quiet centre. I'm wrapped again in that cloud of silence that descended when Dad died, but this time I've summoned it back. It's nicer in here. It's comfortable.

It's there on Tuesday. Even when Jamie tries to introduce me to the new kid, Ahmed, who smiles when Jamie tries really hard to pronounce his name right, and then says it again himself in this warm, soft voice, and gives me his hand to shake while Jamie smiles, and they both keep smiling at me as I walk away. It's still there, like a soft blanket.

And again, on Wednesday, when Jamie and Ahmed are in the canteen, talking. And when they walk straight past me at the window as I'm looking out at the drizzle, at the last few wet leaves clinging to the trees, the cloud is there, helping me. I'm glad they don't stop and try to talk to me. I'm glad they don't see me.

And that afternoon, in English, when Mrs Burgoyne asks me a question that I don't hear, and when she doesn't ask me again, I know the cloud's still there. As I walk out of the room, I'm glad she doesn't ask me to stay behind like she could have if I wasn't inside the cloud. I'm glad she just looks at me with those pitying eyes again, with *the look*, with eyes that follow me all the way out of the room.

On Thursday, I just nod when Mr Walters says he expects to see me for more catch-up work in his after-school session. When I arrive, I sit in the same seat. Vince and Alan watch me cross the room. Alan smiles. Vince doesn't. I'm vaguely aware of another figure in the back row, probably the other one – Brandon – head on the desk and covered with a coat.

It's the same as last week: Mr Walters reads his newspaper; I work through a few pages of the A Level text book, this time on genetics; the others do whatever it is they have to do. And again, at the same time, Mr Walters goes out to make his tea.

Alan is at my desk in a flash. 'I see you've been on the website.'

'What?' I ask, realising I'm out of the habit of speaking again; I'm far too loud. Vince turns around, bares his teeth.

'The videos. You were on there a few times this week. I can tell. Monday night, or very early Tuesday morning – you not sleeping or something?' For the briefest of seconds, his concern seems genuine. 'And again yesterday evening. My brother set up this thing.' He takes his phone out. On the screen are rows of digits and symbols. 'These are dates and times, and these are computer addresses. This one's you, I think.' He points to a string of numbers. 'I don't really get it. He's a fucking genius with computers, my brother. It's what he did when he was in.' Alan's grin is so genuine it's almost infectious.

'In?' A horse whisper this time. I'm reeling from my week of silence being broken by such enthusiasm.

'In the army. Before he left.'

I hadn't meant to go back to that site. And I didn't watch any videos, just stared at the screen, at a dozen or so thumbnails, freezeframes of streets at night, the back of a few hooded heads.

'This is you, I think.' He points again to the string of numbers. I'm not sure he's pointing to the same one as last time. 'Like I said, I'm not sure how it works. But did you see this?' He opens a new window on his phone. It's a local news website, with a headline 'Increasing Hate-Crime Threatens Families' and a picture of some houses. I recognise them as the ones on Jamie's estate. There's something written in red paint on one of the garage doors, but I can't read it. Alan jerks the phone back into his pocket as Mr Walters comes back into the room.

'Alan?'

'Sorry, Sir, just asking Josh about something.' He stays at my bench, casually leaning on it with his elbow. 'I'm really interested in,' he leans further over, staring at the page of the textbook, 'gun-etics. Gun attacks? Is that in Biology sir?'

Vince makes his fingers into a gun and shoots Alan. Alan's mock-death is carried off with lots of moaning and chest clutching, until Vince puts his finger-barrel to Alan's head and finishes him off.

'You mean *genetics*, Alan, you foul and devious cretin. Don't get involved, Josh. Alan is a foul and devious cretin.'

'Aw, Sir, and I thought you liked me.'

'And for my sins, Alan, I do. I too must be a cretin.'

Alan begins to sidle back to his seat. Mr Walters warms to his theme.

'For some reason, Alan, I do in truth see some value in you. Some faint glimmer of hope that, contrary to your own insidious actions—'

'What's insidious mean, Sir?' Vince pipes up.

'It means bad, Vince. Bad and getting worse. Contrary to Alan's insidious actions, I do believe there resides within him the ability to be a decent human being and to live a long and purposeful life.'

'Is immigration insidious, Sir? Like that new Muslim kid?'

'That, Vince, is another matter for which we have no time. Pack your things. I'll see you next week.' He looks over my shoulder, to the back bench and the figure under the coat. 'You too, Dana, for what good it's done you.'

I spin around so fast my stool wobbles violently, just in time to see the door close behind her.

TWENTY THREE

I can't avoid Alan and Vince this week. They stay and talk to Mr Walters for a while and I leave first, trying to glimpse which way Dana might have gone, but she's too quick. I run to one end of the corridor and quickly conclude that she must have gone the other way. I hear Mr Walters' raised voice behind me as Vince and Alan leave the room.

They catch up with me as I emerge from the science block into the seemingly endless drizzle. I was right. Dana must have taken the other exit. There's no sign of her.

'Not trying to avoid us again, Milton?' Vince snarls as he knocks past me.

'I told you, Vinny, Josh is one of us.' Alan's on my other shoulder. 'He knows what these insidious people can do. What they're capable of. Don't you Josh?'

I know that any change in speed or direction isn't an option.

'He knows what these scum can do, first hand. He's been *affected*.'

That word, used like that, where had I heard that before? I keep walking, my eyes on the floor.

'Josh knows what these murdering mudskins do.

Don't you, Josh? How they worship a god who says murder is OK, expected even, in his name? It's like a death cult.'

Vince is so close I can smell the damp, cigarette scent of his breath. I feel it rolling, dark and oily, over my hair and down the side of my face.

'Josh has been on the front lines. He's a casualty. And now there's one of them here. A filthy murderer parading around in our school, in Josh's school. Isn't there, Josh?'

I can feel the stitches in my coat pockets starting to stretch and gape as I push my hands deeper, harder into them. But I don't look up.

'One of those mudskins with blood on his filthy hands.'

I ache for the cloud to come back down and take me, to wrap me up again. I urge it to come and surround me with silence again. I keep walking.

'Josh is angry, Vince. He's angry and he's right to be angry. It's disgusting that the school's let it happen, given the circumstances. It makes you sick, right, Josh?'

I want the world to turn vague, to unhook and float away. But it won't. It's clear and it's hard and it's right in front of me, pressing against the tip of my nose.

'It makes me sick, Josh. Watching him walk around like it's all OK. Like it's all forgotten. I can't imagine how it must be for you.'

And it feels like I'm falling into the hardness and the clearness. Falling so fast I want to scream but I can't.

'I can't imagine being you, Josh. One of those people walking around your town. Going to your school. One of those mudskins who killed your dad.'

Then something snaps and I'm running, running hard, my bag thudding into my back, my lungs burning, my legs trying to break the realness of the pavement and the puddles, the pure fire in my stomach rising higher and higher, the prickling sweat under my arms. Vince runs after me and I don't care, then I hear Alan call him back like a bad dog. The last thing I hear Alan say is 'See you on Sunday!' But I'm not listening, just running, running, and I don't know where I'm running to.

Until I do.

TWENTY FOUR

When I was eight, we went to my grandma's funeral – my dad's mum. It was an open casket, and she had been made up to look healthy and glowing. But Dad's coffin at Westminster Abbey had been closed. There was nothing in it anyway. It was just for the ceremony, glowing with polish but completely empty.

At his private funeral, the week before the Westminster Abbey one, we'd stood around Dad's actual closed coffin as they lowered it into the ground of the woodland cemetery. As the first handful of cold earth landed on the dark wood, and the noise of its landing became muffled by the earth we threw on next, it got even more closed. And then we planted a tree.

I sometimes wonder – if all the thirty-nine people who died that day had trees planted for them, how big a forest would that make?

Not a very big one.

Dad's tree is still pretty young and limp. There's a cylinder of dirty, once-transparent plastic around the bottom of it to keep it from being eaten by deer.

They get a lot of deer in the woodland cemetery.

I don't come here very much. I know I should do

more often, with Mum, but I don't know what I'd do or what good I'd be. I don't know what I'd say to him.

I don't know what you say to a tree.

He's under there, somewhere. In the ground. The roots won't have got to him yet, so I guess there's not much of Dad in the tree. I dreamt, a while ago, that the tree was wearing all of Dad's clothes; a clean, white shirt that smelled like ironing; one of his old-fashioned ties with the little flowers on that I used to try and count when I was younger; the polished, black shoes with tiny holes in that he'd wear to work if he had important meetings.

I still haven't dreamt about Dad properly, just the tree. I told this to Mum a while back, and she told me it was normal. She'd had the same dream over and over again about carrying his pannier bag around. It was the pannier that he always took to work, either to the office or if he was off to London; the one that had always sat in the hallway at home every evening before bed, every morning before he left, until it was lost along with him. She was trying to find him so she could give it back. Her counsellor had told her it might be ages until he started coming to her in dreams. She might hear his voice in the background, or see his things, but that he – the whole of him – wouldn't come for a while. She said – the counsellor – that it's only after we've let go of the objects around the person that the memory of that person will become clear again. And then he'll come and see us in our dreams.

Mum said it made it easier, knowing that he'd come back when she was ready for him. But I don't know. Like so many things at the moment, I'm not sure. I just want to see Dad. Especially now.

I want to ask him what I should do. If he's angry at me. If he's OK down there under the tree. But I can't. I stand, useless, watching the bare twigs flop around in the wind.

It's started properly raining now, heavy and slow, the wind starting to build behind it. As I stand, looking, the heat in my stomach and chest slowly cooling, the pain in my legs subsiding, I notice that the tree isn't completely bare. There's one leaf left, a big one, brown and hand-shaped, its five long, curled fingers waving, flailing. The kind of leaf you only get on this sort of tree.

But I don't know what kind of tree this is.

'I don't know what tree this is,' I say aloud.

Suddenly, the fact of not knowing what tree it is that marks Dad's grave is the worst thing I've ever admitted, and tears spring up, hot and stinging, running down my cheeks, over the bruise that's starting to fade, and drop to the ground at my feet.

I cry harder when I think that this is all I can give him, just a few drops of my hot, angry tears that blur with the rain and fall slowly through the earth to his body, down there somewhere underneath the tree and its roots.

What will he do with those?

And without thinking I lash out at the first thing I can.

And I watch as the last leaf of Dad's tree, ripped and shredded, is caught on a gust of wind and lifts into the grey sky.

TWENTY FIVE

When I get home, I can still feel the raw rings around my eyes – no need to look in the mirror. Mum doesn't take much convincing, and I don't go to school the next day.

I sleep in late, and wake to a cup of tea on the bedside table that's already gone cold. I can hear Mum clattering around downstairs. I feel strangely cleaner than yesterday. Yesterday, I felt covered and caked in thick mud from the moment I left Dad's tree until the moment, who knows how many hours later, when I fell into bed. Today, my head doesn't feel groggy anymore; everything is less fuzzy.

After a shower, I go downstairs. Since Dana's visit, Mum's gone back to burning the toast, but I'm not hungry anyway and it's too late for breakfast. She's taken the day off work. She often does on Fridays.

'Do you want to come with me this weekend, love?'

'Where?'

'Nanna and Grandad's. They've not seen you for months, Josh. It'd be nice if you came.'

I think about the prospect of spending another weekend on the sofa watching bad TV, or staring at the rain running down the windows. Or, worse, staring at the screen of my laptop; at the website I know I'll go back to if left alone.

'OK.'

In the car we listen to the radio for a while until the news comes on and Mum turns it off. We sit in silence. I pull my phone out of my pocket and plug in my headphones. Mum gives me that look where I think she's going to say something, but maybe she's forgotten how and her eyes return to watching the road. The red lights and headlamps of the cars on the motorway all repeat for a second in the raindrops before the mechanical arm wipes the windscreen clear, only to build back up again.

After a few minutes, I'm bored. I pop open the glove box. First aid kit, a couple of spare bulbs, can of energy drink that must be years old by now. Dad's things. I smile.

'Your dad always was a practical man. Prepared for anything. Even if he didn't like driving, he did it properly!'

I nod, take my headphones out.

'He'd have been glad to see you yesterday.'

I pause, shocked into silence. How did she know?

'Whatever I may be at the moment, Josh, I'm still your mother. And mothers know.'

This is one of the ways I remember her, my mum, back before she was like she is now: hands on the steering wheel, eyes dead ahead. But I was always in the back seat, surrounded by sleeping bags and boxes of camping equipment as we headed down through France, or up through Welsh mountains, or to any number of holidays or weekends away. They were always her idea. Dad would be sitting where I am now as I sweated it out in the back. Dad's hand would idly rest on the back of Mum's neck, giving her an occasional rub and he'd ask if she wanted him to take over. She always said no, which was a good thing as Dad was invariably asleep within a few minutes of asking her. Me and Mum would talk then, in slightly hushed whispers, about everything. She was surprisingly good at football tactics and pulled no punches when talking about the weaknesses of the rest of my team. We talked about school and her work and my friends, about what we'd do when we got where we were going. She loved – at these times – to set me little challenges for our trip, like 'spot five new kinds of tree a day' or 'wake up early and record the first birdsong on your phone'. I loved completing them, and we'd talk on the way home, while Dad slept, about what I'd seen, or heard, or collected.

But we don't do that anymore.

She turns the radio on again, the news having safely finished. We listen in silence for the rest of the journey.

Nanna and Grandad's house is probably like all Nannas' and Grandads' houses in the world. From the kerb, the net curtains hang neat and quiet in the windows, and there's always a couple of empty milk bottles on the front step. Inside, after you've taken your shoes off in the porch and walked into the hallway with its bright carpet, there is that reassuring grandparent smell – mostly dust and laundry with a bit of cooking thrown in. Things will never change here, and walking in makes me feel like I'm six years old again: warm and comfortable.

Grandad's coming in through the back door from the garden, his jumper wet at the neck where his coat wasn't done all the way up, grey trousers tucked into mottled brown socks. The only time I've ever seen him dressed differently was their Golden Wedding Anniversary about three years ago; that day he was wearing a light blue suit and tie. He looked very uncomfortable, especially when Nanna kept sticking his hair down every few minutes and generally making a fuss.

Almost at the same moment, Nanna comes into the hallway from the living room – the front room, they call it. The sitting room is at the back, in the conservatory. She's got her cleaning apron on, duster in her hand. They both say 'Hello dear,' to Mum at the same time.

Then they spot me.

Since I can remember, Grandad's always squeezed

my shoulder to say hello, giving it a little shake, like he's rocking you backwards and forwards. He never does a full hug – the shoulder squeeze is as close as he gets. Well, almost. He used to do it to Dad too, but he'd shake his hand as well as squeeze his shoulder, rocking him backwards and forwards in rhythm with the handshake. Since Dad died, I've been granted this full handshake and shoulder version as if I'm an adult. This time, the squeeze is so hard it almost hurts, and it lasts for much longer too. I'm rocked so much I almost fall backwards, then I actually do stumble forward a bit into Grandad. It's almost a hug. Nanna's greeting is less restrained as she ticks off all the clichés on the Nanna list; cheek tugging, kisses, hugs, holding me at arm's length to look at me, commenting on how much I've grown. The whole thing takes about five minutes.

We sit around their big kitchen table and have a cup of tea. Nanna's made more flapjack and keeps apologising that there isn't enough (even though the deep tin is brim-full of little, bitesize squares). She didn't know I was coming. She'll have to stretch the joint out (lamb tonight) but it should be fine if Grandad can bring in a few more leeks and carrots from the veggie patch.

I answer all their questions about school, about how my friends are, and manage to keep my blushes to a minimum when they ask about the still-just-visible bruise on my cheek. I can't control the blushes when they ask about Dana though – Mum must have told them – and Grandad gives me some brief advice about women.

'Don't try to understand them, Josh. Just be as nice as you can be.'

Nanna hits him with the duster.

'Thanks, Grandad. I'll keep that in mind.'

As Mum talks to Grandad about his garden, Nanna busies herself with putting more freshly boiled water in the teapot and re-filling the plate of flapjacks from the seemingly bottomless tin. I've forgotten just how orderly this house is, how well everything seems to sit with everything else. There's the porcelain salt and pepper pots in the middle of the table, shaped like a boy and girl. Nanna always places them so they look as if they're holding hands. On the top shelf of the dresser, in front of the posh plates that never get used, stand the same row of my school pictures, from Year One right up until the one from last spring. And the people in the room as well; they fold into kitchen chairs like it's the most natural place to be in the world.

I watch Mum as she talks with Grandad. Mostly she's listening. He tells her about the right time to 'put the garden to bed', what needs covering for the winter and what needs leaving, when to get your early potatoes in. I think of Dana's garden; how it doesn't seem to need much looking after. From how she talks about it, everything just seems to happen on its own.

Mum is always sad, but even though she's smiling at her father, nodding along and asking questions, she seems sadder here than she does at home. Nanna comes and puts a hand on her shoulder and asks whether Grandad could do aubergines again next year, or if she'll have to make do with courgettes, courgettes, courgettes again as normal.

Maybe that's why Mum looks so sad. For her, there is no 'as normal' anymore. She grew up in this house, surrounded by its warmth, its everything fitting with everything else: the people, the furniture, everything so solid, secure, immovable. She probably thought this would be how she and Dad would end up. And then, for her, for both of us, it's like someone took that future and shook it so hard that all the pieces have flown apart. All those pieces that used to fit are now so far away from each other that it's impossible to remember what fitted with what.

And there are some very big pieces missing altogether.

Dinner that night tastes like old times, and afterwards, as hasn't happened for years, Nanna gets the photo albums out.

'I don't suppose anyone has these anymore, do they?' she ponders, as she always does, lifting the heavy, leather-bound book from its almost sacred place on the bookshelf. 'With all of the internets and Face-whatsit-webs, no one prints photos anymore, do they?'

'No, Nanna,' I say, smiling.

'Now shuffle up, and let Nanna embarrass you with old-fashioned technology.'

We look at some of my old birthday pictures from when I was a toddler. I can just about recognise myself in the bright-eyed, blond child staring out from the cellophane wallet the picture is held in. There are other children around me, few of whom I recognise, most of whom I haven't seen since. Not long after my fifth birthday, we moved away from Nanna and Grandad's town to where we live now.

There are pictures of steam trains, and me looking proud on the platform. Pictures of walks on the beach at what seem ridiculous times of year to visit the seaside, especially considering how far away it is. Pictures of me and Mum and Nanna and Grandad on a big, fallen tree in the middle of a field somewhere. And lots of lots of pictures of Dad. His arm over my shoulder as I'm painting, me sitting on his lap as he talks to someone out of shot, him and Mum in the background, cuddling, as I'm racing Grandad across a park.

And then there are the blank spaces, at the back. 'This one's for your sixteenth birthday, if you'll let us come,' says Nanna with a nudge. 'And this for your first driving lesson, first trip to the pub, first girlfriend...'

After the laughing stops, we put the album away. There's a show on TV about celebrities that Nanna always insists on watching.

That night, in the bed that Mum used to sleep in, I dream once more of Dad's tree. It's on its own in a big field, and there are very small people climbing it. They all get to a certain point, then jump off and start climbing from the bottom again. The more I watch, the more it looks like a trail of ants going up and up the tree. I panic and start to brush them away with my hand, but then they're all climbing on me, jumping off my arms and starting again at my legs. And then I don't have legs anymore, but a trunk, and branches for arms, and I can't stop the tiny ant people as they climb and jump, climb and jump, climb and jump.

TWENTY SIX

We're halfway up the hill behind Nanna and Grandad's house, squelching through mud and hunched against the wind that, thankfully, isn't full of rain this morning. I've borrowed a pair of Grandad's wellies; the fact that they almost fit me drew more squeals from Nanna about how much I'd grown. Further ahead, Mum's talking with Nanna, their arms linked as they negotiate the bigger puddles. Grandad and I are a little slower. My feet aren't quite as sure as I'd like in these big boots that knock against my knees, and he keeps stopping and poking the undergrowth with a stick.

'Mushroom season, Josh,' he keeps explaining. 'It's a good, damp one this year, but a touch too cold I'd say.' He ushers me down into a ditch to show me a line of what look like eggs, stood in a neat little row all along a rotting tree-stump. 'Puffballs. When they get ripe, they'll explode.'

I can't pretend I'm that interested. When he starts talking about 'mycology', and how the 'mycelium' is actually a giant web of interconnected fibres that can span huge areas, I know I should be a little more enthusiastic. For some reason, probably the Thursday sessions, my interest in biology isn't very high at the moment.

As we get towards the top of the hill, the scrubby woods give way to more sandy terrain, with low gorse bushes speckled with yellow flowers. Grandad picks one and pops it in his mouth.

'Want one?'

I shake my head.

'Now, look at this, Josh!' He's stooped at the side of a larger gorse bush, his fingers holding back a tuft of grass at the base of what is, actually, quite an impressive mushroom. It looks like the ones in kids' books – a flat, red disc on the top of a long, straight stem, covered in little white flecks. The edge is starting to curl back on itself, and the white bits underneath are going slightly orange. Beneath it, there's a slightly smaller version, it's top not yet flat, but even redder, even shinier, like a snooker ball.

'Can we eat those?' I ask.

'Only if you want a quick way to shuffle off this mortal coil,' Grandad replies. 'These are *fly agarics*, Josh. Very poisonous indeed. Best left alone, but very good for looking at.'

I nod, trying to look interested.

As we watch, a small black beetle crawls over the rim of the smaller one's top. It twitches this way and that before it's joined by another one. Under the gorse bush, there's a small bird hopping around, probably trying to keep out of the wind. I wonder what it would be like to be a small creature; a creature small enough that this mushroom, or this gorse bush, could be my whole world.

'Yep, kill you straight off, these buggers will.' Grandad wakes me from my daydream. 'Or they'll make you very high. Now let's catch up.'

The question I was going to ask rides the wave of my surprise and comes out as a splutter. 'Grandad?'

Yes, Josh? Grandad doesn't miss a beat, his eyes sparkling with humour.

I regather my composure. 'If I wanted to plant something now that would come up early in the spring, what kind of thing should I plant?'

'To flower early in the spring? Easy. Narcissi.'

'What?'

'Daffodils.'

'Oh. The yellow ones?'

'Or you can get white varieties. Orange trumpets. Gorgeous.'

'So I'd plant the seeds now?'

'They don't come from seeds. Well, they do, but most people grow them from bulbs.'

I suddenly remember planting bulbs with Mum when I was very young. We'd put them in pots and soil and leave them on a high shelf in the shed over the winter. Then, in the spring, when they were starting to sprout a thin, green finger, we'd put moss all around the bottom and a few stones and give them to Dad's parents on their annual visit, and to Nanna for her birthday in February. I ask Grandad what they were.

'Hyacinths.'

'Higher synths?'

'Yes, very pretty purple ones they were, mostly, though they come in all colours. And the smell. Very strong. You wouldn't want too many in a room at once!' Grandad smiles.

'Can you grow them outside?' I continue.

'You can, but they're not as easy as daffs.'

'Where could I get some?'

'Ah, now that I can help you with.'

After lunch, we go to Grandad's shed. It's completely different from our dark and spider-infested cave. His is bright, with a long bench than runs beneath big windows along one wooden wall. It smells of wood sap and dried earth; like everywhere else in their house, it's warm, like a hug.

From underneath the bench, Grandad pulls out a cardboard box that's full of small, brown spheres. They look like onions.

'Now, you've probably only got a few weeks left before it's too cold to plant these,' he says, placing a dozen or so in a paper bag. 'Push them quite deep into the ground – about twice the length of your index finger. You don't want the frost to get them or they won't flower. Your mother will enjoy seeing these come up.'

'Yeah. Thanks Grandad.'

Back in Mum's old room, I put the bag of bulbs carefully in the bottom of my backpack.

That afternoon, Mum and I drive home in comfortable silence. The radio, on low, is playing cheerful, forgettable pop songs. The tub on my knee is once again full of flapjacks (Nanna did a new batch while we were having lunch) and I munch away, two at a time, for most of the two-hour journey. I find it easier now to see why Mum does this long drive at least twice every week. I feel somehow fuller than I did on Friday morning. And it's not just the flapjack.

When we pull up at home, it's started raining again. As Mum goes to open the front door, she almost trips on something that's poking out from under the doormat. 'Get that for me please, love. It's probably a phone book or something. Straight in the bin.'

But when I pull it out it's got my name on it. I empty its contents onto the kitchen table. An A Level Biology textbook.

'Isn't that thoughtful? He's right, Josh. Your dad would be proud of how well you're doing at school. Mr Walters has really brought you on.'

I smile and see there's a piece of paper tucked into the front. I pull it out. Something's written in the same handwriting as the envelope. It's not Mr Walters' handwriting either. This looks like it's been done with a pen tied to the end of a very long stick.

Sunday, 8:30, Function Room at The Crown.

And then it comes back, the last thing that Alan shouted after me last week.

See you on Sunday.

The feeling of fullness starts to drain away.

TWENTY SEVEN

The rain gets heavier that afternoon, and doesn't lift on Sunday either, so there's no way I can get to Dana's garden to plant those bulbs. Instead, I watch a film with Mum – an awful, animated kids' film – and spend some time reading before I do my homework. I find a little bit in the Biology textbook about mushrooms. Apparently, fungi (which is their proper name) are really useful in nature as they help dead matter to decompose. And some have something called a 'symbiotic relationship', which means that the plant or tree they grow on actually benefits from their being there. But they can be a nuisance when they are 'saprobial', which means they kill the thing they live on.

And then, after tea, which is always early on a Sunday, it's eight o'clock.

I know the Crown; it's a pub not far from here. About a ten-minute walk. Mum is upstairs in the bathroom. She always has a long bath on a Sunday evening, then goes straight to bed after shouting 'good night' down the stairs. So if I went out, she wouldn't notice.

But why am I even thinking about going?

It's something connected to Alan, and what Alan was

saying about Ahmed on Thursday. It's got a lot to do with that website. Which means it's got a lot to do with Carl.

Despite this, I watch the clock slowly turn towards half past eight, and my legs start twitching. My fingers start to drum on my desk. Maybe if Carl's there I'll see Dana.

I'm not going to go, I decide.

But I have to say it out loud to myself. More than once.

I'm still talking when I realise that I've opened my laptop and clicked on the email link again to the website of videos.

Before, I'd just looked at the pictures. But now I look at what else is there. In the top right corner, there's the outline of a lion's head with *White Lions* written underneath it. Down the left-hand side, there's the normal list of different parts of the website, also written in white. The one I'm on, 'What We Do', is underlined. I click on the top one, which says 'About'. An error message pops up – *You are about to leave a secure connection. Do you wish to continue?* – I click 'yes'.

This page is mostly text. *The White Lions are a group of people who love their country*, it begins. At the top of the page, an animated St George's flag flutters in a digital wind. *We love our country passionately, and are prepared to do whatever we must do to protect it. We are deeply proud of who we are and what we stand for, and we know that the generations before us, who also fought to defend what was rightfully theirs, would be proud of us. We feel they walk among us every day, and we honour their memory in our ongoing struggle.*

At the bottom of the page is a small, red flower. A poppy. The cursor changes when I hover over it, and after I hold it there for a second or so, a little white box comes up that says 'read more'. I click it.

It's a long page of text and I start to scan through it. I pause over one of the statistics highlighted in a bold font: **Only 9% of Britons can truly say they belong here.** *That's less than 10% of our beautiful nation who haven't yet been poisoned by incomers and lesser species.* I read about how the last official invasion of Great Britain was in 1066, but since then millions of people have come to these shores (*our shores*) uninvited. *Under a pretext of weakness and the flag of surrender*, the article continues, *they set about changing our country, our culture, our colour, from the inside out.* There are lots of bits about purity and impurity.

Further down, there are sections about specific people – local councillors and business people, their bios say – that I've never heard of before. Their names always have three sets of brackets around them. Their children are named, too. Some of them have the names of local schools listed alongside. I skip through this all quite quickly.

Then there's the part about the terror attacks. All of them seem to be there; every single one documented.

There's the first one, *the first act of war* they call it, with the planes and the Twin Towers that happened before I was born, then a few more before 7/7, which is also a kind of hazy memory for me. I can't have been much older than three or four maybe. Then they are listed, hyperlinked; the streak of smaller-scale machete and knife rampages, the cars driven into groups of pedestrians. And, finally, the one that killed Dad. The hyperlink is the same blue as all the others. I don't know why but I feel somehow like it should be different. I click it. And there are the pictures – ones I've seen a hundred times on the news – pictures of police and ambulance crews, of scores and scores of injured and walking wounded. Some close-ups, some taken from a distance, some of piles of rubble, of angry orange explosions, or twisted and blackened metal.

But there are other pictures too – ones I haven't seen before – of the smoke still rising from burnt-out train carriages, of bloodied arms or legs sticking out from the rubble, twisted and unnatural like branches caught in a flood. Pictures of ambulance crews zipping up body bags around the remains of what used to be people. I spend a few minutes clicking through them numbly before I realise what I'm hunting for. None of the pictures are of Dad. But there's one that I stare at for I don't know how long – it's a picture taken from one end of an exploded tube train, the roof ripped off and the strip lighting from the tunnel shining into what's left of the carriage. Along the length of it, amongst all of the buckled seats and ripped fabric, there are bodies. In the blood that spatters the foreground, there are footprints. The caption reads *epicentre of the blast*.

I look at it for a long time, not really seeing it. For some reason I can't focus on any of the details, even though I want to strain my eyes over every distended limb or part of a face, looking for Dad.

I try to return to the video page, but it's blocked. A message on the website says *site under construction*. I go back to the email, click the link, and once again the dozen thumbnail images appear on my screen. I want to see again that look in Carl's eyes – the look that says there's something you can do about this to feel better.

I click one of the thumbnails.

Once again, the familiar bumpy camera work. The person holding the phone is running. They cross a normal, residential road towards a parked car. The camera drops slightly as the cameraman – Alan again? – crouches down. You can see a bit of the car bonnet at the bottom of the screen.

From the left of the shot, two more people appear. They're running in a kind of half-crouch, and looking left and right. Their hoods are up and I can't see their faces. They run straight across the road and up the driveway of the house that's in the middle of the image. One stops next to the car – a big white 4x4. Both of them put their hands down inside the zipped-up fronts of their coats and, almost perfectly synchronised, they pull out cans of spray paint, shaking them furiously. Huge, red shapes start to appear on the white garage door and along the side of the 4x4. Because it's raining, the shapes start to disintegrate almost immediately, leaving a pinkish curtain of paint and water.

One of the men wipes the garage door with his arm, then starts again. Seeing that it's working, the other does the same on the car bonnet. The shapes this time are more distinct. Letters.

Leave

The front door opens, and a woman comes out. She has one foot on her front step, another still in the house, and she's waving frantically with one arm. One of the hooded men takes a step towards the woman in the doorway, and she seems to shrink back, but her arm is still waving, and you can see her lips moving as she shouts at the hooded man. She steps quickly inside her house and slams the door just as one of the cans of spray paint bounces off it. The other man stamps on his can then throws it, erupting with paint, onto the roof of the car. The paint runs over the windscreen, the bonnet, the sides, like a veil of blood. The two hooded men then turn, sprinting away from the house, back the way they had come. They run out of the left of the shot. The camera goes shaky again as its holder stands up and begins to run in the opposite direction.

The video ends. The screen with the thumbnails returns.

I click on another.

In this one, the camera is in the middle of a group of people. They are shouting, raising their fists towards something that I can't see.

I pick up my headphones, and shouts of 'Murderers' fill my ears.

The camera turns a little, over the heads of a few more people. For a split second, like the camera has been dropped, it tilts down and I see Alan's face staring straight at me. But it's almost too quick to register, and I'm looking over the top of about fifteen people, past the signs that they're waving, across a road. It's a town – or a part of town – that I don't recognise, but the people shouting seem to be behind some kind of fence, like the metal railings they put up for spectators to stand behind at marathons and things. Across the road there is a building behind a larger set of gates and fences – permanent ones, enclosing the building in a way that looks claustrophobic, as if it wasn't originally designed to be fenced in. Behind the fences, the building is a faded white, with a steep roof. On the wall facing the road, the words '*Jamia Masjid*' are visible below a picture of a crescent moon and a star.

As I watch, the doors of the building open, and the volume of the people near the camera gets almost unbearable. I have to pull the headphones away from my ears a little. Some people come out of the building, and start to walk towards the gates, moving as if to open them. They step back when a bottle smashes against the fence a metre or so to their left, and the camera swings around to see where it came from. Suddenly, more bottles are thrown, and the camera swings back as one of them flies over the top of the fence and hits the wall of the building. The people at the gates are by now moving quickly to get back inside. The doors close and a cheer goes up through the crowd.

Then the camera starts shaking violently, and what seems to be a police officer's hand, the arm glowing in that familiar neon yellow, reaches towards it.

The video ends, this time with a title card – 'We must secure the existence of our people and a future for white children – 14 Words.'

I'm still staring at this screen, headphones on, when I realise Mum is standing in the doorway. I slam the laptop closed as she steps into the room.

'Are you alright, love? I've been calling you for ages. Done your homework?'

What did she see? 'Bit of English to finish off. I'm doing it now.'

'I fell asleep in the bath. I'm off to bed now. I can barely keep my eyes open. What were you watching?'

Nothing. She saw nothing. 'Nothing Mum, just some school research stuff. English homework, like I said.'

'Well, don't stay up too late.' And she's gone, closing the door gently behind her.

TWENTY EIGHT

'Thanks for not coming to watch this weekend, mate. We won five-nil!'

Jamie finds me first thing on Monday morning. He's glowing. Apparently, he scored a hat-trick, including one direct from a corner. I don't mention the apparent competence of the opposition's goalkeeper, and let him enjoy his glory.

'You do Burgoyne's homework?'

We'd had to write a response to a Thomas Hardy poem about war. The poem was from the point of view of a soldier who was talking about his experience and how strange it is trying to shoot someone that, if you'd met them in a pub or something, you might get along with quite well.

'Yeah, you?'

'A bit. Didn't really get it. Wrote something about the soldier not really liking war. It'll do.'

After Mum had gone to bed last night, I'd written about two hundred words explaining how the soldier was clearly just bad at his job, and that in wartime it was treasonous to consider the humanity of your enemy; if you were fighting for your country, it was your patriotic duty to kill those who threatened your home and way of life. I'd finished it with the words from that title card; that the only things that matter are protecting the existence of our people and a future for our children.

But I don't tell Jamie this.

From across the playground, the new kid, Ahmed, is walking towards us. Jamie raises a hand in greeting.

'And this is the man who made it all possible,' says Jamie, clapping Ahmed on the back. Ahmed smiles, looking slightly embarrassed. 'This guy endured wind and freezing temperatures to cheer me, to cheer us, to victory.'

'You like football?' I ask.

'Yes, very much!' Ahmed replies. Again that warm, soft voice. 'I've been a Man City fan for years. Since I can remember. Though my father was always annoyed with this. He thought I should follow Al Ittihad, like him.'

'Al who?' My face is steel, strong, impassive.

'Al Ittihad, best team in Syria, or were. They're from my hometown, Halab.'

Again I look blank, shrug my shoulders.

'Aleppo. Here, it's called Aleppo.'

'So why not call it Aleppo?' From the corner of my eyes – which are levelled hard at Ahmed – I see Jamie's jaw tense, his forehead furrow. I know this is a ridiculous argument, but there's no way I'm backing down.

'It's just pronunciation, I guess.'

'Well, you're in England now.'

Jamie steps forward to speak, but Ahmed smiles – a wide and generous grin. 'Yeah, I'd noticed. I've been here for years and still can't seem to get it right. Maybe you could teach me?'

Trying too hard, Jamie latches onto Ahmed's joke and laughs. 'Come on, that was the bell.'

They walk just ahead of me. All the way to lessons I stare at the back of Ahmed's head.

I barely notice the morning go by. I keep trying to work out what I'm supposed to do. Jamie sits next to Ahmed in all of the lessons, the teachers rearranging the seating plan to make it possible. It's not that I have to move, but I find myself getting angry anyway. A small fire has sparked up at the bottom of my stomach and it's hungry for fuel. Everything I feed it seems to make it hungrier and hungrier. I find myself following Jamie and his new best friend to the canteen at lunch and sitting with them. There's something about the warmth and humour of Ahmed's voice that I know I should like, but the fire in my stomach swallows it and grows hotter and hotter.

And the embarrassment of how I acted earlier, the way I spoke to him, the anger that came out of nowhere, all because of the name of a place in *his country*! Surely he gets to call it what he wants. I don't know what I was thinking, but all that shame keeps coming back to me and feeding the fire even more.

By the end of the day, it's a white-hot furnace.

TWENTY NINE

On the walk home, I'm suddenly aware of a strong grip on my arm. Vince, the attack dog, appears beside me as if out of nowhere. The fire inside me almost makes me take a swing at him to make him let go. I check myself just in time.

'Alan wants a word,' he grunts.

Alan is waiting around the back of the Tesco garage, taking occasional lungfuls from an e-cigarette. Our conversation is punctuated by the sounds of younger kids coming out of the shop and laughing with each other as they tear into their sweets and energy drinks. It's one of those shops that has a 'two school children at a time' sign, but no one takes any notice of it, and the staff never say anything either.

'Didn't see you last night then?'

I shrug, unsure at first as to what he's talking about.

'Get that book I sent you? Nicked it from Walters' desk. Thought you'd like it.'

Of course the book came from Alan, not Mr Walters. My relief is stopped when I realise this means Alan knows where I live. So does Carl.

'Tell me, is there anything in that textbook about

different species of humanity and how they shouldn't be allowed to breed with each other?'

'Don't know, haven't looked yet.'

'Ah! I'm sure there isn't – but it's a scientific fact that we need to start talking about. Natural differences. In intelligence and stuff. My brother says the government has silenced all the people that say it's true because they don't want to deal with the riots in the streets. But that'll happen anyway when everyone realises they've been lied to. Maybe you'll be the scientist who makes it all go off. Brings truth back to the world.'

'OK.' It's the best I can offer.

'So you won't find it in textbooks. And not on the news either, unless you start looking at the *right* news.'

I'm not sure what I'm supposed to say – there aren't really any questions to answer – but I can still feel the imprint of Vince's fingers on my arm like teeth, so I feel like I have to say something. I say, 'I looked at more of that website.'

'I know. That's one of the places you'll start to find the truth. What did you think of it?'

'Yeah, it was OK.'

'It's the most honest thing you'll find around here.'

A cloud of vapour peels from Alan's mouth into the sky. We watch it rise.

Alan continues, 'There are people watching us, Josh. You know what I mean? People. Watching. They don't want you to know a lot of things. They think you won't be able to handle it and you'll just get angry. But you know what I say? I say anger is *good*.'

I struggle to think how this constant, bone-deep heat could ever be good. I want to rip things up and run and run and run until my legs can't anymore. Then I think of Carl's eyes again, at the end of that video. The word that comes to mind to describe them now is *satisfied*.

'But it's a good job we're watching too. I saw you talking to that new Muslim kid. The one your mate Jamie's hanging around with.'

There's a pause. I hold Alan's probing stare and try not to look away, to point my fire at him.

'You did good,' Alan smiles. 'Kind of.' Vince laughs – a cold, angry laugh.

'What do you mean?'

'You *challenged* him, Josh. You didn't let him assume he could walk all over us without some kind of a *challenge*. You didn't just lie on your back like your mate Jamie when he was told he had to be his "buddy". You didn't let some reprobate species of humanity tickle your belly. You showed strength. We need more people like you.'

'For what?'

'For the Lions. If you're interested. No need to answer now. You know where we meet. I'll send you some more truth in the meantime. I've got your email.'

As Alan stops talking, a car – loud, black and with

tinted windows – pulls around the back of the garage and comes to an abrupt halt. The driver's window glides down.

It's Carl.

My cheek starts to pulse again and I quickly turn away and look at the floor.

'Oi!' And then again, a few seconds later, 'Oi!'

I turn around, slowly.

'How's the face?' Carl's eyes are hard. He says the words more like an accusation than a question.

'… fine,' I manage.

Carl is emerging from the car, uncoiling himself from the deep cup of the driver's seat and stepping towards me. 'Let's have a look at you.' His hand takes a firm grip of my chin and tilts my head backwards, his fingers probing the still-raw flesh under my cheekbone. He jerks my head the other way, looks again.

I try not to catch his eye, blinking up at the massing clouds.

'Looks alright. Healing well. What you using on it?'

The words catch in my throat. 'Suh… Some antiseptic stuff.'

'Keep going with it. You'll be fine.' He lets go of my head, but he's not finished yet. His hands land heavily on my shoulders. I feel his fingers curl into my shoulder blades, his thumbs hard in the gap above my collarbones. 'Now look,' he fixes me with his eyes.

I try to focus on something the other side of him.

Alan has climbed into Carl's seat and is toying with the radio. The volume suddenly jumps, the car vibrating with the hum of bass. Carl's head snaps round and he gives a kind of whistle, his bottom lip behind his top teeth. Alan sheepishly turns the volume down and removes himself from the driving seat.

'Fuckin' child,' Carl continues, the burr of his voice softening. 'Look, I'm sorry about the face, right?'

He seems to expect me to nod. I do so.

'But you watch yourself with her. With Dana. She's got issues, y'know? Needs a hand keeping on the straight and narrow. She's not to do what she did. She knows that. But if she's taken a shine to you, I need your help keeping her in line. 'K?'

Again I nod. Inside my head there's a smaller version of me thrashing his arms and legs around, livid.

'Good man. Come over here a minute.' He puts an arm around my shoulder and leads me to the edge of the hard standing behind the garage. There's a low brick wall and, beyond that, the ground falls away sharply so there's a view across the backs of houses, a few scraps of green space before the railway line rises up on its embankment. There's a goods train on the track, waiting to go through a red light, its haphazard arrangement of containers – blue, red, yellow, green – all rusting equally at the edges.

Carl's other hand goes to the chest pocket of his white shirt, pulls out a packet of cigarettes. He flicks his

136

wrist and one pops out of the top. He gestures towards me with it.

'No, thanks.'

'Wise man.' He puts the end in his mouth and returns the pack to his shirt pocket and rummages for matches or a lighter. I notice that the back part of his hand is blotched with white scarring that disappears up the inside of his sleeve. He sees me looking at it.

'Battle scars,' he says. 'Burns.' Unbuttoning his cuff, Carl rolls up his sleeve to reveal the blanched and hairless flesh rising in a series of angry ridges and ripples up the length of his arm. There are places where the muscles seem wasted away. There's a kind of crater in his forearm. You can see the gap between the bones. 'They did this to me. Afghanistan.'

I'd seen this kind of injury before. At the big funeral for Dad and the other victims, there had been survivors of previous attacks who had spoken to us afterwards.

'It was an IED,' Carl continues. 'You know what that is?'

Yes, I know. Improvised Explosive Device. I nod.

'Of course you know. It was by the roadside, hidden in a kid's toy. Our unit were passing when it went off. A fucking kid's toy. That's sick, isn't it? I was at the front, a way past it. Everything went black then I woke up under a pile of rubble a few minutes later. Some of the unit weren't so lucky though. I got these trying to pull them clear.' He rolls his sleeve back down, re-buttons the cuff.

The goods train jerks itself into movement, pulling slowly away and out of town.

'When Dana told me who you were, after I'd hit you, I felt guilty. I know what you've been through. I've lost people too. To *them*.'

I hear the crackle of Carl's cigarette tip and he inhales deeply. He breathes out slowly, a thin line of smoke disappearing into the middle distance of the housing estate below us.

'For a little while, Josh, I didn't know what to do. Then I found something. I'm telling you this because you know how it is, don't you? You know that anger, that heat? I can help you. Give you a way of living with it. A way to do something with it. A way to honour your dad's memory.'

'Excuse me, you can't smoke here.' It's a woman's voice. We both turn as she walks towards us from a door at the back of the garage. 'This is a garage, there's petrol here and gas cylinders in that cage over there. You can't smoke here.'

Carl takes another deliberate and slow draw on his cigarette. The closer the woman gets to Carl, the more she seems to doubt her confidence.

'Look, you can't do that here. Please extinguish it, or leave. Please.'

Carl casually flicks the still burning cigarette towards the woman. It bounces off her legs as she jumps back, a small hole in the shin of her tights. She stamps on the glowing butt.

'Excuse me…' but her voice falters.

Carl stalks towards his car. 'Don't worry about me, love. It's them you should be keeping an eye on.'

The woman's head spins to where Carl points. A group of three kids, one of them black, about to enter the shop. She makes straight for them, 'Just two at a time, please.' She makes the black girl wait outside, then stands in the doorway and glares when the girl scuffs her feet on the newspaper racks.

Alan is standing behind the open back door of Carl's car, his e-cigarette aloft. 'Told you you should get one of these, bro. You can do it anywhere. Look,' and he sends another cloud of vapour skywards.

'Get in, you prick. And turn that stupid thing off. It smells like a slag's toilet.'

The engine guns, the music blaring again.

'See you around, Josh.' Then Carl gestures with his hand, holding it out of the window, pointing downwards, fanning out his fingers and making a circle with his thumb and index finger. The window begins to roll up again as Alan and Vince get in the back. I glimpse someone else in the front passenger seat: long hair, school uniform, looking straight forwards.

Dana.

THIRTY

By the time I get home, there's an email from Alan with a list of links to websites. I click on a few. They've all got the same words in a lot of their headlines: words like 'invasion' and 'epidemic', and more medical-sounding words like 'spreading' and 'infection'.

There are more articles with words like 'heroes' and 'citizens' and 'protection'. Like the others, they all look like a normal newspaper websites, but I've not heard of the names before. I click on one article called *Hero Soldiers Told to Wait for Housing Behind Immigrants*. The story is about a couple of soldiers who had left the army and had been placed on the bottom of the list for council housing. There were pictures of them sitting on their childhood beds at their parents' houses. It looked ridiculous, these big, muscly, tattooed men perched on top of Spiderman duvet covers, pictures of cars on the walls. There was a quote from one of the soldiers at the top of the article: 'it's demeaning and dehumanising to line up at the job centre behind the kind of people who might have been shooting at you out there.' The article goes on to describe the estimated 7000 ex-Servicemen who are thought to be homeless in Britain, and the disgrace – that word again – of the government's policy of putting immigrants to the top of the list for things like housing and healthcare.

I get to the end of the article and realise my fist is clenched hard on the mouse. The final picture shows a smiling family – mum, dad, and four kids – standing outside a terraced house. The caption reads *Helped first and furthest*. Their skin isn't white.

I click a link to another, similar article and have to double take. It's from the local paper and the big, colour picture shows Carl, undressed to the waist. The scarring I'd seen earlier travels over his shoulder and engulfs almost one half of his torso. His good arm shows several military tattoos. The article explains how Carl was discharged from the army on medical grounds, despite wanting to return to the front lines. Because of his discharge, he won't receive the benefits he would have received had he completed his term of service and he, like the men in the previous article, was back living with his mum and brother. Another picture shows Alan and Carl sitting either side of their mum, a tired-looking woman who doesn't look that much older than Carl, in what I assume is their living room. I scan to the bottom of the article and find the following.

Readers will remember Carl from a story we ran a year ago. Carl's unit was attacked in Afghanistan by a roadside IED. Three men were killed in the explosion and two further victims were kidnapped and subsequently executed by so called Islamic State. Carl, the unit's technical reconnaissance officer, survived only because he was partially covered by rubble and probably considered dead. He received a medal for bravery, pulling the bodies of his comrades from the centre of the blast.

I read this paragraph several times before moving on.

Another website has a huge banner across the top in childlike handwriting, saying 'Hey, It's Just an Opinion!' Below this are loads of memes, cartoons of frogs and short videos. I don't really get most of them, except the ones of a man with a bomb in the top of his turban. There was a video that went viral a year or so ago, just a looped clip of the guy who presents a TV show making a weird noise. It got funnier the more you watched it. Maybe these videos are like that. I click on a few things and come to a really retro arcade-style game where the turbaned man is running around a network of caves, and you – as an American GI – have to catch him before he collects all of the gold coins. I play this for a while before Mum comes home. The anger slowly subsides.

I sidle into the kitchen as she's putting dinner in the microwave. Mum never cooks on a Monday evening – it's enough just facing a new week, she always says. I don't mind much. There's something about microwave food that's reassuringly safe.

'Mum…?' I start.

She's leaning on the sideboard, her shoulders heavy.

She doesn't look up or respond, and I get the impression she hasn't heard me come in or speak.

'Tea?' I ask, a little louder, picking up the kettle.

She nods, slowly.

I move past her to the sink, catch the scent of cigarettes. Maybe it's Carl's smoke on me.

'Good day?' I ask over the loudness of the tap.

Mum lifts herself a little, puts her hands on her cheeks and hold them there as if she's trying to put herself back together before she turns around. It's at this point that I worry she's been crying. Perhaps I shouldn't have come downstairs.

Her eyes are a little red when she turns around a second or two later, but there are no tears, which is good. 'No, not really. You?'

'Not that bad. Why? What happened?'

'Nothing to worry about. Just a new person starting at work who they want me to train.'

'Oh.'

'It's fine, really.' Mum shakes her hands in front of her, the way she does when she's trying to flick away all the bad thoughts. 'It'll be good in the long run as I can give her things to do to ease my work-load, but it was exhausting, being with her all day today. Just....' She tails off, the exhaustion clear in her voice.

'Was she not very nice?'

'No. The opposite. She was lovely.' Mum's voice is flat. She's staring at the floor.

The kettle starts to make its almost-boiling noise, I click it off before it starts to roar and get one of Mum's latest fruit infusions from her jar, put it in the mug (looping the bag label's string through the handle, like Dad taught me) and pour on the water, then put the kettle back on to boil for my English Breakfast.

As I clink and potter around with teaspoons, soggy teabags and milk, Mum stands leaning against the sideboard, her eyes open but registering nothing. There's a background hum from the microwave, its orange light behind Mum's head like a strange halo.

'There you go, Mum.' I place her mug next to her, far enough away from her elbow that, if she jerks, she won't knock it over.

'What? Oh, thanks love.' She did jerk, as I thought. The mug remains safe.

But when the microwave pings, Mum spins too fast and her hand knocks the mug off the sideboard onto the floor where it explodes in a bomb of steam and china. I go straight for the kitchen towel as she jumps out of the spray, wincing as it splashes her legs. I throw sheet after sheet of kitchen towel on the floor and Mum dabs them around with the end of her shoes until we've created something like a dam around the worst of the spill. Then I get the dustpan and brush from under the sink and gather up the tiny fingernails of white china that are all over the floor, empty them inside the dam, then use the small, purple brush to slowly make the dam smaller, mopping up the water and gathering the broken crockery together before emptying it all from the dustpan into an empty cereal box that was waiting on the side to be recycled. The whole thing happens in silence and takes less than a minute.

When I get back in from putting the cereal box – still steaming – straight in the outside bin, Mum is sitting at the table.

'Another tea?'

'Thanks love.' She offers a weak smile. She looks at the trail of footprints my wet socks have brought in from outside. 'Oh goodness Josh, your feet! Did you hurt yourself?'

'No Mum, I'm OK.'

'That was so stupid of me. I can't even look after myself this evening and now you're ripping your feet to shreds because of me.'

'Mum, I'm fine. Don't worry.'

'It's ridiculous Josh, how incapable your mother is. I'm sorry. I really am.'

'Forget about it Mum. I'll make you another cup.'

As we talk, I take two plates from the cupboard and empty the contents of the microwave containers onto them. Chicken jalfrezi. The kettle is still hot enough for Mum's tea, and I bring it to the table with her plate, then go back for my plate and the cutlery.

'And this thing at work,' Mum continues. 'This woman. She was lovely. Pleasant as could be. Polite, smiling, really friendly, asking about you and school. She's got a son your age who's just started there. Ahmed, he's called. Do you know him?'

I go tense. 'I think so, yeah. Seen him around.'

'She's into yoga, and cooking, and walking. We really have so much in common. And she's just so *keen* you know? So eager to do well. She reminds me of … well, of *me* about five years ago when I started there. And what she must have been through… But I just couldn't give her anything back. I was completely numb today, like most Mondays. And I know she'll take some of my stuff, which will make things easier. But I couldn't shift this idea…'

'What idea?'

'This notion, that…'

'That what, Mum?'

Mum pauses for a moment, her fork halfway to her mouth. 'That she could easily replace me. That she'll take all my work and be so much more capable than me that the firm can finally offload me. Which they've wanted to do for ages. Ever since…'

For a while, we eat in silence.

'Mum?'

'Hmmm?'

'If they got rid of you, we could sue them, right? For discrimination?'

'It wouldn't be discrimination, Josh. And it's not going to happen. It's just me being daft.'

'But it does happen, you know.'

'What are you talking about, Josh?'

'… well, people are losing out to them all over the place at the moment. Jobs, housing, healthcare. People who are from here, people who deserve better are being put to the back of the queue and told to shut up while they, people who don't belong here, people who don't deserve it, all go first.'

Mum puts her fork down. 'Josh, you're confusing me. What are you talking about? Them? I've had a long day and feel wretched, so less cryptic would be good, please.'

'Immigrants. This woman, Ahmed's mum, she—'

'So you do know Ahmed?'

'Yeah, a bit, but his mum's taking your job, and they've taken a house on the estate near Jamie's that probably should have been given to someone else as well. And they're taking over, slowly, getting their foot in the door so they can turn this into the country they want, and then none of it will be ours anymore.' Even as I speak them, the words don't sound entirely like my own. This is anger talking, the white heat creeping out. 'So what I'm saying is, it's discrimination if they start taking from us and giving to them. It's racist. We should do something about it, right? After what happened to Dad, it should be us who …'

Mum's fork clatters against the edge of her plate. I stop. Mum looks at me for a long time. A very long

147

time. And I can see tears are starting to rise up in the corners of her eyes. Again, I want very much to be back upstairs in the safety of my room.

But all she says, very quietly, is 'Don't you ever use your dad's…' Then she tails off.

We sit in silence for what feels like ages. Then she stands up and leaves.

I hear her bedroom door close upstairs and stare at the wisps of steam rising slowly from her second undrunk mug of tea.

THIRTY ONE

It's the thud of the front door closing that wakes me up the next morning. I'm vaguely aware of Mum's car engine dwindling into the distance, then I realise it must be late and I sit bolt upright.

It is late. Very.

I quickly pull on my uniform and run downstairs – almost at the same time – ready to throw a glass of water down my throat and grab a slice of bread, when I stop myself. Why rush? If Mum wanted me to go to school, she would have woken me up.

On the table, there's a note. *Get some more rest. See you when I get home. Mum x.*

Vindicated, I wander into the lounge and slump down in front of the tail end of breakfast television, scrolling through the channels of news and lifestyle shows. There are hospital closures, accidents, a couple of celebrity babies, and a hyper-intelligent cat who can talk to her owner through text messages she types with a massive, homemade keypad. There are six buttons on it – one for food, one for treats, three for different toys or games, and one that just has a big heart on it. The man who owns the cat is sitting on the uncomfortable-looking sofa in the studio and saying that the cat tells him she loves him at least six times every day, and both presenters are smiling at the fat tabby asleep on his lap.

I get up only to make tea, collect biscuits, and – once – to change out of my uniform and put my dressing gown on.

Just after eleven o'clock, there's a knock on the door. I freeze. Thankfully I didn't open the curtains so they can't see I'm in here. They might be able to hear the TV though. It's probably just the postman; he knows to put parcels in the shed if there's no one home.

A few seconds later, I hear the side gate open on its squeaking hinges. Just the postman after all. I relax again and go back to focussing on whether the couple on TV will buy the house with a garden big enough for their dogs but not enough bedrooms, or the one with a granny-annexe and near to woodland walks. Watching TV with Mum has started to wear off on me, I think.

A huge thud at the back window makes me jump almost a foot in the air. Behind the flat palm that made the thud is a grinning, demonic-looking skull – teeth bared and nostrils wide open. I'm rooted to the spot in sheer panic.

As I watch, unable to look away, another skull hovers up to the glass, grinning.

'Josh! Let us in!' It's Alan. It takes another second to realise the hideous face is Vince. Both their heads are freshly shaved.

Alan taps something else against the glass, making

a cutting, metallic sound. It's a beer bottle. He holds up three more in his other hand. 'Hey! Skiver!' his smile broadens. 'Look what we found in your shed!'

After I've let them in and Alan and Vince have drunk a beer each at the kitchen table in a single, long swallow, they start talking.

'Noticed you weren't in today. Thought we come and pay you a breaktime visit, after we'd sorted our hair out.' Vince swallows a belch, runs a hand across his stubbled head.

'Just a flying one though. Vince has got a meeting this afternoon he can't miss.'

'Head's detention. Dump-tackled some immigrant kid from St Martin's in the rugby game last week and got sent off. Head was watching. Thinks I did it on purpose.' Vince spits into the top of his empty beer bottle.

'You did do it on purpose, Vince,' Alan clarifies. 'You told me right from the start of the game you were going to do it, as soon as you saw him. Why they still let you play is a fucking mystery.'

'Well, whatever. They'd get murdered without me.' Vince is worrying at the top of another beer with the edge of his key-ring, then jerks his head at me when he realises what he's said. 'Oh.'

There's no apology, but is this Vince's way of at least softening a bit? I pass it off with a shrug.

Alan thumps my arm. 'What's your story, Skiver? You look at those other websites yet?'

'Yeah, some.' I take a sip of my beer. On an empty stomach, it almost comes up again. I swallow it for the second time.

'That Jeff's Place one is hilarious, yeah?' Alan is leaning forward, hitting the table with his first as he speaks. 'It's brilliant there are places in the world where people still find these things funny, right? That this political correct, woke bullshit hasn't got to everyone. It's just refreshing that there's a place where no one's getting offended and kicking off because they take something the wrong way.'

I nod. I don't want to, but I do.

'You should check out that Reich series,' Alan continues. 'This guy was putting them up on YouTube, but then YouTube banned him so the guys who run Jeff's gave him a home, but basically he's playing all the historical FPS games on the market, but he's reskinned them to play as the bad guys. So he's the Nazis, or the Germans, or the Communists or whatever, and on the voice-over, he's just ripping in to all the so-called good guys he's killing because they probably would've gone home and married a black girl or something, or would've started a business and employed only migrant workers. It's hilarious. And he's, like, head-shot kills, *every* time.

I'm going to grab some more of these, OK?' He waves his empty bottle.

I look anywhere in the room but at Vince, making up for his momentary thaw, who stares at me with unwavering eyes until Alan returns with another four beers. He opens two and puts one in front of me.

'Come on Zulu warrior. Drink up! You don't have to go to work today!'

The next mouthful I take feels like it's stripping the lining of my oesophagus as it goes down. I take another, and wince slightly less.

When my eyes stop streaming, I see that Alan is still standing up, looking at a picture on the wall. Taken a few years ago, it shows me, Mum and Dad standing in some autumn woods near Nanna and Grandad's house. We're all smiling in the way you do for family photos.

'Is that him then, your dad?' Alan points with the top of his bottle.

'Yeah.' I feel blood pounding in my ears.

'He looks like a real good bloke.'

'He... He was, yeah.'

'I was thinking about him the other night. About what a hero he is.'

Vince raises his bottle towards the picture too. 'To the fallen,' he says.

'Vince thinks so too, don't you, Vince? Your dad was a soldier in a war he didn't even know was going on. He gave his life to show we won't be forced into being cowardly, ugly, anti-white puppies for a bunch of bearded bullies that hide in their gated mosques and synagogues and whatever.'

Just like the last time that Alan spoke about Dad, I feel myself growing hotter and hotter, unwilling to listen. But some of the words are starting to get through.

'His sacrifice was the greatest that anyone can make, Josh. Do you know that?'

I feel myself nodding, the knot too tight in my throat to be able to speak.

'To sacrifice yourself for a country that you love, a way of life you believe in. His name should be on the memorials, you know?'

Again, I nod.

'And the worst thing we can do, Josh – the *worst* thing – is to forget that sacrifice. To let the vile, invidious bastards who want to change this country and our culture do so.' There's something about Alan's words that sound rehearsed. Scripted almost. 'They're doing it from the inside out. You know that, you've read about it. It's happening, right? Even here! In our little town! They're here, Josh, and they're trying to push us out. It makes me sick. Physically sick.' Alan sits down again, he clinks his bottle against mine. 'To your dad, Josh.'

Vince does the same.

I swallow the rest of the bottle in one gulp.

THIRTY TWO

I don't know whose idea it is to go back to school, but while I'm upstairs changing again, Alan and Vince find a small bottle of vodka in the back of a cabinet in the lounge, and they pass it between themselves as we walk along the main road, giving me the occasional sip and pats on the back to aid my choking.

'Right. Hardest punch you ever took,' Alan says.

'Easy,' replies Vince. 'Stepdad. Prick.' He spits into the gutter.

'Don't think we need to ask Josh, do we?' Alan laughs as he pats the side of my face, which is starting to go slightly numb. 'Unless your dad ever hit you?'

I reel at this, stopping in my tracks and fixing Alan with a stare I didn't know I had. 'No.'

''Course not. He doesn't look the type anyway.'

I haven't stopped staring at him.

'Hey, easy, Josh. Just asking. Friends? You're lucky, you know. That he didn't used to. Makes him a bit of a rarity, far as I'm concerned.'

We walk in silence for a minute or so before Alan continues.

'For me it was Carl, too. Hey, you know what Josh? Carl said he didn't expect you to get up after the first punch. When you did, he was a bit impressed, he said.'

I smile, despite myself.

'Tough fucker aren't you?'

'Maybe. So why'd he hit you?'

'He gets these … I don't know. They're *dreams* I guess. But he's not asleep. Sometimes I find him when I get back from school sitting on the edge of his bed, or my bed – we share a room you know – and he's just… staring. Staring at the wall. This one time I came home and found him like that and went to make him a cup of tea for when he came round, and when I got downstairs I heard this wailing from our room. Sounded like some bitch or something. So I run back upstairs and he's still sitting there, but yelling. He's clawing at his scars and there's water running down his face – sweat, tears, whatever. And so I go to grab his arm and stop him. But he picks me up like I'm nothing, throws me against the wall. I don't think he even saw me, so I get up and try again. This time he's a bit more… *there*, a bit more present in his eyes, and he does see me. But I don't think he knew it was me because he lets me have it with this massive right hook that sends me flying into the wall again. I went so fast I left a dent in the plasterboard. It's still there. Vince has seen it – it's the exact size of my head, right, Vince?'

Vince laughs his growling laugh, tips more vodka down his throat. 'Yeah. Fuckin' legend.'

'But he's alright, my brother.' Alan puts a hand on the back of my neck as he says this. 'He's alright now. He's found a way to get better. To make everything better. He'll be fine.'

Again, I feel like Alan's words are rehearsed, and that they're not meant solely for me.

THIRTY THREE

We arrive at school a few minutes before the start of lunchtime and wait in the bushes opposite the front gates, wrapped in conspiracy and laughing occasionally, until we hear the bell. Once the front playground has started to fill up, we slip quickly into the crowd and stand over a group of Year Eights until they get up and give us their picnic bench.

For the first time, it feels good to not be wearing the cloud. I feel powerful, in control, and most of all, I feel visible. And the people who can all see me now know that I'm powerful.

I've still not eaten anything and my stomach is churning, so I mutter something about this and go inside to the canteen, emerging a few minutes later with two slices of pizza which I devour rapidly. Feeling slightly better, I look up to see what Alan and Vince are talking about, and am surprised to see that Dana has joined us.

'Hi,' I splutter, bits of pizza spraying everywhere.

She looks at me in shock, then something that might be pity, then finally anger. Then she leaves.

'Alright, Josh, maybe don't be quite so charming next time, eh?' Alan laughs.

Last lesson that afternoon is English. My head is aching and I'm ridiculously thirsty, excusing myself twice in Ms Yawl's Geography lesson so I could suck at the water in the bathroom tap like my life depended on it. I'm hoping Mrs Burgoyne will let me sit quietly like she normally does, but maybe because I have to ask to borrow a pen and some paper (I forgot to bring my schoolbag), she has other ideas.

'Josh, your point of view on the narrator in Thomas Hardy's poem last week was very interesting. Could you explain it to us, please?'

'Pardon?' My voice catches in my throat, so the word comes out half gurgled and half squeaked. There's a short roar of laughter from the class.

'Thank you, everyone.' The class settles again quickly. Mrs Burgoyne has a habit of never raising her voice, so every time she almost threatens to shout, everyone goes very quiet. 'You said that you questioned the narrator's professionalism, Josh. How so?'

'I can't remember, Miss.'

'What a pity. I've got your homework here. You say that he lacks professionalism. Your words, 'the job of any soldier is to do their duty and protect their country. If insidious sentiments like friendship start to cloud the soldier's judgement, he is unable to perform his duties effectively.' What does insidious mean, Josh?'

'It means bad and getting worse, Miss.'

'Quite so. You don't think that recognition of one's enemy as human is a fundamentally human response in the soldier's situation?'

'I don't know, Miss. I've never been to war.' I want to ask her whether the man who murdered my dad looked at him in the second before detonating his backpack. Did he recognise *him* as human?

Mrs Burgoyne continues, her voice cutting through the small ripple of laughter from around the room. 'You don't think that the soldier could have been coerced or manipulated into signing up? We looked at the propaganda from the first world war last week – dehumanising the enemy, turning the whole thing into sport – couldn't the soldier's attitude be a realisation of "the old lie"?'

Mrs Burgoyne raises her arms and conducts the class through a slow intonation of *dulce et decorum est pro patria mori*.

'Maybe,' I say. 'But…'

'But what, Josh?'

I want to say something about how the soldier was clearly a willing participant, and that Mrs Burgoyne didn't know the first thing about being a soldier in a war you didn't know you were fighting. But I don't. Instead I say, 'It's just … I think that the enemy *should* be dehumanised, really.'

Mrs Burgoyne's brow furrows. The room stills to an

expectant quiet. The teacher folds her arms across her chest, says, 'Go on.'

'Isn't it the same with any war, Miss? Any war, once it's started, has to be won. Otherwise you lose. And if you start seeing the enemy as being people like you, then you must be starting to become like the enemy.'

There are a few giggles here. Mrs Burgoyne quells them with a hand. 'I'm not sure I understand, Josh.'

'So, if you're looking at the enemy and you think they are like you, if you don't know the difference, then maybe you are the enemy already.'

'I think that's the point, Josh. That there are no natural enemies. There are no inherently good people and bad people, right people and wrong people; that we're all the same. War insists on a false categorisation from which nobody emerges well.'

'But that's not true Miss, is it? There are people who want to kill us because of the way we live, or what we believe, because they think their way is better. They *are* our enemies. Religious organisations. Terrorists. How can they not be our enemies?'

I see Mrs Burgoyne flinch when I use the T-word. 'But Thomas Hardy wouldn't have known anything about that, would he now?' She's smiling. She thinks I'm going to stop now and opens her mouth to speak.

In my head, I cut her off and tell her about the research I did for this homework. I tell her that Hardy knew all about this kind of thing. In my head I say that, when Hardy was a kid, the whole Crimean war was fought over the rights of Christian minorities to access the holy lands in the Ottoman Empire. We didn't want to see them fall into Russian hands which would have excluded our people from practising their faith. And the Boer War, which Hardy was writing about in 1902, was about being British. The Boer didn't like the British, and wanted to take what the British had. So if the British soldier is looking at a Boer soldier and thinking they might be the same, then that soldier is a traitor to his country because that Boer soldier doesn't like the way that British people live and would do anything to destroy it. In my head I tell Mrs Burgoyne that, if the soldier comes home from war thinking he shares something with his enemies, then the war has been lost, because his culture and his children's future is all at risk because he'll let it wash away like, like ... like sand from a beach. He'd have been better dying for his country and making a sacrifice that would make his children proud to be British, rather than coming home and letting his country and his culture erode beneath his feet. In my head I'm on my feet now, almost yelling that Hardy's 'hero' is anything but. He's a bad soldier – the worst soldier you can be, because he's not only failed to keep the enemy out, he's actually let the enemy's way of thinking in. And once you let the enemy in, it's almost impossible to get rid of them.

But I say none of this. All of my well-thought-through logic and truth are useless here. I remember what Alan said about the people watching us. My actual response to Mrs Burgoyne is too loud, overly sarcastic. 'You're right, Miss. We all need to stop killing each other and be nice to people.'

At the back of the class, one kid starts a slow, ironic hand-clap, but he stops almost immediately under the cold look of Mrs Burgoyne. Jamie, a few rows in front of me, has turned around in his seat and is staring at me with a complete lack of recognition.

On the walk home, which takes a long time, I stop twice to be sick into a bush, and once over someone's garden wall.

THIRTY FOUR

News of my outburst in English, which is already a thin and hazy memory to me, must have gotten around pretty quickly; next day, a few people call me 'Soldier' in the corridors.

Alan and Vince have gone back to keeping their distance, but that's fine. I am starting to realise that I can call on them if I need them and that they'd have my back. I'm confident of that. In a way, I'm oddly proud of my new, strangely earned nickname. We're all soldiers, the three of us.

I spend breaktime on my phone, looking at more gifs and cartoons of the fat, green frog. There's a few that I'd probably get in trouble for looking at in school, but maybe that's part of what makes them funny, too. I thumb through them, smiling. There's always loads of memes going around at school, so I don't see why this is different. Maybe some people would find this really offensive. But I don't mind who sees them over my shoulder. There's nothing that can stop me looking at them. It's my right. And it's my right to find them funny. Alan says it's good to look at them because it shows we can do what we want even if some people would be offended. And it's their problem if they get offended. They don't have any right to tell us we can't find these things funny. It's powerful, laughter. It's the one thing they can't take away. The frog is dressed up in a Nazi uniform and going out shopping, or has a white hood on and is sticking a thumb up in front of a burning cross. The funniest ones are the ones of the man with the bomb in his turban being chased by GIs in mirror sunglasses who are about three times the size of him. The GIs can't fit into the caves that the bomber keeps hiding in. In one, the bomber runs into a mousehole in an old Tom & Jerry cartoon, chased by Jerry the cat.

At lunchtime, I find Dana in the canteen, eating on her own. I sit down next to her. She rolls her eyes but doesn't get up.

'Hi,' I start.

'What?'

'I'm sorry about the other day, at my house—'

'Keep your voice down! I shouldn't have been there, you know?' Dana's eyes dart around the room, as if there are spies listening to her every word. She's right too.

'It's not a problem. You were really … honest with me. And I got a bit upset. But I think I'm getting better now. I think I'm finding a way through it. A way to deal with it.' There's a part of me that is amazed at how I'm finding words for things at the moment – things I found difficult to talk about up until a few weeks ago are suddenly flowing out of my mouth. Well, maybe not flowing, but they're definitely coming out. It's refreshing, liberating even, to be so visible. To be out of the cloud.

'You have no idea what you're finding, Josh.'

'What do you mean?'

'Do you know what kind of stuff you're getting into?'

'Yeah, I'm finding the truth. And I'm getting less afraid of talking about it.'

'I heard about English yesterday. Everyone's talking about it. Maybe it's best you keep—'

'Alright, Soldier!' Vince sits down heavily on my right. Alan slaps me on the back – a little too hard maybe – and slides in on my left. 'What're you talking about?'

'Nothing.' Dana hastily starts to stack things on her tray, making moves to leave.

'Hey, D, stay a while.'

'No, I've got a detention with Amber again.'

'You should try being good for a change. Like Josh here.'

'Yeah, well…' Dana flashes her eyes at me once more as she turns to leave, barging past a group of younger kids as she does so.

'Josh, I hear you told Burgoyne some truth yesterday?'

'Yeah, I s'pose so. She wanted me to believe some kind of nonsense about—'

'I'll stop you there.' Alan's voice is harsh, firm. For a second I see how much like his brother he is. 'Look,

Josh, I like you. You know that, right? But the thing is with these liberal cucks is that they're in control at the moment. And any time someone says something they don't like, they feel a need to react.'

On my other flank, Vince is moving closer, his left arm pinning my right elbow against my side.

'Which makes trouble we don't need. You're new to this, and it's not your fault, but you've got to learn that you can't just spout off about things in public. There will be consequences. We can't be close to you, can't help you, if you bring attention we don't want. Our whole operation might be blown. Do you understand?'

Alan is smiling. I smile back, 'Yeah, sure. I get it. No more truth in class. OK.' I reach for my phone in my pocket, 'Hey, check these out, they're really—'

Alan interrupts me, his firm hand holds mine down. 'Good. And you'll also understand why this next bit has to happen too.'

The 'next bit' all happens too fast for me to keep up with, but Vince shouts something very loud and the next thing I know I'm underneath the table in the dining hall, my hand still on the phone in my pocket. Some of my food is on top of me and the rest, when I struggle out and up onto the right side of the bench, is spread across half of the room. You can hear a pin drop, and everyone is looking in my direction. I am surprised at the slow drip of blood spotting onto my shirt and the scattered chips and peas in front of me, and more surprised when I realise that the blood is coming from my nose, which suddenly starts to hurt. A lot. The ringing in my ears grows steadily louder as I turn around to collect my bag and coat. Vince is still holding the tray he hit me with, and as I bend down, he hits me again, sending me back underneath the table. From here, I watch Vince and Alan's feet slowly make their way towards the door as no one makes any attempt to stop them.

They are far too visible for that.

THIRTY FIVE

In Miss Amber's room, they want me to write a report of the incident. The blood has stopped now, and I've told them that I don't need to go to hospital. Despite this, they've phoned Mum to tell her what happened, and that she should keep an eye on me at home.

'So you were sitting there, eating lunch, when Vince and Alan came up and attacked you? Out of nowhere?'

'Yes. No, not Alan. It was Vince who hit me. With the tray I think.'

'And Alan didn't touch you?'

'No.'

'And did either of them say anything to you at all?'

'I ... I don't remember. It all happened so quickly.'

'It's OK, Josh. Just keep calm and try to write down exactly what happened.'

After a few false starts – a combination of my shaking hand and me not knowing what I should say – Miss Amber takes the pen herself and goes back to asking me questions.

'So, you came into the canteen and sat down by yourself at a table, is that right?'

'Yes.' I thought it was definitely a good idea not to mention Dana, whose look at me as I passed her in

Miss Amber's doorway at the end of lunchtime was a mixture of shock and disgust.

'Then what, Josh?'

'Alan and Vince came past me, and … and I think my bag must have been sticking out.'

'Your bag?'

'Yes, my bag was sticking out, and my coat, and I think Alan or Vince must have tripped on it and spilled their food, then Vince took my tray and when I tried to stop him it hit me in the nose.'

'People say they saw Alan Almes talking to you for a minute before the incident, Josh. That he was muttering something to you. Is that not right?'

'No Miss, it must be when he fell over and sat down next to me as he fell.'

'As he tripped over your bag?'

'Yeah, and spilled his food. He said something about how he should take my food because I tripped him up. Then I said no, so Vince tried to take my tray.'

'Vince didn't trip up, though.'

'No, just Alan.'

After a bit more questioning, I manage to come up with a passable story which explains the food everywhere, the bloody nose, and me ending up under the table. Miss Amber seems satisfied, typing up the notes into an email which she explains she is sending to the behavioural unit. She clicks 'send' with a very precise 'and there.'

'I know you will anyway Josh, but stay away from those two, OK?'

'Yes, Miss.'

'I don't just mean for a few days, but in general. They're not good news for anyone. I know Mr Walters has put you in his Thursday sessions for extra work, which we're all very happy with; it's just unfortunate that he can't find a separate evening for you.'

'It's fine, Miss. The Thursdays I mean.'

'That's good of you, Josh, and you've got your head screwed on right, we know that. It's just…'

Somehow, I know she's thinking about the English class yesterday. Whether she's heard the story from students or from Mrs Burgoyne I don't know, but I know she knows what was said. What I said.

'Yesterday. You were behaving a little strangely in class. Mrs Burgoyne has emailed me…'

'Yeah, sorry. I was playing devil's advocate.'

'What do you mean, Josh?'

'Well, I don't want to upset Mrs Burgoyne, but I sometimes feel that we have to just agree with what we're being told. And I wanted to see if I could argue against that for a change.'

'You picked a strange subject for your experiment, Josh. Mrs Burgoyne's a little worried about some of the … sentiments you were showing in your homework.'

'It was ironic, Miss. It was supposed to be funny.' I offer my best, bloody-nosed smile.

'OK. If you say so, but be careful where you're getting your ideas from, Josh. And any more trouble from those two, you let me know, please.'

'Yes, Miss.'

'Right, back to your lessons then. And remember, keep away from those two boys.'

THIRTY SIX

I'm powering homeward, hands pushing against the stitches in my coat pocket. I understand why what happened had to happen, and I'm amused on one level at how easily I managed to slip through Miss Amber's net. But there's still a sense of being wronged – by Alan and Vince, by the school, by everything else – that's smoking like a small bonfire in my chest. Not quite the anger of a few days ago, but it's not like it's nothing either.

Jamie has to put a hand on my shoulder to slow me down, and I wheel around. A couple of younger students almost walk into us as we stop, abruptly, in the middle of the pavement. I glare at them, my eyes spitting sparks as they speed off up the street.

'What?' I demand.

'Jeez, Josh. What's the problem with you at the moment? First Monday, then English yesterday after turning up in some weird mood, and now this lunchtime thing? How's your nose? It looks…'

Over Jamie's shoulder, I see Ahmed getting into the back of what must be his mum's car, pulled into the side of the road. A white BMW 4x4, quite new. It looks familiar. Then it clicks. It's the car from the video. The red paint has been completely removed.

'Josh? Are you listening? What's the matter?'

'Nothing. Leave it.'

'No. I'm worried about you, and I get the feeling you're about to blow up or something.'

'What, like "explode"? Great joke.' It doesn't feel like me speaking anymore.

'You know that's not what I meant.'

What I don't need right now, what I really don't need, is someone calm, concerned and loyal. Someone like Jamie. I want to be angry. I want the feeling I've enjoyed for the last few days to come back. The smouldering bonfire is growing by the second. I fan the flames. Every time I open my mouth, I belch out great clouds of black smoke. I want people to choke on them, to struggle to breathe.

But Jamie just stands there, unaffected. Which is worse.

'Leave me alone, Jamie.' I jut my chin over his shoulder, towards the BMW that has now rejoined the crawl of parent traffic along the main road. 'Go back to your—'

'What?' Jamie interrupts me. Deep down, the part of me that isn't fire is glad he does. So glad. 'Go back to my what?'

I stare at him. I want the fire to pass on to him, to set his hair alight. 'You know.'

'No, I don't. And I don't think you know either.' He pauses for a second. His eyes soften. 'What happened this weekend? We missed you at the rec. It was great when you came last week. Everyone said so. What did you do?'

I want to tell him that it was the best weekend for ages, that I spent the weekend feeling like myself again, and that I came home with things to plant in a garden; things that would grow into something that someone might like. I want to tell him that I felt, for a while, a feeling like I fitted in somewhere, fitted in with all the the pictures and salt and pepper shakers, all the other stuff that is what family is. But when I came home, all I felt was that that wasn't possible. Because everything that is my family has been taken away from me, and that I can't have any of it anymore, and that I don't fit in with what's left over.

I want to make him understand that all of this is feeding a bonfire so big in my stomach, my chest, my limbs; a bonfire that burns so hot that I can't touch anyone, and when it's burning I don't feel like me. When the fire is burning I feel like something bigger, something more powerful.

And I want to tell him that the thing that is burning feels good.

And I want to tell him that this scares me.

THIRTY SEVEN

'Hi, love. Look who I ran into on the driveway.' Mum is coming in with the shopping. I walk through from the kitchen to help her.

'Took one for the team yesterday, Josh? If you'll pardon the expression. How's the nose?' Mr Walters face appears behind Mum in the doorway. He smiles, two shopping bags in each hand.

'It's OK, thanks.' The shock at seeing him here is overtaken by my manners. He looks somehow different outside of school. Somehow smaller without his room around him, but taking up more space.

'Mr Walters says you missed the session this afternoon. Is that right?'

'Not to worry, Josh, I'm sure you had other homework to be getting on with. English or something.' I'm not sure, but I think Mr Walters winks at me.

'Yeah. Right.' My weak reply.

'Not to worry at all. I was looking for that textbook so I could bring it by. I pass your house on the way home. But I couldn't find the one you were using.'

'It's here, Sir. Upstairs. I must have put it in my bag after last week. Sorry.'

'Never apologise for keenness, Josh. I was grabbing

a spare from my boot when your mum pulled into the driveway.'

'Oh. OK.' I'm unsure why I'm owed such a technical explanation.

Mr Walters has dumped the shopping bags on the kitchen table. Mum's gone out for the others. We're alone. He stands with his hands on his hips, looking awkward.

'So, here we are. A bit weird, having your teacher in your house, isn't it?'

I smile, shrug.

Mum's voice from the hallway breaks the silence. 'All done. Thank you, Mr Walters, for your help. And can I just say thanks again for looking out for Josh. He's really responding to the Biology work. It's brilliant you've taken an interest.'

'Just doin' ma job.' His cowboy accent is truly awful, but Mum laughs delightedly. 'I'll be on my way now though. See you tomorrow then, Josh. Mrs Milton.'

As he leaves, Mum puts out a hand to pat the air a few inches from where his arm had just been. Turning, she walks back to the kitchen. 'Thursday already, eh? You been home long, Love?'

'Yes Mum, since school finished.'

I haven't. In a bid to avoid Alan and Vince as instructed, I'd gone back to the burial ground again and sat for a while by Dad's tree as it got dark. I'd apologised, in a kind of half-whispered, half-thought way, for how much I'd let him down in the last few years by not doing anything about his murder. I told him how he must have been ashamed of me for not recognising what he'd done, and for how I'd just carried on as usual without realising that he'd died in an ongoing war which I hadn't even known about. I'd explained that I knew now, and that I was going to change. The rising wind had howled its approval, and I'd pushed against my nose again, wincing through the pain and making it bleed fresh onto the tree's deepening roots. Just a few drops. Perhaps now he'd come to me in my dreams.

I'd told Dad what I was learning, and read to him some stuff from the websites about the movement of the mob and the anger. About how we are being weakened from within, and about how we need to expose the lies of society through humour – I know now why the frog, Pepe (I know his name now), is such a powerful symbol.

I'd told him about the things I'd been learning from the White Lions site and others, explained how the mainstream media aren't reporting on all the actions that are happening up and down the country in an accurate way; about how their words like 'hate crime' and 'racially motivated attacks' are being spun by their mainstream bias because they are owned by the same people who want to eradicate us. I'd told my dad exactly what Carl tells people on the site. 'This is why we use their tactics, Dad. Fakery and irony and treating nothing we do as serious. If we do that, they can't pin us down and we stay one step ahead.'

'But it is serious, deeply serious. But we always remain, on the outside, unserious. It's by treating our beliefs as a joke that we show how serious we are.'

I'd explained all of this to my father, fully convinced I'd understood.

That's where I'd been, not at home.

'Pizza for dinner this evening, love?'

'Yes, Mum.'

'Any homework?'

'No, Mum.'

'You're a good boy, Josh.'

'Yes, Mum.'

THIRTY EIGHT

Friday. On the way home, I stop at the point on the road with the bent stinging nettle, where the bushes and undergrowth grow to a height against an unseen wall.

The nettles look a little bit trampled today – a larger than normal hole in the green. Still almost indistinguishable, but definitely *there*.

Checking I'm not seen, I step through, careful not to make too much damage.

The gate is locked. I look up into the canopy of the bush. It looks climbable enough. Leaving my backpack against the wall, I start to push up through the leaves. The bottom layers have hardened yellow and brown. Some tip cold water onto me as I climb, small reservoirs trapped in their crinkled cups. The top of the wall, when I reach it, is still a good distance beneath the top of the bush. I crawl a little way along it, the mortar crumbling under my palms, before emerging into a place where I can see into the garden.

Dana is there. She hasn't seen me yet. She is using a small spade to turn the soil in one of the beds. I've watched Grandad do this countless times, and she has the same, smooth action, leaning into the top of the spade, the arch of her foot meeting the shaft and its angle with the top of the blade – Grandad calls it the shoulder – and wedging the blade into the soil. When she leans into the handle, standing entirely on her spade foot, there is a rasping shuck as the spade drives into the ground. Watching her, it's as if she and the spade are the same creature.

After a few minutes of watching, she stops turning the soil and begins cutting the turf where it meets the bed. She cuts a straight, clean line. The spade, with Dana steering it, moves quicker – a series of neat little slices. There's a piece of string set up as a guide, but from up here I can see it's not quite straight – it leans slightly away from parallel with the wall. I want to call out and tell her, but something about her actions, how self-contained they are, suggest she's in a different universe all together. She won't hear me.

As I watch, she starts to sing to herself, softly. Not a song I recognise, but one which seems to match the rhythm with which she works. She pushes the spade in, lifts it, lines up against the string and sinks the blade again in time to her singing.

> *Go to sleep, little baby.*
> *Go to sleep, little baby.*
> *Everybody's gone in the cotton and the corn*
> *Didn't leave nobody but the baby.*

As quietly as I can, I climb back down the inside of the bush.

'I know you're there, Josh.'

Not quietly enough.

I pick up my bag and wait for the door to open, which is does with a violent jerk. Dana's head is in the opening, her eyes hard, all wall.

'Were you watching me?'

'No. Yes. Sorry. I—'

'Do you get thrills from that kind of thing? Are you one of those perverts who likes watching people?'

'No. I—'

'Did Carl send you?'

'No. But—'

'But what?'

A blackbird fills the silence from somewhere inside the garden.

'Are you coming in then, now you're here?' The door gives an inch, and Dana steps back.

I creep through, the smell of turned earth sharper down here than it was from up on the wall.

'What are you doing?'

'Tidying up. Sorting out the dead leaves, digging in some compost for the spring. I'm late this year, what with … everything. There's a box in the far corner; rake up all these leaves and put them in there.'

The box is a relatively large bin made of planks of wood hammered to spikes in the ground. It's behind a bush. When I take the lid off, a warm, sweet-sour steam wafts gently upwards from the rotting leaves already inside. Before long, I have to take my coat off. The work keeps me warm and busy for about twenty minutes, and when I'm finished there isn't a leaf left on the grass. I enjoy the mindless thoroughness of the job.

Almost without speaking, Dana and I take the lower planks from the leaf bin and she digs out a small pile of rich, deep brown earth. A few worms are coiling and uncoiling on the top of the heap. She fetches a large bucket, which I fill and carry to wherever in the garden she points. We then mix the bucket-soil with the ground-soil until they're indistinguishable.

Next, she goes to one of the many shrubs and bushes and, using what look like short, curved scissors with long handles, she starts to clip off branches and twigs, checking the length of each section before deciding whether or not to trim it. Wordlessly, I gather the offcuts and put them in the bin with the leaves.

After an hour or so, seemingly convinced of my work ethic or compliance, Dana pulls a vacuum flask from the pocket of her coat which is hanging over an upright spade, pours a stream of brown liquid into the lid, and offers it to me. She has decided, it seems, that the huge, unspoken things between us have grown small enough to let us speak.

'Do you want some or not?' she asks when I don't move.

The hot chocolate is gloriously warm, rich and creamy. I smack my lips and pass the lid back. 'Thanks. That was brilliant.'

'You're not bad at this. You seem to know what you're doing.' Dana pours herself a cupful.

'I watch my grandad a lot. Or used to. And Mum and Dad used to do a bit, too. They made me help a few times. I never used to enjoy it. But this time it was good. I feel … I don't know…'

'Grounded.'

'Yeah, that's it.'

'Like you've given something back. Like you belong a bit more.'

'Yeah. Exactly.'

Dana drinks her hot chocolate slowly, thinking something over.

'How are you?' I ask.

'Fine. Why?' Her question is accusatory, sharp.

'Just … asking. Being polite.'

Suddenly, she turns on me. 'Have you got any idea what you're getting into? Who you're hanging around with?'

'God, will you stop going on about it?' Dana's constant attacks are starting to get to me. 'Anyway, I thought you were on board with all this … stuff. He is your boyfriend, after all.'

She looks away. 'I told you about that.'

'About Carl? You said something about being lowered down a well.'

'So you were listening then, that day in your room. Just…'

'Just what?'

'Just didn't *do* anything about it.'

'What was I supposed to do?'

The warmth of the hot chocolate is curdled by another heat, the anger rising again. 'You'd just told me I was absolutely fine about my dad being murdered and how much you admired that.'

Dana's testy, angular demeanour is rubbing off on me.

'That's not what I meant.'

'And your boyfriend had already hit me once, so I didn't fancy another black eye. I was probably justified in having a few problems with your boyfriend on my mind.'

'Stop calling him that. He's not that.'

'What? Your boyfriend? *You* call him that. Don't you?'

'You know what he's like. You've seen him *in action*. He has a way of making you … *be* someone he wants you to be. Of making you … *do* things.'

'So you don't believe in what he does? In all of the—'

'What do you think?' Dana's question lashes into me. 'You think I'm one of you *soldiers*? Some nasty, violent kid who gets a kick out of hurting people, like

Vince? Do you think I'm like his wet sack of a brother? But don't let me stop you, "Soldier". I bet they're dead pleased to have you on board.'

'I'm not on board,' I protest.

'You're doing a fucking good job of pretending.' Dana downs the rest of her drink and slams the lid back on the vacuum flask. 'What are you doing here, Josh? Why are you spying on me? Why are you turning up to my place – *my place* – as if it's yours as well? Why do you think you're being *helpful*?'

'Do you want me to go?'

'God! Josh! You really don't get it, do you?' Dana is shouting now. 'No. I don't want you to go! Where's your backbone? Stand up to me, for God's sake! Stop being such a pushover!'

I pick up my coat and head for the door in the corner, my face burning.

'Josh. I'm sorry. I'm not good with people. For some reason I say the wrong thing. I don't know, maybe I want everything to go to shit.' She laughs, half-heartedly.

I turn. Behind her crumbled wall of aggression and capability, Dana stands looking like a lost thing. Her shoulders droop, and a light breeze could blow her over.

'Please stay.'

So I do. The nick and slice of turf at the edge of the beds, the slick roll of cold, wet soil on the end of my fork, the call and return of blackbirds inside the garden and beyond. These are the only sounds of the evening.

THIRTY NINE

Dana and I leave the garden a long time after the sun goes down.

'Will he be angry at you, for being out?'

'He's away at the moment. On "business". Out of town.' Something in the way she says 'business' sounds disdainful, sneered. 'He's got something he needs to prepare for, apparently.'

'That's something, at least.'

Dana smiles, 'Yeah. I guess.'

She turns the opposite way to me at the main road, the fork and shovel slung over one shoulder, a plastic bag of other tools in the other hand.

'High-ho,' I offer, weakly.

She laughs, turns back and we share a clumsy hug. She essentially armless, me trying not to get mud on her back. 'Thanks. For your help.' She nods towards the garden.

'No problem.' A short silence, a car or two passing on the road, the sweep of their headlights catching Dana's eyes. 'So...'

'Yeah. So.'

'See you Monday?'

'Yeah.'

And she's gone.

Mum spends from Friday night until midday on Sunday at Nanna and Grandad's. I survive on toast, microwave meals, and commenting on the forums of the websites that Alan and Carl have sent me. Mum and I spend Sunday afternoon and the best part of the evening avoiding each other until, after her bath, her bedroom door clicks closed at about half past seven.

Five minutes later, I step out of the front door.

The things that Dana said have buzzed around my head all weekend. But something in the websites I'd spent most of Saturday looking at – something in the pictures, the headlines and videos – had sat on top of her words and kind of squashed the air out of them. The White Lions seem like a kind of calling. I know they can make me feel better.

The Crown is about a fifteen-minute walk, and I set out through the drizzling rain. The wind is picking up again, whipping the droplets into my face despite how tightly the toggles on my hood are drawn. But there's a well-stoked fire in my stomach, despite Dana's warnings, fanned by excitement. I don't feel the cold.

The pub looms up as I turn the last corner. A single bulb, somewhat forlorn, points at the sign that swings in the wind. There's not much light coming around the thick curtains at the windows either. A pair of orange points glowing in the smokers' shelter to one side trace patterns in the air – up, glow brighter, down again. It's 7:52. I'm early, and don't know what to expect. Nervousness keeps me standing in the covered bus stop across the road for a few minutes more.

The two orange cigarette ends drop to the floor almost in unison. I give it two more minutes, then cross the road.

The function room is accessed around the side of the building, but I hear my name hissed from the main doorway as I walk past. Dana grabs my arm and pulls me back towards the smoking shelter.

'What are you doing?' Her hair is wet, plastered to her head.

'I was… Aren't you here to—'

'This is dangerous. Too dangerous. These are not nice people, Josh. I told you that. What are you doing here?'

'Aren't you here as well?' I ask, a little mystified.

'It's different for me. I can't… Look, I don't have long. You don't have to be here. You could walk away now. Walk away now, please, Josh. No one will know. I won't say I saw you.'

'What do you mean? I thought you were with us?'

'Us? Who the fuck is us, Josh? Didn't you hear anything I said on Friday? You're sounding like them and it's scary. It's only been, what, a month? Less? That's all it took.'

'All it took for what?'

'Is that you, Soldier? Hiding from the rain? Afraid you'll melt?' It's Alan's now familiar voice. 'Come on, they're starting.'

I look back at Dana, and even from a few feet away I have trouble making her out where she's slipped backwards into the shadows. She shakes her head at me, almost imperceptibly.

'Yeah, coming,' I say, and follow Alan and Vince through the heavy, wooden door and up a flight of stairs, the red and black carpet almost worn through in the bowed middle of each step.

Inside, the room is warmed by several gas heaters but has not quite shrugged off the smell of damp. Dotted around the room are several tables with a few stools at each, their coverings as worn as the carpet. At least one stool at each table is occupied. In all, there are about twenty people here. I sit with Alan and Vince at a table against the left-hand wall. At the front of the room, a small group of five or six men huddle around two of the other tables that they've pushed together; there's a sheet of paper spread out on the table, and they keep pointing at it. One of the men is Carl.

Seeing Carl up there, I feel suddenly that Dana was right, in a way. I try to remember that feeling of power that came from looking at the websites, the frog memes, but it's not there anymore. It's different, somehow, in real life. And I don't know what Vince would do if I just left. Or Carl. I tell myself that I owe this to Dad. But something in my stomach is saying I need to get out.

I mutter something about needing a piss and follow the toilet signs down a narrow corridor that smells even worse than the meeting room. Luckily, the toilet's empty, and I sit down in the one cubicle. The lock's broken, and the door opens outwards, so I have to hold it closed. Hopefully, I think, I'll have a few minutes to myself to get my head together. To man up a bit.

But I'm out of luck.

A man comes in, whistling. He makes straight for the urinal and lets out a loud sigh. I try to keep as quiet as I can. There's only a thin plastic panel between us.

'How you doin' in there fella?'

He can't be talking to me, can he?

'First time nerves is it? Don't worry, Son, You'll be alright. Saw you come in.'

He is talking to me. My heart is pounding in my ears.

'These lads are alright, Kid. Best bunch I've met to tell the truth. Especially Carl. He's a diamond. Bit scary to look at though, eh?' He laughs a laugh that turns into a cough.

I hear his fly zipper, then a moment later the tap starts running.

'Look, I'll tell you a story.'

The loud moan of the hand drier starts up. Then stops.

'First time I came here I was like you. Unsure, nervous, all that stuff. Wasn't sure why I'd bothered, tell the truth. I drink downstairs see, and was just a bit curious I guess. So I wandered up here one night to see what was up.'

There's a creak as the man leans on the frame of the cubicle, his voice closer to the door.

'Wasn't that impressed at first, lots of language being used I wasn't used to hearing, things I'd been told you weren't allowed to say, you know? So I thought about getting up and leaving. Told myself I would, too, when they stopped for a break. Was telling myself I was going to have to find somewhere else to drink, all that nonsense going on up here. But do you know what happened?'

There's a pause. I can't fill it.

'Well, I'll tell you. Soon as Carl finished talking, he comes up to me and offers to buy me a pint. Sits down with me for a long while and has a talk with me. Just me. There's plenty of people in the room trying to catch his eye, but he talks to me, a fella he's never met before. Don't mind saying but it made me feel a bit special, you know?'

Yes, I know.

'And he doesn't say much either. Just asks me questions and listens to the answers. Actually listens. So I told him about me, my life, all that. And then I stayed. Simple as that. To be honest with you I don't much care for the kind of things they talk about here. I could take it or leave it, but after the big lads have all finished lecturing, it's the chat that comes after that I like. That's what you'll find here, Kid. Friendship. And we all need that, don't we?'

My fingers slip on the door and it opens a fraction of an inch. Through the small opening, I see the back of a blue knitted jumper, fraying at the elbows. Faded jeans. The man is facing the opposite wall. I ease the door closed again. The hinges creak loudly.

'So do you know Carl quite well then? Like, hang out with him and stuff?' My question surprises me. So does the low voice I try to put on when I ask it.

'Well, not so much really, apart from these meetings. But we always have a drink after. There's not a lot of friendship going around at the moment. People are suspicious of everyone. Seem like everyone's scared of each other I'd say. And anyway, even if it is only once a month, at least it's something to do, eh? What else you going to spend your Sunday night doing, except sitting in a toilet?'

He laughs again, then coughs.

'Tell the truth, I'm not always a hundred per cent convinced Carl's got his head screwed on right, but it's his opinion and he's entitled to it. Anyway, I'm going to get back in before they start. Don't know what nonsense they're going to talk about tonight, but they seem pretty excited. Maybe we'll have a chat after it's done, eh? If you come out, that is?'

There's another laugh, and a creak as the man removes his weight from the door frame. I hear his footsteps cross the bathroom, the door open then close again. I give it half a minute before I come out.

I run my hands under cold water at the cracked sink, looking at myself in the mirror. I can see my father's eyes looking back at me somewhere behind my own. Or at least that's what I want to see. Just listen, I tell myself. What else have you got to do on a Sunday evening?

On my way back into the room, the man in the blue jumper and jeans catches my eye. His face has a sort of open expression. But his eyes seem to be somewhere else. He's on his own at a table, two large cokes in front of him. He picks one up and raises it in my direction, offering it to me.

'Cheers,' I say. That deep voice again. It's not my voice, but it makes me feel … better, somehow.

'Catch up in a bit then, eh?' The man asks. His eyes have an almost desperate quality. 'My name's Dan, by the way.'

'Sure. Nice to meet you, Dan. I'm Josh.' We clink glasses. I make my way back to Alan and Vince's table, walking a bit taller.

A few minutes later, Dana slips in and sits on her own in a table in the far corner. She doesn't look at me as she crosses the room. She doesn't look at anyone. At the front table, Carl turns and watches her cross the room. For a horrible second I think he's seen me looking at her, but he simply nods at our table – Alan nods back – and Carl goes back to his conversation with the others.

'Can you feel it, Josh? That buzz in the air?' Alan can hardly keep still. 'Something's going to happen tonight. It's all about you, Poster-boy!'

I don't know what he's talking about, but there is, despite the smell, something electric in the atmosphere. In ones, twos and occasionally threes, the men in the room are talking in hunched groups or to those men on other tables, raising their pint glasses and clinking them together. And looking at me.

'Right lads, we're gonna make a start.' A man steps to the centre of the room and a hush descends immediately. He's wearing all black, but stands out a mile. From the ripped ends of his black T-shirt, full-length sleeve tattoos of skulls and hammers run down to his wrists. Creeping above the line of his collar towards his left ear, a union flag. On the other side, a pair of crossed hammers.

As if responding to some unspoken cue, the whole room stands at once. It takes me a few seconds to realise I should stand up too. Everyone's got their hands across their chests, like they're taking some kind of oath.

The man at the front of the room barks a few words, then everyone replies together. I don't know what they're saying, or what I should say, but I stand there with my hand on my chest and try to mutter something. There's a little bit that I do recognise: the 14 words from the end of the videos. I think I get about half of it right.

Everyone sits down again, the energy in the room doubled in intensity.

'As you know,' the man at the front continues, 'Carl's got some stuff to feed back on the last few national meetings in London. Then he's got some news about what's coming up here soon.'

There are a few cheers and whoops, shouts of 'Go on, Carl!' which the frontman silences with a smile. He continues, 'Once again gentlemen, it's very good to see so many soldiers here this evening. It's good to know that there are still good people in this town who love their country and are willing to protect it.' His eyes flick to me at that moment, finding me in a heartbeat. Like he knew I was here. 'For our children. And now, Carl.'

Carl steps up. He also bears a sleeve of inked hammers, skulls and flags. I didn't notice them under his shirt last week, and they must be recent as they weren't in the article photograph either. 'Before I start, I'd like to welcome a new soldier to the ranks. Someone we've been expecting. Gents, this is Josh.'

I freeze as all the eyes in the room are on me in a second. Just able to return their gazes for a second each, I see many other tattoos of crossed hammers, many blue-inked knuckles wrapped around beer glasses as Carl continues.

'Josh's story is known to most of you, and it's with pleasure that I welcome him here. He's made a step towards doing something about what happened to him. About what's been taken from him. And you know what he's been through, so make him feel welcome. We're going to help you. We're all here for you, alright Josh?'

I realise this is a question, and nod rapidly. The other men nod back, more than a few cross their arms in front of their chest, revealing a tattooed hammer on each forearm. Alan pats me on the back.

'Anyway, the National Committee are pretty happy with the groundswell at the moment, and how that's continued for the last year or so,' Carl continues. 'We've kept the momentum going locally, even in the smaller backwaters, like here, where there's no centre to base a movement around. I know a lot of us are part of various football lads' groups, but we've kept our end up without the traditional pull of a big team. So firstly, from them, well done. We'll carry on with the leafletting we've been doing, keep talking to the same groups, and keep up the agitations at the weekends.' There's a small cheer at this. 'But Barney…?'

A huge man with a shaved head looks up, 'Yes Carl?'

'Remember to keep it PG before the watershed OK? There were kids in that pub last Friday. It's not good that their safety ends up dominating the press on the issue.'

'Right you are, Boss.'

'Good work on the choice of target though – sounds like those three ... gentlemen ... won't be coming through again, on business or pleasure.'

'My business, my pleasure,' smiles the man called Barney. There's a low cheer, and a smattering of applause.

Carl holds the attention of the room in the same way that good teachers keep control of their classes at school. After every few things that he says, he makes a joke or a comment about someone in front of him. The result is a funny kind of glow that goes from person to person around the damp-smelling room, almost like Carl is a kind of lighthouse, casting light on each person in turn. It's warm in the light, and you listen very hard to what's being said, because you think that will make the light fall on you again. It reminds me, for some reason, of the Thursday evenings in Mr Walters' classroom.

So I listen very hard to talk about national actions: a march that took place in London last weekend – peaceful, unfortunately, but with good opportunities to network with other groups; an online campaign to encourage younger members to get out from behind their computers and be more active – Alan and Vince get some light for that one; and finally the news that the White Lions' plan has been given the go ahead by the national committee. 'Martin thinks it's good. Sketchy around the edges, but the core is pure gold, he said. And you know what that means.'

Again, cheering. Everyone seems to know who Martin is, except me.

Everyone in the room is leaning further forward on their elbows. There are eager looks between a few of the men. Carl scans the room with narrowed eyes, fully aware that everyone is giving him their undivided attention, like some wild animal, waiting for the rest of the pack to show respect, and milking it when he gets it. A pair of older guys towards the back of the room are talking quickly to each other under their breath. Carl stares hard at them until they realise and cease speaking immediately. He could rip their throats out. He is leonine, impressive. I'm rivetted to the spot, ready to hear what the fiercest man in the room has to say.

'It's been disappointing,' Carl begins, his voice changed and barely above a hissed whisper, 'that so many of our recent actions have not seen the participation of more than a handful of this group's members.'

The quiet in the room gets, somehow, even quieter. People are afraid even to cough or move their hands. Drinks go un-drunk on the table tops.

'Who is it that goes out on patrol in the evenings, keeping our streets safe? Who is it that has been taking our message straight to the root of our country's problem? Which of you can say that in the last year he's done anything more than waving a flag at a couple of demonstrations?'

With this last question, Carl seems to look directly

at several people in the room at the same time. Their eyes lower, meekly. The man called Barney says, 'Too fucking right.'

Carl continues, 'So if any of you have lost your appetite for this war, I'll say what I've said a hundred times. There's the door. If you can't stomach what needs to be done, if you are too selfish to commit, if you are putting your own interests above those of this beautiful country, above doing what's right for Josh, then get out. Now.'

In the seemingly endless silence that follows, nobody moves. All eyes are on me and I can barely breathe. I see Dan in his blue jumper, nodding.

'Good,' Carl's voice is even quieter now; a rasping, guttural croak. 'Because this thing we're going to do, for our country, for Josh, is going to include all of us. You are all necessary. You all have a role to play.'

Every time I hear my name it's like an electric fist in my stomach, tightening. Under the table, I can feel Alan's leg bouncing in nervous excitement. Vince sits with his arms crossed, looking as always like a dog at heel. I can feel my heart racing in my chest and I'm reminded again of Dana's story. Not about Carl but about her father, about the well. I feel like I'm hanging over a dark hole, and someone has been lowering me down slowly all evening. The more I've listened, the deeper I've gone.

And in the musty room of that pub, when Carl tells

us his plan, someone lets go of the rope that was holding me. I fall head first, and so fast that my mouth packs with rushing air. I can't even scream.

FORTY

Monday morning, and I wake up in my own bed, not entirely certain of how I got there. My bedside clock says it's just after 5am, but I know I won't be going back to sleep.

I roll over in the darkness of the first day of December and stare at the ceiling, last night replaying in front of my eyes as vividly as it did when it first happened. As vividly as it replayed again and again all night. I've barely slept; every time I drifted into a kind of sleep I'd be met by the faces of those men, swimming out of the blackness to snarl at me. Some invisible 'Martin' behind them all. Every time oblivion threatened to welcome me, Carl's hissing voice told me again the details of what they were planning to do.

I shiver beneath the duvet. Dana was right. I shouldn't have been there.

But I was. So, wrapping the covers around me, I shuffle over to my desk and open my laptop. I open one of the many sites that are now saved in my browser and start looking for the justification that I need.

I find what I'm looking for after a few clicks.

The pictures of the blown-out tube train float on the screen in the darkness of my bedroom. The whole room is lit by their blue-grey glow as I stare again past the twisted remains of seats, looking for what I thought I saw last time.

The pictures haven't changed – they've been waiting for me patiently, holding their secrets. The blood in the foreground has the same pattern as I remember – blurred footprints. The buckled metal of the seats, the smashed over-head lighting; everything is just as it was.

I increase the image size and use the scroll-wheel to pick through the pictures section by section, like a search and rescue party sifting through a snowy field. But I'm not looking for survivors.

I zoom in on a section of the train which must have been at the centre of the blast. The sides of the carriage are split and you can see the walls of the tunnel itself, the dim lights shining weakly between the ripped tin-can edges of buckled steel.

When the pixels start to separate from each other, and the whole screen looks like a collage of grey and brown squares, I zoom in even further. Eventually, just one square fills the centre of the screen. It is a very dark square, almost black. It is the colour of Dad's pannier bag, and it will do.

I stare at it for a long time.

That single, black square hangs in my vision all day. I use it to block out the memories of last night; the looks on the faces of those men as they heard about what was going to happen, about what Carl was going to do. What he was going to make us all do.

About the thing that Martin said was pure gold. Whoever Martin is.

English passes behind this black square. So does Maths after break, and Geography before lunchtime. I spend these lessons staring at this black square in my mind. Later, it blocks out all the noise and jostling of the canteen. The same as I get my lunch. I sit at the window again and stare at the black square, imagining that it has been printed out on a huge piece of paper and stuck to the glass. It's not quite enough, so I imagine living inside of the square, being enveloped by it, letting it take up all the space and sound around me.

But it's still not enough. Every now and again, Carl's face will get through the cracks where the black square isn't black enough, or isn't complete enough. Sometimes it's his voice, disembodied and quiet, slithering into my ear. And there are thoughts I can't keep out: not those of Carl or Alan or Vince or the other men, but my thoughts.

I don't go, that afternoon, to my biology lesson. I spend almost two hours in the end cubicle of the boys' toilets, staring at the wall and flushing the chain whenever the silence gets too loud.

On the way home, I drift along with the tide of people heading away from school. The traffic is at its usual almost-standstill, the drone of queueing engines oddly soothing. It is raining lightly. I think Ahmed waved to me as he got into his mum's white 4x4, but I'm not certain. I'm not even certain of where I'm going, or of what I will do when I get there.

I'm not sure, either, of what Jamie says when he puts a hand on my shoulder to stop me. All I know is that I want to get away. I want nothing so badly as to go back to that screen with that single, black square that may or not be Dad and to stare at it with all my being until everything else fades away.

But Jamie is asking me questions. His face seems to show a look of concern. He is taking me by both shoulders and shaking me gently, stooping slightly so he can look into my eyes.

I want him to go away.

I don't hit him so much as push him. It's not as if I swing a flaming fist into his cheek to give him a bruise and spill red blood all down one side of his face, like mine.

It's not like that.

Instead, I place both hands on his chest and shove as hard as I can, to get him away from me.

And then I'm fully awake, the black square lifted, and I'm seeing everything very, very clearly.

I see Jamie step backwards, his startled face lost as he struggles to keep his balance. He takes one, two, three steps. Backwards.

Towards the road.

The traffic still isn't moving very quickly and, behind the wheel of her white 4x4, Ahmed's mum sees Jamie coming before he steps off the kerb and starts falling backwards. She stops in plenty of time. But we both watch, our faces similarly frozen, as Jamie bounces against the back end of a red car in front of hers, his arms desperate for some kind of solid surface to push against. We watch the red car, unaware of what is happening, creep slowly forward in the flow of traffic and I see through her windscreen Ahmed's mum's mouth held in a perfect O, her eyes wide, as Jamie starts to slip sideways and fall into the gap between her car and the red one in front.

In the passenger seat, Ahmed's eyes are glued to his phone screen, but because she has been watching, Ahmed's mum reacts quickly, braking hard to bring her car to a stop safely in front of Jamie, who sits in the road, staring at me in disbelief. Ahmed flinches, his head jerking up. He takes it all in. He sees Jamie in the road. He sees me.

But the cyclist, riding fast down the inside of the stationary traffic, his headphones loud, his mind elsewhere, does not see any of it. He doesn't see me. He doesn't see Jamie lying in the road.

He passes the white 4x4 at speed.

His front wheel ploughs into Jamie's leg.

The bike stops. The cyclist doesn't. He turns a complete somersault over the handlebars, through the air above Jamie's head, towards the back of the red car.

Before the dull thud of the cyclist's body striking the red car's tailgate, before the sound of tinkling glass, before the slow tick of the bike's still-spinning wheel coming to a stop in the seconds afterwards – before all of these things, there is the worst sound of all: the crack as Jamie's leg breaks.

FORTY ONE

I imagine car doors opened and people shouted and telephone calls were made.

But I wasn't there to hear them.

I imagine a crowd of students gathered around the screaming form of Jamie in the road.

But I wasn't there to see them either.

I was running.

I still am.

As I run, I think I imagine the insistent siren of an ambulance.

But I'm not sure.

None of this feels real anymore. Or maybe it's the opposite; that everything is suddenly far too real.

I get home and up to my bedroom, shutting the door and heading straight to my desk. My laptop. When they come, they might take it away. They might see what's inside.

Without hesitating, I pick it up and go as fast as I can on shaking legs out into the garden, towards the shed. Inside, I put the laptop on the floor and rummage behind the beer stack for a brick.

I wince at the sound of the heavy brick meeting the laptop's aluminium shell. But I raise it again, bringing it down hard. The glass smashes and the computer bends up at the edges. Shards of screen and a few keys leak out where the laptop no longer closes properly.

I hit it again. And again. And again.

But what if it's not enough? What if they can reconstruct what's here?

Grabbing my bag, I stuff the blistered and crumpled machine inside.

Ten minutes later, I'm standing under the hedge, the wrong side of the locked door. I try to climb the wall again, using the branches of the hedge to help. But I'm panicking. It takes a few attempts to get started, and I take the skin off a few knuckles against the wall. After a few deep breaths I try again and manage it. Then I'm pulling myself onto the top of the wall, looking down at what must be a three-metre drop into the garden.

I go backwards, holding onto the top of the wall and easing myself down until my arms are stretched. It's still a metre to the floor.

I land in a flowerbed, on the soft soil that Dana and I turned over on Friday.

Only three days ago.

I slash through the bush in the corner and there it is, the well, still visible in the early evening light. I have to move a few half-rotten planks, the wood crumbling in my fists as I pull at them, the nails at the ends soon giving up and slipping from the wood with a damp screech. I make a big enough hole to post the remains of the laptop through, and I let it go, listening for the crash as it hits the bottom. There's a second sound as all the bits of screen and keys and circuit boards land just after. It is a sound like rain.

I sit for I don't know how long, breathing heavily, clutching my school bag to my chest.

Soon, I'm vaguely aware of a lump in the bottom of the bag. I reach in, past the schoolbooks, my pencil case. My hand lands on a rustling ball of brown paper. Inside, a dozen brown spheres that look like onions.

Grandad's bulbs.

FORTY TWO

When I get back to the house a few hours later, I'm not surprised by the police car that's parked next to Mum's in the driveway, or the voices coming from the sitting room stop as I let myself in.

Mum comes into the hallway. She's been crying. More than usual. She gives me a look which is part pleased-to-see-you, part are-you-ok, and part something else which I don't recognise. She steps back and points, weakly, towards the sitting room. 'There's someone to see you.'

'I know,' I say as I walk past her and, as I do, she puts her hand out to stop me, placing it very gently on my cheek. I smile, weakly.

On the sofa, and taking up most of it with her yellow jacket, bulky vest and an assortment of things around her waist, is a police officer. She stands as I come in.

'Hello Josh.'

'Hi.'

'I think you know why I'm here.'

I nod. 'Is he OK? Jamie?'

'Yes, he'll be fine. He'll stay in hospital overnight, but he'll be out in the morning.'

211

I swallow. 'What about the other one? The boy on the bike?'

The police officer looks at the floor for a second. 'In hospital as well. We'll let you know if there's a change. But it doesn't look good. He wasn't wearing a helmet.'

A pause. A long one. I can hear Mum breathing.

'Why don't you sit down, Josh?' The police officer points to the easy chair in the window.

I notice as I round the room that there are three cups on the coffee table, only one of them still full. Cold.

I sit. The police officer pulls a notebook from a pocket of her vest.

'Jamie says you weren't right today. That you seemed angry. Want to tell me what's going on?'

I sit in silence.

'OK, why don't you talk me through the incident. You were on your way home, and...'

'I pushed him.' I say, bluntly. 'I wanted to hit him but I pushed him instead, and he fell backwards and then the bike came along.'

'Why did you push him, Josh?'

'I wanted him to leave me alone.'

'Was he threatening you in any way?'

'No. He was...' I trail off, aware of how ridiculous it sounds.

'He was what?'

'He was ... being nice. I didn't want him to be nice to me.'

The police officer steals a look at Mum, hovering in the doorway.

'Well, Josh,' Mum speaks. 'It seems that Jamie is still being nice, despite what his parents want. And despite what another witness says. He says that he pushed you first, and that you were playing around and it was an accident.'

I don't look up, but feel my cheeks burning.

'Is that right, Josh?' The police officer asks, her pencil poised above her notepad.

'Yeah,' I manage, hoarsely. 'If that's what he said, that's what happened.'

'The lucky thing for you, Josh, is that Jamie doesn't want to take this any further. He's happy to see this as an accident. Which means the school won't be taking it any further either. However, the fact is that your actions directly caused an injury – quite a serious one – to a cyclist. Whatever the two of you were up to, it was reckless and dangerous. It can't happen again. Do I make myself perfectly clear?'

I almost whisper, 'Yes.'

'We're going to need to speak to you again, at the station. We need to be absolutely certain of what happened before we can take the next steps, if there are any, and as you fled the scene – which doesn't look good at all, by the way – we need your statement quickly. Is that clear?'

Again, a whisper, 'Yes.'

'Mrs Milton, do you think you'd be able to bring Josh along tomorrow, at about 10, so we can get his statement? You'll need to be there with him, I'm afraid. Sorry if it's inconvenient.'

Mum's voice is barely louder than mine, 'That's fine.'

There are a few more exchanges, mostly about where to park and who to ask for at the front desk. When Mum lets the police officer out, I rush upstairs and close my bedroom door. A few minutes later, I hear Mum do the same.

FORTY THREE

The police station is cold – not just the air temperature, but the seats and the cramped reception area and the looks on the faces of the people who walk in and out as we sit in the foyer. It's not really a foyer, just a few plastic chairs and a table covered in ripped magazines wedged into the small space in front of a glass screen. After a few minutes, an officer behind the screen tells us to come through the door. We're taken through to an even colder, even smaller waiting room. The police officers' faces behind their desk are cold as well. So is the tea in the vending machine.

Mum and I don't speak while we sit in the cold chairs, drinking our cold tea, and when the officer from yesterday comes in and greets us it shakes us both from a kind of cold-induced stupor.

We're taken through to another small, square room with greying tiles on every surface and a large sheet of one-way glass on the wall. The officer explains that the interview will be recorded and asks if I understand that I'm not under arrest or caution at this point, but if I want a lawyer I can have one.

I nod.

I tell the tape recorder what happened; that Jamie

and I were mucking around on the way home and it got out of hand. And I say that it was very lucky that the woman driving the car was watching us so closely and that she stopped in time or it could have been much worse. I know that.

And I say about the cyclist not paying attention, and that he had his headphones in or was using his hands free to talk to someone or something. And that he didn't brake before he hit Jamie's leg, and that I think Jamie had been sitting in the road for about three seconds before he was hit, and that I might be wrong about the timings.

And the police officer says that the other reports they've had, including from the driver of the white BMW, all suggest the same, and that the cyclist was on the phone to his girlfriend while he was cycling along, and that he has now woken up in hospital and, despite a few nasty bruises, will probably be OK, and has said he was stupid for not wearing a helmet and that he hopes the driver of the red car doesn't expect him to pay for the damaged lights.

The police officer finishes by repeating that this could have been a lot worse, and that we were all very lucky. She says lots of things about if the traffic wasn't so slow, or if the cyclist wasn't so lucky, or if Jamie and I hadn't been so reckless – she uses that word a lot, reckless – then none of this would have happened.

And with a sigh, shared with Mum, she says I can go.

Unless, she adds, there's anything else I want to tell her.

At this point my heart hammers in my chest, desperate to shout out the truth about what I know. The officer sits on the other side of the desk, looking at me somehow as if she already has a pretty good idea. Maybe she even knows who Martin is. My heart is telling me that this is the place to do it, and the time, but I swallow those thoughts down hard, unable to erase the sight of Carl's fierce eyes, his snake-like, threatening voice, the way that voice has wormed its way inside my head.

And, perhaps, because I know – in another part of me that seems to have stopped working – that the plan needs to go ahead and it's just me that's the problem.

So, with one last searching look from the police officer, we leave the police station and head home. Or at least I think we're going home. But we don't. Mum pulls out onto the main road and starts driving in the opposite direction. Away from home. Away from school.

It takes at least ten minutes to realise where we're going. To realise that we've started following the red 'H' signs at every roundabout.

When I do work it out, my heart hammers at my chest all over again.

FORTY FOUR

Jamie is in his own room on the children's ward. When we go in, he's lying back on a big pile of pillows, watching morning television. Any other situation, and I'd make a joke about the teddy bears on his pillow cases, or the multi-coloured butterflies painted up the walls. His left leg, encased in a blue cast, is propped up on still more teddy-bear pillows. He turns his head as we enter.

'He's still a bit sluggish after the operation, aren't you, Jamie?' says the nurse as she lets us in.

Jamie gives a half-smile – to the nurse and Mum, not to me – and goes back to looking at the TV.

'I'll be outside, Josh. You need to do this,' Mum whispers as the door closes slowly behind me on its sterile hinges.

For a few seconds, we maintain the silence, both staring at the familiar TV studio and the overly smiling presenters.

'Jamie, I—'

'Don't.'

I take a step closer to the bed. 'Does it hurt?' And when there's no response, 'Stupid question. Sorry.'

'That's a start.'

'I don't know what was going on yesterday. I was … out of it. I wasn't myself.'

'And who is that, exactly?' Jamie's eyes level on me now. 'Just who are you, Josh? Because I'm not sure that I really know anymore. One minute you're back to your old self, you're talking again, for the first time since … I don't know when.'

'Yeah, I know.' I feel like I'm being told off by a parent. There's something reassuring about it.

'And then the next minute you're hanging around with that Alan guy and his psycho brother. They're pricks, Josh. Nasty, violent, racist thugs. Do you know what they've been doing to Ahmed?'

'No.'

'Spitting at him in the corridor, stealing his stuff when we're in PE. Not big stuff, just little annoying things like school books or the top of his drink bottle. It's obviously them. And the names they call him. They're unrepeatable.'

It feels like a heavy weight is rising up through my stomach. Like a bucket being pulled from a deep well. There's a sucking vacuum of air behind it, trying to pull it back down, but it's coming, slowly. And I want it to come. I want it to rise up that shaft, back towards daylight. I know the words they're using to Ahmed. And as I talk to Jamie, and the bucket rises, I want to tell him that I hate them too. Each time I hear them it's like a bite taken out of me. Not from my flesh or anywhere like that, but somewhere deeper. And those words aren't even directed at me. I can't even imagine how they make Ahmed feel.

'They keep asking Ahmed what's in his backpack, like they're expecting him to say it's a bomb or something.' Jamie stops short. Gives me a strange look, like he wants me to confirm that my dad's murderer's backpack looked nothing like Ahmed's.

How would I know?

He carries on, his voice dropping, more sympathetic. 'And none of the teachers that overhear it know what to do at all. They just stand there looking disappointed or say something like "that's enough". And the spray paint on his house a few months ago. Did you know about that? That was almost definitely them, even though they were wearing masks.' Jamie's spitting his words out now. 'They're cowards. They don't go to their own lessons any more, just seem to wait around for him. But I get the feeling this is just the start of it.'

I can't speak, the words sticking in my throat. The bucket's getting closer. I can almost see the shimmer on the water, reflecting the sky.

'And then you, the other week, facing him down that morning. It was like you were on their side, Josh. You're not like that. I don't know what poison they're feeding you, but you need to stop.'

'I know,' I manage, eventually. The water is just a trickle, but it will have to do. For now.

'Or someone's going to get hurt.' Jamie smiles a little at his own joke, intended or not.

'Yeah, I'm sorry about that.'

'It wasn't you. Not entirely anyway. It was that guy on the bike that broke my leg. No more goals from the corner flag for a while at least.'

I make a limp attempt at a laugh. We stare at the screen together. The presenters have stopped smiling and are looking seriously straight down the camera lens. Images of a dusty, bombed-out city, smoking in the heat of the sun. The caption reads 'Aleppo, Syria'.

'You know, his dad died out there. Ahmed's, I mean.'

'What?'

'Ahmed's dad. He worked for some kind of charity or something. Legal stuff I think, or maybe medical. Really important, apparently, so they didn't get out when the fighting started – there were too many people they were helping, or maybe they thought it wouldn't last. Ahmed said that one day his dad didn't come home. Nor did a bunch of other guys he worked with. There was no word from any of them for a week, and his mum tried all the hospitals, or what was left of them. Ahmed's parents had made a pact where if that happened, to either of them, then the other would get out, run away. They'd explained all this to Ahmed. Can you imagine that? Being a little kid and your parents sit you down and explain that they might not come home one day?'

221

I can tell that Jamie knows he's close to the line with me. He's looking at me, gauging my response as my mind flashes back to that that last, warm Sunday evening with Dad, the joke about a last-minute holiday. If it were possible to know the future, would I have wanted to know my life was about to change, violently and irrevocably? Would I have wanted to know that he wasn't coming back? Or am I luckier than Ahmed that our tragedy dropped out of a clear blue sky rather than one already full of smoke and falling bombs?

'So that's what they did, Ahmed and his mum. Ahmed won't talk about it, the journey, except he said that they were in a refugee camp in Turkey for a while. And I haven't pushed him. It took them a while, months I think, but they managed to get to the UK and claimed asylum. I think it was pretty hard on them.'

More silence, me dumbstruck. I know that feeling, how every direction you've ever known is suddenly taken away from you and you don't even know up from down. I can't imagine trying to get somewhere, to save yourselves, whilst carrying that grief.

Jamie's picking at the top of his cast. 'They still don't know where Ahmed's dad is.'

I think about that for a moment. No one to bury. No body to mourn.

We look again at the screen, the camera panning across the skyline of what used to be a modern city. People used to go there on holiday. Now it's just piles of rubble and burnt-out cars where the parks and plazas used to be. So much destruction. So much ruin. So many images to zoom in on, looking for a single pixel.

FORTY FIVE

The next time Mum talks to me, it's Thursday.

She asks me to pass the salt.

We're sitting around the kitchen table. Me. Mum.
And Mr Walters.

They'd bumped into each other in the supermarket
again, and this time she'd asked him if he wanted to
stay for tea.

I can barely breathe.

After Mum, Mr Walters and I had put the shopping
away in silence, Mum pulled a lasagne out of the fridge.
Not a shop one, but one she'd made that day. 'Oh, this?
No, nothing special at all. Just knocked it up this
morning!' she'd said, like it was normal. It's not as if
Mum doesn't cook anymore, but the last time she did
lasagne was a long time ago. Over two years ago.

There's a strange, unfamiliar smell mixed in with
the cheese sauce and minced beef. I think Mum's wearing
perfume.

Conversation is hardly free flowing. Mr Walters keeps
trying to include me, asking me about my other subjects,
how I'm feeling about the new year and my exams. He
keeps asking me things when I've just put a fork-load of
food in my mouth. I almost choke a few times.

And Mum keeps apologising for how quiet I'm being, thrusting glances my way that demand I do better. And Mr Walters replies that it's all OK, that most kids nowadays are the same, and that Josh is probably a bit put out, having his teacher in his house.

After dinner, Mr Walters makes his excuses and leaves. This time, Mum puts her hand on his arm after he's put his coat on. She leaves it there for a full three seconds.

I go upstairs to my room.

The next time she speaks to me is on Sunday night. She's later home than usual. Again, she brings a waft of perfume into the house as she enters. And I think she's wearing make-up.

'Are you going to ask me where I've been?'

'Er… Nanna and Grandad's?' I don't mean to sound so sarcastic.

'Josh, I'm going to start seeing someone.' She is trying to sound more confident than she really is.

'OK. Is it Mr Walters?'

She's surprised that I've guessed. 'Yes, Love. It is. But I need you to understand something.'

'That you're not trying to replace Dad?'

'Well, that wasn't how I was going to put it, but yes. Look, I don't know how long this will last, or how far it will go—'

'Mum!'

'We're not … *doing* anything yet.'

'Mum!'

'I want you to know that.'

'Did you consider whether or not I *wanted* to know?'

'Don't be immature, Josh. He's good to talk to, that's all. At the moment. But before we meet again I wanted you to be sure of what was going on.'

'OK. Fine.' I make to leave. The sanctuary of my bedroom has never called so loudly. I know Mum needs some other company than her parents, but with so much rolling around my head, this new information will have to wait its turn.

And if it's making Mum happy, or happier, it can't be a bad thing I suppose.

Even though I know I have to stop Carl, doing it seems, at first glance, to be almost impossible.

At least time is on my side. Carl's plan won't start rolling towards its inevitable conclusion until the new year. The timings have all been worked out intricately. So I know I've got at least a month before anything will happen.

A month to worry and sweat. A month before standing idly by will start to have consequences. A month of Thursday night dinners with my Biology teacher. Mum keeps me in the loop; they meet in the café at the supermarket a few nights a week, and apparently the coffee isn't as bad as you'd think. On Thursdays, Mr Walters comes and helps with the shopping and stays for tea.

I stick to the plan and keep my distance from Alan and Vince at school – Carl said that this is so that the links between us all will go as undetected as possible. They've even been told to stage some kind of high-visibility falling out, which they do one Tuesday lunchtime in mid-December in a routine that reminds me of my own public punishment. Both of them leave the canteen bleeding, and through opposite doors.

I know I shouldn't miss them, but I do. Not Vince, of course. But Alan was at least trying to comfort me. And there was something in his eyes every time he talked about his brother. He clearly worships him, even though he knows, somewhere, that he's broken. I can't help but feel a little pity for him.

So I go back to being pretty much on my own. Jamie, though not as cold as he could be, is understandably distant, and the majority of people are rightly on his side. There are no ends to the offers to carry his bag, or to leave class early with him to navigate through doorways as he gets used to his lumbering crutches. Most of these offers are from girls, which makes me smile. And Jamie's never more wobbly on his feet than when Louisa's helping him.

As I start to plot what needs to be done, and how to do it, I start to feel a little bit like one of the heroes in the books I used to read. I'm the lone fighter in some kind of dystopian universe, all the other kids unable to see what I can see. Alone, I must battle the secret drone army which is holding the world to ransom. On my modified BMX with a sharpened stick, I must save the world.

Fiction is much less scary than real life.

I'm not really allowed any contact with Dana, either. Not that I was ever really allowed to see her anyway. Despite this, I do go a few times to the garden, climbing up onto the top of the wall to look down. She's never there. The ground toughens towards Christmas, the turned earth sinking back to itself and hardening to cold knuckles. I want to drop down, lay a hand on the cold soil, but I wouldn't be able to get out again. Maybe that would be a good thing.

I do see her around school sometimes. Usually outside Miss Amber's office or, some afternoons, I glimpse her from a second-floor classroom, drifting around the edge of the field, out of lessons.

Once, we passed each other in the corridor. It was halfway through a double Biology lesson and I needed to use the toilet. Mr Walters winked at me when I asked if I could go. 'As it's you, Josh,' he'd said. I went bright red. Might as well have worn a sign saying 'Mr Walters <3 my mum' around my neck.

Dana was leaning against the wall outside the

Deputy Head's office. I smiled, about to say 'hello', but was met by a look of panic, a small but certain shake of the head.

That look kept coming back to me for days after that. Something desperate in it, something trapped. Caged. But it was quickly replaced with Carl's narrowed eyes and the calm violence of the other tattooed men. Their cold faces are never far from my thoughts.

And all the while the days go past. I try to work out what to do. I fail.

With no laptop to spend my time on, I go back to evenings with Mum in front of our usual TV – redecoration shows, house-building shows, which-house-should-we-buy shows. We start getting on better again, but there's something about her which is even further away than it was before. Mr Walters starts staying after tea for some TV, or maybe a film. From my room, I hear them laughing. Or Mr Walters is laughing; Mum is definitely giggling.

We're watching something on catch up one evening, just Mum and me, when a home-building project goes hopelessly wrong as the presenter always knew it would. The one-man building team looks at the semi-devastation around his intended five-bedroomed glass box and says, 'Well, it is what it is.'

I look across, but Mum doesn't seem to register it.

Every morning comes with the smell of burnt toast. Mum takes the batteries out of the smoke alarm.

FORTY SIX

One weekend, almost at the end of term, I decide to wander to the recreation ground to watch the team play again – the last match before the Christmas break. Jamie's there, leaning on his crutches, wrapped up against the frost which, on the top pitch right under the trees, has lasted until the middle of the afternoon. Ahmed's with him. They're both sipping from cans of energy drink.

I'm reluctant to join them at first, for lots of reasons, but Jamie sees me and raises a crutch aloft.

'Alright mascot?' he quips, jocular. 'Still don't fancy a game then?'

'You play?' Ahmed asks.

'Played. I used to. Can't seem to get excited by it anymore.'

'It's not easy in this weather to get excited by anything.' Ahmed stamps his feet which are encased in polar-explorer levels of socks and fur. I look at the snow boots, jealous.

'Nice boots.'

'Necessary. I don't know why all the people here don't have a pair. You can pick them up cheap on Ebay.'

'Might have a look.'

'Do you think they'll sell me one for half price?' Jamie looks down at his single shod foot, the other in a blue cast with mismatched football socks pulled over the end. 'I've got two pairs of socks on and my foot's still freezing. It's making my other foot cold just standing next to it.'

We laugh.

For a while, our breath smokes together as we watch the twenty-two figures on the pitch jostle for possession and hunch, almost as one, against the occasional blasts of wind that cut across the recreation ground. Ahmed offers me some of his can, but I shake my head.

'It's worst for the 'keepers,' I say.

'That's where I play. Played, I mean. Back home.' says Ahmed.

'Didn't you play at your last school?' I ask.

'No. They had a full squad. Besides, there were a few … elements … in the team that weren't too friendly. But FIFA's better, and it's never this bloody cold in your bedroom, right?'

We laugh.

'Word of warning,' says Jamie to me. 'Never accept a FIFA challenge from this guy. I thought I'd got good since this,' he pats his cast. 'But Ahmed rinses me, every time.'

Ahmed takes another sip from his can. 'You're such a noob.' When Ahmed laughs, half of his sip comes back out of his nose. Then we're all bent double, laughing.

Jamie regains himself first. 'I've told Ben that Ahmed wants his job. I'll bet he's touching benches quicker than ever now.' Jamie and I explain Ben's changing room idiosyncrasies to Ahmed.

'The centre forward on my team at home used to run and touch every corner flag before kick-off,' Ahmed says.

'Did it help?' I ask.

'Not a bit. He was useless. But his father was the coach. And his older sister was gorgeous and came to every match, so we didn't mind too much.'

We spend a few minutes talking about the relative merits of the female supporters. Mark has two older sisters, neither of whom come to watch. A good share of the others don't have siblings, like me. Apart from that, there's just mums, of which we decide Ben's mum is the best, and that she drives the nicest car.

'Your mum's BMW's not bad though,' says Jamie to Ahmed. 'I got very well acquainted with its back seat!'

'Yes, she said you handled yourself very well, considering. You didn't scream so loudly that you put her off driving. I'm sorry I didn't give up the front seat. Thought you were better off stretching out in the back.'

'Ahmed's mum took me to the hospital when I—'

'You mean when *I*?' I break in.

'Whatever. When my leg got broken.'

'That's really kind,' I say. Ahmed flashes me a smile.

As we talk, two figures emerge from the tree line on the other side of the field. They stand for a moment, looking down the slope towards us, then start to move off to the right.

'We should go,' says Jamie, seeing what I haven't, yet.

Alan and Vince are soon recognisable, trying to knock each other's beanie hats off as they approach the corner flag on the far side of the pitch.

'Yeah, let's go,' says Ahmed. The two of them spin around and head for the footpath almost directly behind us.

'Coming, Josh?'

'Yes,' I say.

Alan and Vince pick up their pace as they walk past the back of the home-team's goalposts. Jamie is moving fast on his crutches, with Ahmed keeping pace. I have to jog to catch up with them, down the narrow alleyway between the houses at the edge of the recreation ground.

We're about halfway along it when a car screeches to a halt at the far end, riding up onto the kerb and blocking us in. It's Carl's. The tinted windows remain up, the engine gunning.

We turn, the way we came blocked by Vince and Alan, who start to walk purposefully down the alleyway.

I swallow, my heart in my throat.

I see Jamie plant himself on his good leg and one crutch, raising his other arm ready to swing.

But Alan raises his hands. 'Easy. We come in peace. Just want a word with one of you.'

Vince's eyes narrow on Ahmed. Mine dart between them. Ahmed is visibly sweating in his many layers.

But, at the last moment, Vince switches his stare to me, and with one of their hands on each shoulder, I'm manhandled quickly to the end of the alleyway, and almost thrown through the open back door of the car, followed by Vince. Alan turns to Jamie and Ahmed, raising his right arm in a salute, and gets in the front.

The car accelerates so quickly I'm pinned into the footwell, unable to get up. When I try, there's the heavy weight of a boot on my shoulder.

'Stay down, Poster-boy,' Vince growls.

FORTY SEVEN

Apparently, there have been emails.

I explain about the incident with the police, and my need to get rid of my laptop. To stop them finding out about the plan, I say.

Carl is not convinced, and as we speed through the suburban streets on the way out of town, each of his gear changes seem like an alternative to twisting my skull from my body.

Carl is beginning to doubt me. No, he says, he has gone past beginning, and since I am not responding to any of the usual channels, it has come to this. After everything they are doing for me, Carl says. After everything they're doing to help me, Carl needs proof of my loyalty. So does Martin. Proof that I am a soldier and that I am willing to do the necessary. Willing to join the fight.

'Words,' he says, 'are not enough. Not anymore.'

After twenty minutes or so we are entering another town. The only way I can tell this is that the streetlights overhead get closer together, the stops and starts of traffic and traffic lights more frequent. Although, still in the footwell, I can't tell where we are at all.

Soon, we come to a stop, and Carl turns off the

engine. He spins around in the driver's seat, his face suddenly just inches above my own. He spits through his teeth as he talks.

'If there's anyone in my army that I don't trust, it makes me very nervous. You see, it's all about trust. I need to trust that you love your country. That you love it enough to do something about it. My brother here thinks you're fine – that you're one of us because of what happened to your dad. I want to believe that. But I'm not sure. See, I've been thinking. If that'd been my dad, I'd have been on a plane or boat straight away, getting a gun and taking the fight to the bastards that killed him. But not you. You wait a few years, getting on with your schoolwork like a coward. Which makes me doubt whether you really care at all. Whether your love is strong enough to *do something about it.*'

With this last, shouted line, Carl grabs my collar, lifting my head to his flashing teeth and showering me with saliva. I try not to flinch, but I can't help it.

'Alan. Hammer.'

Carl holds out his hand as Alan opens the glove box. A second later, a claw hammer is thrust under my nose, the smell of the metal sharp in my nostrils.

'Just ahead of us there is a shop – a charity shop. It sells the donated goods of cowardly, British people to fund the lifestyles of the people who killed your dad. You will take this hammer, you will smash the front windows to shit, and then you will run to your left, straight down the road. There is a bus leaving the bus station in five minutes. Be on it. Alan, bus fare.'

A crumpled five-pound note joins the hammer.

'Do this, and I believe in you. Don't do this, and you'll find yourself on the receiving end of this hammer. Vince, let him up.'

The back door opens and I tumble out onto the pavement, straight into a puddle of icy water. The hammer and the money are in my hand. I stand up, try to gather myself. I pocket the money. The hammer feels like dead weight.

The shop, as described, is opposite. *Refugee Support* is painted in bright yellow letters above a large window. Three mannequins – an adult and two children – fill the display which is trying to be festive, the mannequins dressed in Christmas jumpers and bobble hats.

I start walking. I turn to see Carl watching me through the front window. Alan, next to him, holds a mobile phone up and is watching me through its screen. Remembering the other videos, I'm thankful that my coat has a hood. I raise it.

I cross the road, heading straight for the shop. My mouth is dry and I'm struggling to breathe properly, gasping against the chill in the air. My head feels light, as if I might faint. In my hand, the hammer is unrelenting. I feel the sharp points of its clawed side as it bounces against my jeans.

Let it be quick, I say to myself. Just let it be quick.

I see my reflection in the window and, beyond that, the shop itself. Empty, apart from one member of staff who stands with her back to the window, her cloud of white hair bobbing on top of her bright jumper, her stooped, elderly shoulders. I stand there for a second, the hammer half raised.

The lady turns around.

At first, she smiles at me, thinking me to be a customer, or that I'm reading one of the many posters in the window.

Then she sees the hammer.

I bring it down with as much force as I can just as the wash of terror floods across her face. I raise my left arm as the blow strikes, shielding myself from the shower of shards that explode from the centre of the window. My gloveless hand follows the hammer through its trajectory, through the window, the falling glass all around me. Then I'm raising my hand again, back through the gaping, ragged hole, bringing the hammer down somewhere else. I hear the scream from inside but I keep smashing and smashing, the glass raining down onto the pavement and inside the shop. In what must be the fourth or fifth slash at the window, the hammer slips from my grip, flying straight at the smallest child mannequin and knocking it over. The handle of the hammer is red with blood. My blood. I didn't feel the cuts. I spin on my heels and sprint in the direction I have been told as, behind me, I hear the roar of an engine fading into the distance, going the other way.

The whole thing takes less than ten seconds.

FORTY EIGHT

At the bus station, I wrap my hand in my coat as best I can, which makes paying the driver difficult. I have to reach my left hand across my body to my opposite trouser pocket. My lungs are burning from the run, my legs and head woozy from shock or blood loss or both. Inside the sleeve of my coat, I can feel the warm wetness increasing.

The bus is mercifully empty, and I sit on my own at the back of the lower level. Once the bus pulls out of the bus station, with no blue flashing lights in sight, I gingerly remove my hand from the sleeve.

Two pieces of glass are sticking out of my red right hand. One, about the size of a two pound coin, is wedged into the place where my thumb meets my palm. The other, longer but thinner, sticks out from the knuckle of my middle finger. I take hold of this longer piece first and try to pull. The pain makes my head swim.

Transferring my attention to the other shard, I brace myself as I try to clasp its wet, sticky sides in my left hand. With the smallest possible movements, I ease it clear of my flesh and let it fall to the floor. I'm whimpering like an animal. Sweat is rapidly cooling under my arms and across the top of my back. I feel like I'm congealing in a feverish puddle.

It's another five minutes before I can touch the other piece again; five minutes in which I cradle my hand as the bus lurches around corners and jolts over speed bumps. I grit my teeth, this time gripping the sharp edges of the glass to get a better hold. I feel the bulb of my thumb give way against the shard, and this new pain lessens the pain in my knuckle as I gently pull upwards. I yelp as the glass slips loose, tears filling my eyes. A fresh bloom of blood weeps from the deep gash as the second blade of glass falls to the floor. I wrap my hand tightly inside my coat sleeve again, and lean my forehead against the cool comfort of the window.

The bus journey takes almost an hour. Maybe some people get on and some people get off, but I spend most of the journey with my eyes closed.

It's getting dark as we get to recognisable streets. When we're within walking distance of home, I press the bell and lurch towards the front, my right hand gripped under my left arm. I step from the cold bus into the even colder evening, and am surprised at how quickly the pavement comes up to meet me.

It would be so much easier to lie here all night, but I force myself back to my feet. The bus driver is standing in the door of the bus, shouting something after me as I hobble and stagger down the road. After a while, I hear the bus pull away.

But it isn't over. Not yet.

As I veer towards my driveway and my merciful front door, headlights flash at me from across the road.

'In here. Now.' It's Carl's voice.

It's all I can do to lurch into the back seat. Alan is there, and takes my hand gingerly, unpeeling my fingers and flicking on the door light to get a better look.

'You've really fucked yourself here Josh. You feeling OK?'

I mutter a response; my throat feels like it's full of cotton wool.

'Here.' Alan takes a bottle of water from the footwell, opens it for me. I drink in large gulps, each one seeming to bring new life back into my numbed arm and, with it, more pain. 'Easy. Go slow. Small sips, yeah?'

Alan has a roll of kitchen towel and he's wrapping my hand slowly, making wide circles around the wounds. He's almost tender.

'Don't get blood on my seats.' Carl's eyes are slits in the rear-view mirror.

'He did it though, Bro. Didn't he? Smashed that window right up. Did you see that old bint's face? Priceless!'

'Yeah. I saw.' Carl is quiet for a moment. Alan continues to wrap my hand, slightly tighter now. In the stark white light I see the faintest crimson blush appear on the top layer of paper towel. He admires his handiwork and lays my hand back in my lap.

Carl continues. 'You did alright, soldier. How do you feel?'

'Like shit.'

'It'll pass. Listen. I want you to know I don't do these things lightly. Martin has reservations, and when your superiors give orders, you follow them, right?'

I'd almost forgotten about Martin.

'Told you he was a good soldier,' Alan adds. I'm not sure whether he's talking about me or Carl.

'I'm proud of you, son.' Hearing that word from Carl's mouth is like another wound opening. The pain is electric. 'I'm sorry I said those things about your dad, too. You *are* doing something to honour him.' He turns in his seat, facing me. 'When I was in, y'know in the army, it felt like a family to me. The first one I'd really known. And when … what happened, happened, they were all taken from me. So I know what it's like. The Lions can be your new family, Josh. They're my new family. We can look after you, get you through this, make you feel like you again.'

I already have a family, is what I want to say. But I can only nod.

'I don't tell many people this, but I was the reconnaissance guy on that mission. It was me who was supposed to spot those IEDs, recognise the tricks those bastards were using. But I didn't. I failed.'

Next to me, Alan seems to shiver, almost as if he's willing Carl to stop talking.

He doesn't. 'Five men lost their lives because of me. Five members of my family. Every time I see one of those people it makes me so angry. The people who kidnapped my family, cut their throats on camera and broadcast it to the world like they were cattle, like they were animals. Well, they're less than animals to me. All of them. We should be smashing all their windows in. Ripping down everything they're trying to build in this country. *Our* country. They're trying to take it away from us.' Carl's eyes are hard, cold.

Alan is growing jittery, shaking his head and his body from side to side. Each bounce of his leg rocks the car, sends more stabs of pain through my hand and up into my shoulder.

'So I know how you feel to have lost someone, OK? I know what it's like to be responsible for it. We're *connected* by that, Josh. There's a *link* there. We've both suffered, you and me, because of being *responsible*. And so I don't like doing what I had to do this evening. But I had to. Martin called it. And he's in charge. You understand that, don't you?'

Again, just a single nod.

'One more thing. There's another guy, another Lion, someone I should have been able to trust. You met him. He bought you a drink.'

The man in the blue jumper. Kind face. Lost eyes. Dan.

'He wasn't committed. He wouldn't show his loyalty

like you did today. He was more likely to do a runner. Tell the police. Well I won't tell you what I did so you won't have to lie. Suffice to say he won't be running off anywhere for a while.'

'Running off, yeah.' Vince laughs. A terrible, low growl of a laugh.

Alan is fiddling with the door handle, the window button, a thread on the knee of his jeans.

'I'm glad I didn't have to do that twice.' Carl points a finger at me. 'You find a way to keep in touch, so we can avoid this happening again.' He turns in his seat, reaches awkwardly behind, and places a hand on my shoulder. 'Especially as we're all doing this for you.' Then he turns back towards the road, starts the engine and places both hands tightly on the wheel. 'Now, out.'

For the third time that day, the roar of the engine, the squeal of tyres in the cold air.

At home, I pull the under-stairs cupboard apart looking for the first aid kit. Inside, there are a couple of large bandages. I peel off Alan's effort, careful not to rip the kitchen towel where it's stuck to my skin. I run my hand very briefly under the cold tap to get rid of the worst of the blood and the few scraps of paper that I couldn't peel off. The pain is so deep I almost pass out. What little blood is still coming from the wounds is thicker now, the flow slowing down. It's difficult to bandage my right hand with my left, but I manage it eventually before wiping down the bathroom with the anti-bac wipes that are kept under the sink.

Visions of the shop woman's face, and Dan's – what have they done to him? – swim in front of me as I put my coat, my jumper and T-shirt into the washing machine. Questions come, and I hear them in Dad's voice. What did I do to her? What did Carl do to Dan? I hear again and again her scream, the deafening crash of the glass, feel the weight of the hammer in my hand, which is Carl's hand, covered in my blood, the woman's blood. Dan's blood? What did they do to Dan? Was that for me, too? My legs are about to buckle under me, my stomach lurches to one side. I see my dad pulling glass from his bloody hands. Half of his body is burned away. I'm halfway up the stairs, still standing in front of that shop window. The hammer in my hand is in Dad's hand. He's asking what I've done. He's smashing at glass, screaming in a voice which is the woman's voice. *Responsible*, they scream. *Responsible. Responsible!*

With what feels like the last of my strength, I haul my pale form up the rest of the stairs and pass out on the bed.

FORTY NINE

The next day – a Sunday – I wake up late. Despite the complete black-out for about sixteen hours, I feel like I've barely slept at all. One word has gone around and around my mind: *responsible*. Does Carl think I was responsible for Dad's death? Was I responsible? I try to shrug the thoughts off. I fail. Am I responsible for everything they're doing, now? For Carl's plan? Is it really ... *mine?*

There's just enough time to check I cleaned the bathroom properly (I didn't, but quickly make amends) and to take my clothes from the washing machine before Mum comes home. I've no idea if I managed to get all the blood out, but the coat, jumper and T-shirt are all dark colours, so it shouldn't show too much if I haven't.

I haven't had time to think of a suitable story about my injuries, so have to make one up on the spot.

'I was trying to get a beer from the shed and slipped. I smashed a bottle and it went through my hand.'

Mum is too sympathetic. Perhaps she didn't hear that I was hunting booze. Or maybe it's because of this, or because she wasn't at home but off somewhere with

Mr Walters again. She doesn't even tell me off for not calling her, but demands to look, unwrapping me carefully.

The bleeding has stopped, but both cuts are very deep and seem to scream from my hand like open mouths. When I clench my fist as Mum asks, the deeper one starts to ooze again. Mum gets another bandage from under the stairs.

'Right, in the car. You need stitches.'

I don't argue.

I feel Mum's eyes on me from time to time as we drive to the hospital. I slip in and out of a kind of sleep where my eyes are open, or where my eyes are closed but I can hear everything that's going on; the groan of the engine, the swish of other cars passing by, the happy voice of the radio DJ. That word: responsible.

It's not a long wait in A&E, and the doctor is quite impressed by how clean the cuts are, and how deep, and by how little I seem to be phased by the four numbing injections and the ten stitches – six in the thumb, four in the knuckle – that go towards sealing up my shredded hand.

Back in the car, it feels like my hand is floating – detached from my body. It feels like someone else's hand.

It's when we get home that the questions start. Mum makes two cups of tea and ushers me into the lounge. She even opens a packet of biscuits as a sign, maybe, that she is not a threat.

'How does it feel?' She starts gently, not probing too much.

There's a huge part of me that just wants to spill my guts; to tell her everything that's happened in the past few months and to declare, once and for all, that I'm not coping. I don't want to be responsible. I want to make this all someone else's problem, and be told what to do.

But I don't. Instead, I say, 'It's OK.'

A silence follows. I take a biscuit, pinching it gently between the bound fingers of my right hand.

'Can you tell me what's going on please, Josh?' Mum's voice is starting to quiver already. 'First it was that bruise on your face ... I know you said you fell up the stairs, and I believe you ... but I'm trying to find a place where this all started. Are you getting bullied at school?'

'No, Mum.'

'And you coming out with that line a few weeks back about... about 'us' and 'them', and how what happened to your dad somehow means that—'

'Don't talk about him, please.' I have to really concentrate to stop my voice from cracking.

'Who? Your dad? Why?'

'I just … I don't want to think about him with all of … all of this …'

'All of *what*, Josh?' There's a pause; the silence getting louder the longer it lasts. 'Look, I know what you mean. And I know I've hardly been a model parent since he died.'

I hear Mum swallow, hard. It's the first time I've heard her use those last two words.

'But I need to know what *this* is. I want to help. You're not *you* at the moment, Josh. You've turned into somebody else. And it seems that that bruise on your cheek was the starting point.'

'I fell up the stairs.'

'I know you did, love. But the beer that keeps disappearing from the shed, and the vodka gone from the cabinet, your late-night stints on your computer… And not to mention what happened with you and Jamie. All of those things. What's going on?'

I can't look at Mum. If I take my eyes off of the square inch of carpet between my feet the world will end.

'Are you angry? God knows you've got a right to be angry, Josh. With me, with your dad, with—'

I interrupt. I want her to stop speaking. 'Why would I be angry with Dad? It's not his fault,' I ask, because I also want so much for her to carry on.

'No, it's not. It's no one's fault but the person that did it, Josh. Some small-minded fool who was brainwashed and … I don't know what else. But I've been angry at your dad since it happened.'

'Why?' I think again about Dad's tree, about that final leaf, about my dreams.

'For not being here. For dying. For leaving me, us, on our own. I'm still angry with him. Helplessly angry, sometimes.'

'But you can't blame Dad for—'

'I don't *blame* him. *Of course* I don't. But I'm still angry. Angry that he won't come back. That he's gone forever.' Tears are streaming down Mum's face, falling from her chin into her lap. But her voice doesn't falter, and she's looking straight at me. 'And what makes me angriest is that I can't do anything with that anger.'

'But why not?' I speak through gritted teeth. 'Why can't you do something? No one else is doing anything, and we should be out in the streets demanding—'

'Demanding what, Josh? Blood? Heads on spikes? That's the thinking that killed your dad. Do you really want that thinking to win? I can't do anything with my anger, Josh, because it's toxic. Anger kills things, either straight away or it makes them wither away to nothingness.'

Another long pause. I watch the tears dropping from my own face and seeping into the carpet between my feet.

I'm shocked by my next words. 'I could have stopped it.'

Mum's response is instant, 'Don't you dare start thinking like that.'

'What do you mean?'

'You couldn't have stopped it. Not at all. You couldn't have known, couldn't have imagined. So don't start talking to me about it being your fault.'

'But I...'

'That science test? That conversation you two had about taking the day off, ditching work and doing the gutters? It wasn't real, Josh. It was never an option. It was you two playing together, the way you always did. Every time before he went to London.'

'How do you—'

Mum's eyes are fierce and red. I don't need to finish the question. She's thought those thoughts too. Relived that last night as many times as I have. More. Has made herself responsible for something she couldn't have stopped, hated herself, and come out the other side.

I decide right then what I have to do. It's going to be difficult, turning things around, but I have to do it. I know where things need to go from here. I'm thinking again of the bucket rising slowly up the well, like it was in Jamie's hospital room. Maybe I need help to haul it up the rest of the way. I reach out and take Mum's hand across the coffee table.

'I've shut myself off and I know I have.' Mum starts again after taking a deep breath, as if she's diving back into something. 'I thought it was for the best and I knew it wasn't but I couldn't stop doing it. And I'm sorry. So, so sorry. You seemed to be doing OK. You looked like you were coping with it, moving on. I should have known it was in there, just waiting to get out.'

I hold back, again, from saying just how much has gotten out already.

'And then these last months ... there it is. The anger. But I'm here, Josh. I know I haven't been, but I'm back now. I'll stop seeing Mr Walters if it helps. And I want to help. I need to help.'

'Yeah. Well, you can't.' I speak just above a whisper.

'Why not? There's a poison in you, Josh. And it's a hateful, evil thing. You need to let someone help you or it'll take over. Believe me.'

And I look up then; I look straight into Mum's tear-brimmed eyes that are staring straight back at me and into me and through me.

And it all comes tumbling out.

I tell her about the websites, and the videos, and the drinking, and the pictures of the bombed train and about looking for Dad, and about Ahmed and how I behaved, and about the fight with Jamie and how I broke his leg. And I tell her that I want to stop, and that I want to go back to normal and to un-see all those things and to be me again. I tell her all of it.

Or nearly all of it.

I don't tell her about the hammer.

And I don't tell her about Carl.
And I don't tell her about the plan.
Because there's only so much shame I can live with.

FIFTY

'How long have you been up there?' When she recognises that it's me and not someone else, Dana puts down the garden fork that she's wielding. Her voice is as sharp as the prongs.

'Not long. Sorry. Can I ...?'

'You know where the door is.' She goes back to turning the soil.

'There's a special list for people like you,' she says when I've shut the door behind me. 'People who hide in bushes and look at girls.' Her eyes are still on the earth.

'Sorry. I wanted to see if you were here.'

'Knock on the door then,' her blunt answer. She switches the fork for a small spade, which also looks very sharp.

'What are you doing?'

'Tidying up. Term's over, it's almost Christmas already and this place is still a mess. Might as well fix what we can, eh?'

I know exactly what she means. Although I know what I need to do about Carl's plan, I'm still not sure on how to do it.

'Carl told me what you did, by the way. He made me watch the video.'

I flush red. The story made the local paper – a colour photograph of the smashed window, the old lady from the shop standing outside looking straight down the lens. Luckily she hadn't been hurt, just shaken up. There was an inset picture of the hammer exactly as it has fallen, a few blood-stains on the handle.

'Did you hurt yourself?' Dana makes it sounds like I should have, like I deserve to have been hurt.

I take off my thick glove and show her the bandage, explain where the stitches are.

'Good. Now the Poster-boy's got some war wounds of his own,' observes Dana. I'd thought right.

'Grab that fork. Make yourself useful.'

Even though my hand hurts intensely, I bend to the labour, turning the soil, trying to avoid the slick pink coils of earthworms as I lever the sod into itself.

We lay sheets of newspaper over the turned earth, weigh it down with stones. 'Keeps the frost out,' Dana explains.

We continue working in silence. I draw a strange warmth and comfort from working next to Dana, side by side. Even if she won't talk to me. I'm thinking about nothing else, just the work in front of me, the stones in my palms, the fork in my grip. After a while, my hand stops complaining and goes numb. Maybe it's the cold. My mind kind of goes numb, too. Just a vague foresight of what will grow here in the spring.

After what could have been five minutes or two

hours, Dana speaks again. 'There are things I don't understand.'

'Do you want to do some more revision?'

'Not those kinds of things.' Her look is withering. 'About you, Josh. I take back what I said about you being able to cope with things. You're not coping. Are you?' It sounds like a statement rather than a question.

'How do you mean?'

'I know I tend to say the wrong thing a lot and fuck everything up, so I'm really going to try not to this time. But you have to listen to me. OK?'

I nod.

'You *know* about Carl. I told you about him. He's toxic. He'll get inside your head, under your skin.'

I know she's right, but I can't avoid my anger. 'If he's so bad, why are you still—'

'I said listen. No speaking from you. I'm still here because I can't get away.'

I shrug, still unable to show the understanding she seems so desperate for.

'You really don't get it, do you? He's everywhere. He knows everywhere that I am. Except for here, this place.' She looks around her, at her garden. 'I suppose, in a way, he's always been in here.' She taps her temple. 'My mum and his mum go way back. Mum thinks he's brilliant, so I can't talk to her about it. She starts crying when I try to talk about what he was like before... And what he does to me now... I tried talking to her once but she just said "there are worse men" and walked off.'

Dana props her spade against the wall and sits on the grass, hugging her knees. 'When she was growing up, Mum had lots of run-ins with Social Services. None of them nice, apparently. And she'd do anything to keep them off her back now. Off my back.'

She's addressing the walls as much as me. I get the sense that if I sat next to her she'd lose the ability to speak.

'Like I said before, Carl was very kind to us when we were kids. Little kids, I mean. Hard to believe it now I guess, but he always made sure Mum had what she needed, for me, so the school wouldn't know what was going on with Dad. The police neither. After Dad left I acted up quite a bit. I'd run off to town on my own. Got picked up for shoplifting a few times. This was all in primary school. They were useless, just ruffled my hair and told me not to do it again. And Carl was always there, would straighten things out, turn on the charm when the police brought me home. I think they thought he was my brother. Or step-dad. And he's still doing it – covering our tracks.'

'Covering his own tracks, too.'

'Yeah. So Mum never reports it if I don't come home for a few nights, and she phones in every day to say I'm ill when Carl tells her to. It's like she's working for him. And everyone at school judges me as some kind of slut. All they saw was the jewellery and clothes and stuff that he was giving me, back before… That's why I don't really have friends anymore.'

'What about Miss Amber?'

Dana looks for a second like she's ready to spill blood. 'Even Miss Amber. Especially Miss Amber. I kind of told her about him once, even though she's hated me from the start. I said I had an older boyfriend. She said she'd heard and asked if everything was OK, if there was anything I wanted to tell her. I said no. Maybe she thought I was bragging or something, like my friends did. Maybe she thought it was inevitable. That that's what girls like me do. And now every time I try to talk to her I just get so angry, and all I can do is swear at her, which just makes things worse. So I can't tell her. I can't tell any of them. They're all against me.'

'What about Mr Walters? He's alright, isn't he?' I don't know why I say this. I regret it instantly.

'No. Him neither.' Dana seems to shiver.

'The police?'

'What are they going to do about it? They never did anything when Dad was still around. Or after he left. Maybe they'd care now, about Carl and what he's doing, but why would they bother with someone like me, who….'

I stop turning soil, lean on the fork.

Dana can tell that I've stopped, picks at the grass between her heels, doesn't turn. 'But *you*. For some reason I feel comfortable with you. Talking to you. And *you* can still get out of this, no matter what he's said. I know he's pushed the right buttons with you. He did with me, in the beginning, started talking to me about my dad leaving and how angry I must be and—'

'It's not the same though, is it?' I'm sorry for my flash of anger as soon as it's released. I take it out on the earth, picking up the fork again and ramming it into the ground. My stitched hand starts to sting.

Dana whirls round to look at me now. 'For fuck's sake, Josh. You don't have some kind of trump card on absent fathers, you know. It's really shit that your dad died, and how he died is awful. I get it. We all do. But it doesn't mean that the rest of us without dads can't feel anything too. You had a funeral for your dad. There's probably a place you can go where he's buried or whatever, to remember him. I've got none of that. Just a hole cut out of my life that I'm not allowed to speak about. Just an empty space. No one to bury. No one to mourn.'

'But didn't he put you down a well?'

'I'm not saying he was a good man. Dangling a seven-year-old down a deep hole on a scraggy old rope might sum him up pretty well, and I'm not saying I was as lucky as you were to have loads of memories of him, kindness and love or whatever. But that doesn't mean it doesn't hurt that he's gone. And that he's probably got a new family now and replaced me.'

'What are you saying?'

'Surely he taught you about this stuff, your dad? About being … it sounds stupid saying it, but about being *good*. Just by how he was with you? Do you really think he'd be proud of what you're getting into now?'

'You don't know anything about my dad.'

'No, you're right, I don't. So ask yourself that question. What would he do in your shoes?'

I look down. I've speared a worm on one prong of the fork. Something in me enjoys the way it curls and winds, writhing in a basic kind of agony.

Dana turns away again. 'Look. My dad was a bad guy. He was horrible to my mum, and to me. Not just the putting me down the well thing. He used to knock Mum about a bit, and then he'd apologise by being overly nice to me, playing with me, giving me treats, trips out. If he could see Mum wasn't responding, he'd drop me like a stone. Literally, sometimes. That's why she likes Carl so much – he's protective, see? Or that's what she thinks. He was protective of us after Dad left, especially after he got kicked out of the army.'

'I thought they discharged him; he wanted to go back but they wouldn't let him back in.'

'Kind of. But that's not completely true. He got done for some nasty stuff just after he left the hospital. Him and some others waited around outside a mosque until a youth group finished, then they attacked a few of the kids. Teenagers. Our age. With baseball bats.

Technically he was just a bystander. That's what he told the judge. Didn't hurt anyone, couldn't hold a bat because of the injuries, just watched the others and couldn't get away as quickly. The judge believed him. So he only got a caution for it. But after that there was some drugs stuff as well. The army would've had him back before all that, not front-line, just support stuff, but the drugs got him kicked out. In disgrace.'

I scrape the worm off the fork with my toe, suddenly sorry. I cover it with the next turn of earth.

'Whenever he was on leave, right from when he first signed up, Carl was always coming over and looking in on us. This was just after Dad left. Like I said, Mum's and Carl's families go way back. I guess he sees my mum as like an older sister. He'd always talk to me too, bring me magazines and stuff. I was ten when he went on his first tour and Mum would make me write to him out there. We sent homemade cards at Christmas, recorded videos for when he could get to his emails. He always sent Mum pictures of the letters and cards when they arrived. I used to feel really proud, my drawings stuck up in a tent in a desert somewhere, helping somehow. He really was a good soldier, you know. He told us about his promotions every time he came home, what they were teaching him to do with computers.'

Dana stands up, shivers, picks up her spade and leans into the ground again, neatening the lawn's edges.

'Then, after the bomb happened, his third tour, he

came back … I don't know… different. He started looking at me different too. A couple of years ago this was. And Mum kind of encouraged it in a way. Kept commenting on how nice I looked when he would come over. It was … I don't know. Weird. His scars were really pink back then, and shiny almost. They made me think of those pink sweets you get, the shrimp ones. And he wore these big bandages under his clothes that smelt of hospitals. I didn't know how to act around him, this guy who'd been around for so long. Who had been so good to me. All of a sudden he was someone different. And different up here, too.' She taps her head again.

I move closer to where Dana is digging, turning the soil for the umpteenth time now, lost in the mechanical motion of it as I listen.

'I felt sorry for him in a way. It was like he'd been chewed up and spat out, unwanted. I wanted to make him happy, I guess. In the way that my cards used to. And, like I said, Mum would always call me down when he came over, tell me to stop with my homework or whatever, make jokes about how all that was pointless if you found the right guy.'

'And you think she meant—'

'Of course she did.' Dana's spade slices deep into the wet ground. "Give Carl a kiss hello then" she'd say when I came down, and then say something about what I was wearing, how nice I looked, how I was turning into a young woman. It made me cringe. But I did it.

Paraded myself for him I suppose. It made Mum happier too. A bit. To see him happy. Even though my skin used to crawl whenever he hugged me for a little bit too long.'

'And then…'

'Mum was going out for the night, with Carl's mum,' Dana continues, her voice dropping slightly. Her body is on autopilot, the words finding their own rhythm as she works the spade mechanically, unthinking. 'Carl was at our house. To babysit, Mum said. I was thirteen. Hadn't had a babysitter for years. Looking back, I know Mum planned it. I didn't know she was going out until she was gone, and Carl was in the doorway. I stuck some dinner in the microwave and me and Carl ate on the sofa, watching some old film. I remember the noise his fork made on the plate when he put it down. So deliberate. Then he moved himself closer to me, put his arm around my shoulder. The next thing I knew, his tongue was in my mouth and…'

'You don't have to say this.'

'Yes. I do. It feels … alright, talking to you. Can't tell anyone else anyway.' She paused for a while, wiped her hair out of her eyes and went on. 'And we did it, on my mum's sofa. He was rough at first. Desperate, but then, he kind of got gentler. It hurt. God it hurt. He pulled out after a bit and put a condom on. Then he stopped and it was over. I felt… numb, I guess. At the end he wouldn't stop crying. I couldn't say anything, just lay there underneath him, his head on my chest, stroking the back of his head. I was terrified, waiting for Mum to come home. But when she did, I could smell the booze on her from the front door. She just stuck her head round the door, smiled, then went up to bed.'

Her eyes are fixed on the end of her shovel, sunk a few inches in the black ground. I walk over. My hand finds hers, squeezes it.

'And that was almost two years ago now. I tried to tell Miss Amber, but I couldn't, and that's when it all started going wrong at school, I guess. Though you wouldn't have known that. You had your own stuff to deal with.'

The tears in my eyes are hot and sharp. 'I can't do it. Carl's plan… I—'

'I know. Me neither. But not now. I don't think I can talk anymore.'

I know what she means. For the last ten minutes, it's like her words have been slowly filling a balloon. Any more words today and the balloon would explode.

'But *when*?' The desperation is clear in my voice. Maybe exploding the balloon would be a good thing.

'In the new year. When school goes back. We'll talk then.' Dana is calm, collected, like she's got a plan of her own all figured out. 'We've got time. Some, at least.' I hope she's right.

'I have to go.' My hand is on the lever of the lock when Dana calls me back.

'Josh.' Dana crosses the space between us in a few strides, and throws her arms around my neck. I hug her back. 'Thanks. For listening. And have a good Christmas, OK?'

She closes the door behind me.

FIFTY ONE

Christmas was Dad's thing. And now it's the hardest time of the year.

As soon as Mum finishes work, three days before Christmas Eve, we pack up the car and get out of the house as fast as we can. I don't know if we'll ever be able to spend the holidays at home again, remembering where we used to have the tree, where we used to hang the lights around the windows, or the lights that hung from the front of the house to look like icicles. It's too soon to think about, and Mum is as delicate as a snowflake as we put our cases in the boot in accustomed silence.

We manage one stilted exchange as we get in the car.

'Will you be seeing him, Mr Walters, over Christmas?'

'No, love. We're taking a step back over the holidays.'

'Oh.'

There are no boxes of presents amongst the carload of clothes and duvets. Any present shopping will have to be done in the next few days, from Nanna and Grandad's house.

It doesn't take long before Mum turns off the

constant stream of Christmas songs on the radio. It was always Dad who would sing along, Mum hating it at first, visibly cringing at every 'merry and bright' and each mention of Santa Claus. But eventually, Dad would win her round with his appalling singing voice and sheer enthusiasm. He'd have carols on in the house all the time for the week leading up to Christmas and he'd go through this big charade of putting presents under the tree one by one, pretending to tip-toe into the lounge to place them there while Mum and I were watching TV, and then making a big show of being surprised to find them, like he expected us to believe that some kind, benevolent force had brought them, or that they'd magically appeared as a result of the festive spirit.

Mum and I shared a kind of cynical conspiracy against him, pretending together to ignore what he was doing: the label on the biggest carrot that read 'save this for Rudolf', the way he'd leave pictures around the house that he'd printed from the internet – pictures of watches, suits, expensive road bikes, cars – the words 'maybe this year?' were written on all of them.

But we'd loved it, his energy. And when the big day finally arrived, he'd be almost uncontainable. He'd be really keen for us both to try to guess what was in the multi-coloured boxes – always four or five for me and at least twice as many for Mum – and he'd sit there grinning while we shook and squeezed the parcels, bouncing with enthusiasm, jittery with a breakfast of chocolate coins and fizzy wine inside him. He was absolutely terrible at wrapping though, so there was always the corner of a box sticking out, or a strip of black cardboard where he hadn't cut the paper big enough to go all the way around. Not that it mattered; Dad would always put each present into at least one extra box, making it impossible to tell what was inside. He once gave Mum a pair of diamond earrings in an old washing-machine box, making her climb right down inside to find them taped to the bottom. And when I got my Playstation a few years back, every controller and every cable was wrapped up in a separate package. He'd even taken the power-lead from the plug, putting them both in separate margarine tubs. It took almost an hour to unwrap it all. He didn't stop smiling once.

And now none of that will happen anymore. We've barely bothered with birthdays either these last two years. They remind us of him too much.

The first Christmas was, with a few exceptions, the worst day since Dad had died. Neither of us had left the house for weeks – not since the big funeral – and we didn't realise what day it was until we turned on the TV that morning. Mum screamed – an animal moan – and pulled the TV off the wall where it lay until halfway through January. She went upstairs then, shut herself in her room and didn't come out until the evening, her eyes burning and barely open. I'd sat on the sofa, watching loads of old TV series on my laptop and crying occasionally. The closest I'd got to turkey dinner was eating roast chicken flavour crisps all day.

So this year won't have to do much to improve on that.

We get to Nanna and Grandad's and are greeted immediately by the smell of baking and cooking. There's a stack of mince pies fresh from the oven on a cooling rack, and Nanna isn't happy until I've had three of them with my cup of tea.

Mum nibbles at one, then leans over the kitchen table that we're all sitting at and squeezes my hand, 'After lunch, shopping. OK? I'm going to lie down for a bit.' She takes herself upstairs.

'How's your mum doing, Josh?' Grandad asks.

I'm not sure how to answer. How much do they know about my recent confession? I don't have to wait long to find out.

'We'd like to add our apologies to your mother's,' says Nanna, shuffling in her seat, looking doubly uncomfortable for the fact that she's normally so relaxed. She finally settles in a very upright pose, her fingers bridged on the table, as if she's playing the piano. 'We thought – we all did – that you were coping better than you were. Your mum told us about what's been going on. How's your friend's leg, by the way? Jason, is it?'

'Jamie. He's OK.' But I haven't spoken to Jamie since Vince bundled me into the back of Carl's car. Mum's kept me off for the last few days of school because of my hand.

Grandad's voice is stern, level. 'Good. And this silliness with these websites. These ideas about the world. That's all stopped too has it?'

'Yes.' I don't have to lie about that.

Nanna speaks again. 'We read in the news last week about someone taking a hammer to a charity shop window not far from you. Can you imagine? A hammer! In all my years I've never seen madness like we're seeing at the moment. Never expected that it could get so close to home. The big towns and cities, yes, maybe. But not here, or where you live.'

'Did they catch the person who did it?' My voice almost fails in my throat as I speak.

'Of course not. They never do.'

I think about my own interview at the police station last month, imagine the tape going into a box in a room lined with boxes, never to be seen or heard again.

Nanna continues, 'Only last week I was on the bus, going to the shops, and someone started troubling this Asian lady just in front of me. I always see her on there. She seems lovely. Anyway, after he got off, someone went to check if she was OK, and she said it happens all the time. I'd have liked to have given that man a piece of my mind, only…'

271

Grandad cuts in, 'But the fact is that it's happening all over, Josh. There are dangerous people out there, and they'll tell you anything you want to hear to help them with their toxic, violent aims. They call themselves British; proud patriots. There's nothing British about what they're doing.'

Nanna picks up the thread again. 'It's lucky you didn't fall in with any of them, Josh. Lucky you were just on the outside of all of their lies, looking in. Standing on the tip of the iceberg. Very lucky indeed. We're both so very sorry, your grandad and I, that we weren't there to help you through it all. But we're very glad that it's behind you now, and that you've seen sense again.'

There's a pause before Grandad speaks. 'If you leave a place empty and uncared for, Josh, something will come in and fill it. In a garden so as inside your heart. And the seeds that blow in on the breeze are most often weeds. They'll choke that space if you let them. It's not fair, what happened to you, to your mum, to all of us. But we're sorry we've not helped you care for that empty space that must be inside you. It's good that you were able to tell your mum. Very mature of you to face up to the problem and to let her in. It can feel like a horrible secret, keeping something like that to yourself. You did well in telling her what was going on. And now we're all here to help too.' Another pause, then, 'I know this is a hard time of the year, but your dad would be proud.'

My eyes are so full of tears I can barely see the table in front of me.

Mum and I come back from town that afternoon with several bags from different shops. The only way to manage it was to go through our short Christmas list item by item, single-mindedly tracking down each thing in turn, not minding or caring if we ended up going back to the same shop three or more times. We'd thought about splitting up, but that would have been even harder.

Despite Mum and I both saying that we didn't want anything from each other, there are a few bags that she won't let me look in. We were barely apart all afternoon, so I don't know how she managed to sneak something into a basket without me noticing.

That said, I did manage to find five minutes on my own to buy her some perfume in the department store while she wandered into the women's underwear section looking for 'necessaries'. I've taken a risk and got her the one that Dad used to buy her each year. I'm not sure yet whether I'll put it under the tree. I can't stand her new one, the one she puts on to meet Mr Walters. She doesn't smell like Mum.

Because of walking all the way up and down the high street twice, and doubling back again and again, we're both exhausted, and flop down in front of the TV with more tea and mince pies. There's a red glow around Mum's cheeks. She stares at the screen but she's not really watching.

'That wasn't bad, was it?' I say.

'Not completely unbearable,' she replies a few seconds later; she took a while to realise I asked a question and come out of her trance.

'I think we did quite well there, considering.'

'Yes. Considering.' She reaches across and squeezes my hand. 'Hey, it is what it is.'

'Yup. It is what it is.'

'I meant what I said, Josh. About being here for you now. I'm sorry about the last few... This time of year... it's...'

'It is what it is, Mum.' I smile.

So does she.

FIFTY TWO

And so we get Christmas out of the way. We get through it. We get to the other side.

In the end, I do put Mum's present under the tree. She wells up when she opens it, but that's not unexpected. She gives me a really big hug that leaves a wet patch on my shoulder from her tears. But I think I left one on her, too.

The bags that I wasn't allowed to look in contain, amongst other things, a new coat. I'm glad of this, as the sleeve of my old one, where I didn't get all the blood out from the gashes in my hand, is starting to smell a little bit. My hand itself is healing well. As Nanna used to be a nurse, she offers to change my bandage on Christmas eve; both of the deep cuts have sealed well, she says. They shouldn't scar too badly. The dissolvable stitches are still there, just about, sticking out of the pink flesh like jagged teeth.

At dinner, I'm watched very carefully as I sip a glass of wine. Mum, Nanna and Grandad talk a bit about having responsible, positive role models for alcohol, and that it shouldn't just be a blanket ban. I feel a little light-headed by the time the Christmas pudding gets set on fire, and the smell of the brandy doesn't help.

Nanna's been working on it for months, and she looks a little concerned when Grandad jokes about how much booze is in it. He slaps me on the back, and everyone laughs.

There aren't many more laughs that day though. Mum is a little absent-minded, drifting in and out of conversations and staring out of windows. She wants to keep me close, and she keeps giving me hugs or brushing my cheek or finding fluff to pick off the arms of my Christmas jumper. Nanna and Grandad do their bit with reassuring hands placed on our shoulders whenever necessary. Apart from the big dinner that Nanna's made – which is incredible – we spend most of the day watching TV, or old Christmas movies on DVD.

Grandad bustles me out of the house for a quick stroll through the crisp, blue air of early evening. There are a few kids wheeling around on what must be new bikes – not as many as there used to be, says Grandad – and we spend forty minutes or so stomping around, not really talking much before he lets me go back home, my new coat 'thoroughly road tested'.

As the day darkens quickly and the evening draws in, we settle into our various contemplations in the lounge. I start stripping the tree of any chocolate I can find, Nanna and Mum both start reading their big, hardback novels they gave each other that morning, and Grandad starts flicking through a new version of *The Gardener's Yearbook*, drawing circles with a pencil around new varieties of veg he might try. After an hour or so of this, I ask if he's got any books about growing flowers. He looks confused for a moment, about to ask me – perhaps – why I'd bother with that and not vegetables. Then he gets out of his seat and goes to his study.

When he comes back, he drops a huge book into my lap that must weigh a couple of kilograms. I leaf through it, idly. Remembering what Dana said about the first flowers to come up in her garden, I flip to the index and look up the word 'crocuses'. One of the pages that's listed shows a small clump of leafless trees with tiny white and purple flowers growing out of the grass at their base. The caption reads *stand of sycamores with snowdrops and crocuses: an early display for a woodland garden*. The shapes of the small trees look familiar, but I'm not sure why.

Grandad's still standing, looking over at me. He nods. 'He'd like that, I'd say.'

But it's the first time all day when I haven't been thinking about Dad.

FIFTY THREE

The day after Boxing Day, we load the car up again with twice as much stuff as we came with. The thing I've been trying not to say or think about has wound itself around the bottom of my stomach, twisting it into strange shapes. Christmas distracted it, but now it's back with force and not happy that it's been ignored.

Back home again, Mum opens the front door and I stagger in with arms laden. The blue skies of the last few days had been giving way to cloud while we drove, and now it's a race to unpack the car before the rain starts, bitter and cold.

A few trips each and we manage it, the first pellets of sleety drizzle landing against the kitchen window as Mum puts the kettle on. I take a few bags of my things upstairs, then take a seat at the kitchen table.

'Something there. Your name on it.'

I pick up the care-worn envelope, see my name on the front, and open it. A Christmas card – sparkly, laughably ugly – falls out. It looks like something that's been kept under a mattress for a decade or two.

'Tasteful,' says Mum. 'Who's it from?'

I open it. A simple message. *Communicate on this from now on.* A SIM card is sellotaped to the inside.

'Dana. You know, that girl who came over to revise a while ago.' I'm almost shocked at how easily the lie comes.

'Yes, I remember. She seemed nice. Did you send her one?'

'No.'

'Well, maybe you should send her a New Year's one.'

'They don't do New Year's cards.'

'No, I suppose not. Just kisses at midnight.' Mum gives me a wink and takes her tea through to the living room.

In my room, I struggle against the panic taking hold. The face of the old woman in the charity shop looms up again; the feel of Vince's boots against the side of my face; Carl. If I don't plug this SIM into my phone and show I'm listening, ready, then something will happen like last time.

My hands are quivering as I unplug the battery, place the small plastic card in the slot. They're shaking so much I drop my own SIM, and then hit my head on the edge of my desk trying to retrieve it.

It gets no better as I wait for the phone to turn on again.

Almost as soon as it does so, a new message alert pops up. It's an invitation to join a closed group. I agree, and a wall of messages fills the screen. Everyone is identified only by phone number, and I guess that – like me – they're all using SIMs that they've been sent.

I scroll through, but it's just people greeting each other, just pictures and slogans.

I say 'just'. I have forgotten why I ever found any of this funny. Cartoons of Nazis and concentration camps crudely drawn; short, looped videos of people crying in a way that's supposed to sound weird and therefore funny. I've heard and seen enough people cry in the past few years to know that it's never funny, that complete loss of control, the descent into such all-encompassing sadness that you lose any kind of grip on yourself and how you 'should' be acting.

After realising there's nothing I need to do to keep up appearances, I write 'Happy New Year' and turn the phone off again, then swap the SIMs over. I place the new one – the secret one – carefully in the drawer of my bedside cabinet. Thinking of a better idea, I get some Blu-Tac from a poster on my wall and stick it to the side of the drawer, right in the back corner so you have to put your whole arm inside up to the elbow to get to it.

I tell myself that I'll check it's there every three days.

FIFTY FOUR

The problem of how to spend the next week and a half until school starts again is solved, in part, by a ring at the door the next day.

It's Jamie.

Mum invites him in and he swings along the hallway on his crutches, giving me a quick and unfixable look as I come down the stairs. He's telling Mum that the cast will be off in a few weeks, and he's had a lovely Christmas thanks, and that he wanted to talk to me about something if that's OK.

'Of course, I'll leave you to it.' Mum disappears upstairs.

'Hi,' I say, weakly.

'My mum said I needed to get out of the house. I thought about not coming here, but then there I was, hobbling up to your door.'

'Are you alright?'

'Not bad. This thing comes off soon.' He taps his cast.

'I heard. Two weeks.'

'Two weeks.'

We sit in silence for a while.

'Did you have a good Christmas?'

'I didn't drop in for a polite but meaningless chat, Josh.'

'No. Of course.'

'That thing that happened a few weeks ago. That was really weird.'

'I know.'

'I can't force you to tell me what's going on. I don't want another broken leg.' There's the faintest glimmer of a smile. 'But I don't know what to do. You weren't exactly complaining about being dragged off, and—'

'It wasn't the best thing that's happened to me either,' I hiss, aware that Mum might hear us. 'I didn't know that was going to happen.'

'I want to walk you through the things I'm thinking, Josh. Stop me at any point. You get dragged off with a group of guys who are known thugs – violent, racist ones – and then you don't come back to school. No one's heard anything from you, even Dana.'

'You spoke to her?'

'Yeah. I'm worried. And what's that bandage on your hand? What happened? Did you fight back?'

'No. They didn't do that. Christmas pudding accident.'

'And then, on the same Monday you don't come to school, there's a story in the *Gazette* about a Refugee Support shop getting vandalised. And a picture of a hammer in the window covered in a lot of blood. And I can't help thinking that…'

Perhaps Jamie stops as he sees the tears in my eyes.

'You're joking, right? So, your hand… That was—'

'They made me. I didn't want to.'

'Does it make a difference?'

I think for a while, before replying, 'It has to.'

'I'm not sure I know what that means. So are you a racist or not?'

'No.' I say, emphatically.

'Oh. So you're just doing racist things. With racists.'

'No. I… There's something that's going to happen. Something—'

'What?'

'Something bad. Really bad if it all happens how they want it to and—'

'And what? You're going to bring it down from the inside?'

'I … well…'

'Come on Josh, who do you think you are? Some kind of MI5 trained super-kid with gadgets and a fucking walkie-talkie? If you know something you need to tell someone, people, *police people*, quickly. We don't live in some film world where kids get to save the day all the time and walk away wiping the dust off their hands while the baddies get put in jail.'

'I know, but—'

'No, Josh. It's dangerous. Really fucking dangerous.' He leans over the table. 'These people you're hanging around with are really. Fucking. Dangerous.'

'How would you know?' I sound angrier than I meant to, again.

'Ahmed's been—'

'Ahmed! Having one friend who happens to be Muslim doesn't make you some kind of ambassador, Jamie. You don't have to wear him like a badge!'

Jamie ignores me, shuts his eyes and carries on. 'Ahmed's been showing me some stuff online about these patriotic groups. It's the White Lions around here, right? That's Carl's outfit?'

I'm startled for a second. 'Yeah. How did you…'

'It's the internet, Josh, not a closed circle. The Lions aren't too bad, compared to some of them. A few marches, some fights. But the bigger groups keep upping the ante. Ahmed's part of some kind of group that monitors far-right behaviour. He told me about it, and I can't remember how it works exactly, but some of the reports coming in sound really scary. Coordinated attacks, firebombs, stuff that makes you feel sick. Or should. And they're on the rise.'

The creature in my gut is writhing. I'm back in that imaginary well again, being dropped deeper and deeper, struggling to breathe. I keep doubting whether the world that I left at the top of the well is still there. Things are getting so unrecognisable, I'm beginning to wonder if the world that I left was ever really there at all.

Jamie continues, 'If you know something, Josh, you need to do something about it.'

'I know. I will. We will.'

'We? Who's "we"?'

'Me and … Dana.'

'Dana? Carl's girlfriend Dana?'

'She's not his girlfriend. She's…'

'She's not *your* girlfriend is she?'

'Are you talking about Dana?' Mum is standing in the doorway. I didn't hear her come back down the stairs. 'I didn't know she was your girlfriend, Love?'

'She's not my girlfriend!' All of my frustration pours out in one bellow.

Mum and Jamie are stunned into silence.

'I … think I'll be on my way, Mrs Milton.'

'It was lovely to see you, Jamie. Have a happy New Year.'

'You too, Mrs Milton.'

'I'll see you out,' I mutter.

I walk with Jamie down the drive. At the pavement, he spins on his crutches. 'Get some help, Josh. The police, that's what they're for. You don't fix this on your own. Especially not… You're not right at the moment. I thought you were, but…'

'Yeah, so did everyone.' I shrug my shoulders.

'If you need me, you know where I am. OK?'

'Yeah, thanks. I'll sort it out. Get it sorted, I mean.'

'Happy New Year, yeah?'

'Yeah. Happy New Year.'

Yes, I do know where Jamie is. He's safe. And

that's exactly where he needs to stay. At the top of the well.

FIFTY FIVE

School goes back on a Thursday. My hand is a lot better. It still aches a bit, but I can pretty much move it normally. I can feel the stitches tugging a bit under the bandage, but it's not as uncomfortable as it was.

Not because I want to, but to keep up appearances, I drag myself along to Mr Walters' classroom at the end of the day. My legs get heavier with each step closer to the door.

I'm the first to arrive. Mr Walters looks up as I enter. 'Happy New Year, Josh.'

I take up my usual seat.

'I've given Alan and Vince – and Brandon I suppose – a stay of execution this week. Turning over a new leaf and all. I expect they're off causing havoc somewhere, no doubt earning their spot on these hallowed stools for the rest of the year.'

'Oh…' I don't think I can last an hour here on my own.

'There's no reason for you to stick around either, I suppose.'

Perhaps I swing my bag onto my back too quickly, perhaps it's the relief on my face, or maybe it's because my eyes dart straight to the door like something hunted.

Whatever it is, Mr Walters sits up in his seat and puts his newspaper to one side.

'But as you are here.'

His chair, as he stands up, rolls backwards into the wall and knocks three marker pens from their tray under the board.

'Maybe we could have a little talk.'

He comes around the front of the desk, perches on the front of it. His fingers wrap around the edge of the desk like talons.

'Have a seat, Josh.'

He indicates the stool in front of him. I sit down.

'I've… I've spoken to your mum. She's told me what you've been dealing with. The websites, the rhetoric. Your dad would be—'

'Don't.' My voice is louder than it should be. But this time I don't care.

'Excuse me?'

'Don't bring him into this.' Remembering where I am, I add a 'Please'.

I feel his stare on the top of my head as I stare into my lap, unable to meet his eye.

'OK. That's fine. I'm sorry. I wish you'd have talked to someone before you started looking at all these things. They're *dangerous*, you know.'

'Yes, I know.'

'I'd like to think, perhaps, that I'm not completely distant from you, Josh.'

I pull at my bandaged thumb until it starts to really hurt, the wound opening up a little.

'I'm here if you need me, OK?'

'Yeah. Thanks.'

'I'm here to stop you from breaking. If there's anything…' He squats down, his face across the bench just inches from my own. Coffee and stale cigarettes, cheap aftershave. 'Anything at all. We all need comfort, sometimes. Someone we can count on.'

His voice is little more than a whisper, now.

'I know you've missed that, Josh. Being able to rely on someone. But I'm here.' There's a long pause before he changes tack, 'How was Christmas? Get what you wanted?'

'No. Can I go now,' I do look at him then, hard and steady and direct. 'Sir?'

He stands up, taken aback. Shocked, even. 'Yes, Josh. You can go. But you know what to do if you need anything.'

The stool clatters to the floor as I grab my stuff and bolt for the door.

Yes, I know what I have to do.

FIFTY SIX

Friday's Biology lesson comes around too quickly. I can't shake the memory of Mr Walters' 'chat'.

It doesn't seem to be playing on his mind though. 'Right then, eager young minds,' he booms. 'Today we have a new addition. I'm sure you all know Ahmed already. Quite distinctive around here is young Ahmed. Anyway, he's been moved up into top set this term, so let's welcome him.'

There's a low drone of 'Hi, Ahmed'.

Mr Walters continues. 'Ahmed, you picked a grand day to join us. Today is experiment day, and we're going to look at the calorific content of this variety of healthy Christmas snacks, all leftovers from the Walters' family hoard this year.' Mr Walters pours, from a cardboard box onto his desk, a bright waterfall of rustling, plastic-wrapped goodies: selection boxes, bags of chocolate coins, giant candy cane packets full of brightly coloured sweets, even a couple of huge, round, red-and-white striped lollipops.

There's a palpable buzz in the room as everyone leans in a little closer.

'Josh, please remind us of what a calorie is.'

I murmur, 'The energy needed to raise the temperature of a litre of water by one degree centigrade.'

'A textbook answer, young man.' He seems to have forgiven me then. 'So class, we'll be setting fire to these tasty nibbles and seeing how much juice they've got in them, how fat they've made us over Christmas, so that when we look at exercise this term, you'll all know how much lard you have to lose. List of equipment and how to assemble the experiment is on your worksheets, along with a table to record your results. Ahmed, I'm afraid I couldn't track down any Knafeh or Halawet el jibn for you.'

'Thank you, Sir. It's not a problem.' Ahmed smiles, but he seems embarrassed at having been singled out. I know that look. It's probably plastered all over my face.

'Shukraan, Ahmed. Shukraan. I've put you with Josh today. It's your first experiment and he's the best we can offer to show you how we do things up here in the top set.' Mr Walters turns his attention back to the room. 'Right then everyone, look at the board to find your partner, then come and pick something to burn. Ahmed. Here, try one of these.' He throws one of the giant lollies at Ahmed.

There are 'aws' of disappointment as the other kids see one of the top targets go.

'Yes, Sir.' Ahmed catches the sweet in one hand, then looks at me sitting a few rows behind him.

I don't catch his eye as I slip off my stool and go to collect the equipment.

A few minutes later, and we're all set up. A beaker

of water sits on a tripod, a weighed fragment of the lolly clamped beneath it and, further up the clamp stand, a thermometer held in the water. To one side, the Bunsen burner's orange flame dances slowly. We worked in silence, Ahmed and I, and it's clear that he knows his way around the equipment as well as I do. We're waiting for the rest of the class to get to this stage.

'Right everyone,' Mr Walters' voice booms across the lab. 'Everyone stop and look at Josh's table.'

Everyone turns, the flicker of our burner caught in twenty-odd pairs of safety goggles.

'Look what they've done with their thermometer. It's sat in the middle of the water, not resting at the bottom. Someone please tell me why that's a good move.'

Silence.

'Fine. Go on then Josh. Tell us why you did it.'

'It was Ahmed's idea, Sir. Not mine.'

Mr Walters seems slightly taken aback.

'It's so you take the temperature of the water, rather than the temperature of the glass at the bottom of the beaker, Sir.' Ahmed's voice is clear, confident. 'Otherwise the readings will be artificially high, given that the flame is in direct contact with the Pyrex.'

There's a short pause before Mr Walters replies. 'Yes, well. In future, if you can set things up as per the instructions and diagram on the board that would be great, Ahmed. Otherwise you're going to skew the class's data. Josh, could you set it right please.'

'Yes, Sir.' I adjust the thermometer, dropping it a few centimetres lower in the beaker.

Ahmed fiddles with the Bunsen's collar, the flame flashing blue, growling, then flicking back orange again. 'We should be doing this properly,' he says.

'Yeah, we need some kind of guard around the flame, right? Otherwise all the heat's going to spill out the sides.'

'Exactly.'

'Gives us something to put in the evaluation I guess.'

We sit in silence again.

'That was mean, what he did to you just then.' I readjust the thermometer again, moving it back to the centre of the water.

I feel the tension in Ahmed slacken a little.

'He's alright though, Mr Walters. What were your teachers like at home?' I wonder if 'home' is the wrong word. I add, by way of correction, 'In Halab?'

Ahmed smiles. 'Hey, you remembered. Not Aleppo. They were fine I guess. Like here. Some want to be your friend, some want to stay as far away as possible. Some good, some bad.'

'Did they all do the thing where they stand at the classroom door and say hello when you're coming in?'

'Sometimes. Some stayed at their desks as we filed in silently. Some met us at the door. There were handshakes as well from some of them.'

'Wasn't that really awkward?' I try to imagine a compulsory handshake from Mr Glynn, our greasy history teacher.

'Depends on the teacher, you know?' Ahmed goes back to fiddling with the Bunsen burner.

'Sorry. I guess you don't like talking about it.'

'Not really, no.'

'And when you get singled out, like earlier, it…'

'It makes it even worse. Yes.'

'Funny, isn't it,' I say. 'How people think they can show they understand how you feel just by using a few words you might recognise. Words they probably googled anyway. They think they can somehow jump into your head and make a connection—'

'And then everything will be fine. Yeah, I've noticed how some of them do that.'

From the other side of the room, Mr Walters threatens a few boys with detentions if they keep eating the experiment.

I continue. 'And all it does is push you further out. Further away.'

There's another pause before Ahmed speaks. 'I don't know. What would they use if they didn't use words? And isn't it maybe better that they at least try?'

'So what do you think about Walters? Is he a good one or a bad one?'

Ahmed turns the burner to a blue roar, pinning the lolly above it. The sweet's red surface blackens, begins to bubble as the flame takes on a greenish tinge. 'I haven't made up my mind yet.'

When I plug in the secret SIM that night, there's a message from a number which must be Carl. Two words is all he needs. *Phase one.*

And I go along with it. I have to. For now.

That weekend and for the few weekends after, Ahmed, Jamie and I stand together on the touchline at the rec, shouting encouragement, laughing, complaining about the cold. And I lend Ahmed a few homeworks and old essays in English. He still has a few problems with writing in English, especially the really formal stuff. I'm better at English than Jamie, and I can kind of explain to him where he's going wrong; the places where the normal rules don't apply.

And we talk, then, about all the other places in England where the normal rules don't apply; how to start conversations, *where* to start conversations, what it means when people say 'maybe' or 'perhaps'. Ahmed reads a lot, and I recommend a bunch of books, lend him a few of my own. In only a few weeks, we're texting about characters, plots, the right thing to do when you enter a public toilet and there's only one urinal free. We share links to Youtube videos. He asks me why it's actually funny to watch montages of the guys from

Masterchef making a bunch of weird noises. I say I don't know, but we both agree it's hilarious. It's like we're becoming friends.

And I'm enjoying it. For the first time in ages, it doesn't hurt to smile.

Every three days, Carl asks for updates about the condition of 'the package' and whether it's ready for 'delivery'.

I don't think Jamie's convinced that what he refers to only as 'the stuff from last year' is over. On the one occasion that he brings it up, we're outside the public toilet on the high street, waiting for Ahmed. It's a Sunday, late January.

'Is it sorted then?'

'Yeah, nearly.'

'What does that mean?'

'It means yes, it's sorted.'

'Police?'

'Yes.'

It's not time for the police yet. A small lie at this stage is necessary. Jamie doesn't see through it, but he can see its edges; I think this is why he's always wary of me. Whenever I see Ahmed, it's the three of us, Jamie always arriving at the place we've arranged to meet a few minutes earlier than I do. He claimed he was quicker on his crutches than he planned to be, but since the cast came off a few weeks ago and he's been walking almost normally again, he's still always a few minutes ahead of me.

Ahmed comes out of the toilet, wiping his hands on his trousers.

'Only one urinal,' he says to me. 'So I used the cubicle, just like you said.'

'Good work. You're almost a native, mate.'

And we all laugh.

I see Dana often.

On bright days, when the ground isn't too wet, we spread out an old tarpaulin in her garden and just sit together, sometimes talking, sometimes just watching the clouds. Sometimes, we watch the clouds until they start to fade, and watch our breath instead, clouding in front of us and drifting away.

The crocuses have started to come up. Small green shoots blooming white, purple and pink, their little yellow stamen like tongues of fire. They're just like Dana described, all those months ago. And there are snowdrops too, along the border, near the well.

At some point, on one of the evenings when we're lying there, her hand finds my hand and holds it.

When we talk, it's about what we should do. Despite her certainty before the holidays, she has little more idea than I do. Perhaps she knew that certainty from her was exactly what I needed. I'm grateful for that. We both agree that we'll have to talk to the police – I know

Jamie isn't wrong – but we need to get our timing right. Phase one means different things for different people. There's a lot of things that need to be 'sourced' – a coordinated list of items bought by different people from different shops, never more than one item per person. There are things to be booked and hired and organised and scheduled, to which the same rules apply.

Carl's keeping Dana at arm's length, she says. She's finding it hard to talk to him, and can't work out what things are in place, and which aren't. He only sees her at her house, turning up late at night, unannounced. I think that's why she just wants to sit, or lie, and be quiet when we're together. A short time after the hand-holding, she starts falling asleep leaning into my shoulder.

I feel like we're in stasis, as if time's been put on pause for a while. For the last few weeks of January, even the teachers ease off a bit about exam preparation. Whether or not they're as exhausted as we are, or whether they're easing off now ready for a big push after half term I don't know, but it feels like everywhere there is one long inhalation of breath.

And, to tell the truth, I'm enjoying it. All this time with Dana, not worrying about what's coming – almost avoiding it on purpose. We call each other over to every new bud or shoot that we find in the garden, both trying to spot the first new thing – tiny as it may be – when we open the wooden door at the end of almost every day after school.

Mum thinks I'm revising in the library.

In a way, maybe I am.

But at the back of my mind, and Dana's, we know it can't last.

It's the supposedly 'poetic' part of Carl's plan that this 'act of love' for his country will happen on Valentine's Day, so we're both aware that we don't have much time. Despite that, we need the police to see exactly what's going on when they make their move. Too early, and there'll be no evidence. Too late, and…

I can't think about that.

Alan and Vince stalk the corridors at school like hyenas. They catch my eye from time to time, but we're all sworn to avoid contact. It's only on Thursdays that I see them. I can't find an excuse not to go back to that classroom each week, and my heart pounds in my chest for the full hour as I sit at the back and try to work through the textbook. I have to keep everything as normal as possible. On the outside at least. Mostly I just stare at the words, none of them registering, and make a quick exit as soon as I can. To avoid being followed, I make random circuits of the school buildings before walking home.

It's on one of these circuits that I see Ahmed, on his own, in one of the IT labs in the technology block. He's sitting at a computer, a screen of numbers in front of him, typing away at the keyboard. I watch him through the glass screen in the door for a few minutes, until he leans back in his chair, stretching.

He smiles as I walk in.

'Josh! Not detention, surely?'

'No, extra Biology. You?'

'Coding club.' He looks around the empty computer room. 'Great turn out, as normal.' He's pretty good at sarcasm.

'No teacher?'

'Miss Fring left a few minutes ago. She says as long as I'm out when the caretakers come, she's happy for me to carry on.'

'Oh. What are you doing?' I look at the screen, but nothing about it makes the smallest bit of sense.

'Nothing really, just playing around. Check this out.' Ahmed opens another browser tab, shows me a video of a football match. I don't recognise the kits. 'Al Ittihad,' Ahmed explains. 'In the red.'

The shots are mostly of the crowd, people waving flags, standing on concrete barriers and singing. Every now and then, a police officer or some military personnel with a baton, or a machine gun. The pitch is dusty, and I don't get much sense of what's going on. The camera only catches the celebrations for one of the goals.

When the video finishes, Ahmed rubs his eyes. 'We won 2 – 1.'

'Well done. Where are they – you – in the league now?'

'Oh, that doesn't matter, really. It's just … well, that was the first football match in Aleppo for five years. Last time I went to that stadium was with my father.'

'Oh.' I don't know what to say. I put a hand on his shoulder.

After a few seconds, Ahmed shrugs me off, closes down the window, and the screen of numbers and code flashes up again. In the bottom corner is what looks like a chat box, but I don't get a chance to read it before Ahmed shuts down the computer. I get a slight feeling that there's something Ahmed doesn't want me to know about. 'Ready to go?'

'I didn't know you were into this stuff.' I gesture at some computers in general.

'Sometimes it's useful.'

There's a pause while I stand in the doorway, unsure of how to leave.

'Hey, I think we go the same way home, right?' Ahmed shrugs on his coat, picks up his bag.

'Yeah, I think so.'

We walk together between the school buildings, not speaking. Me and Ahmed get on great online, or texting. But this is the first time we've been alone together in real life, and for some reason it's awkward. As we head for the main gates, one of the recycling bins has rolled out of place and sits partly blocking our path; we both stop walking at the same time to let the other one through the gap. We laugh, but not because it's funny. It's a stuttering laugh, and I get an odd feeling that we're carrying something between us. Like we're both held down by this immense weight. That it's somehow shared.

We fall silently back into step with each other as we head towards the main road, picking our way around the puddles on the path beside the school drive.

'Hey, check that out.'

I can't see what Ahmed has seen, but he immediately vaults the handrail at the side of the path. Slowly, in a low crouch, he crosses the drive, heading for the uneven row of fence panels on the other side where the gardens of the neighbouring houses all end. Then I spot it. On top of one of them, at about eye height, sits a small brown bird with a red chest. A robin.

'I have seen them sometimes in Syria, but they aren't so brave as here.' Ahmed looks back at me as he talks, his eyes alive in the early evening light. 'They live in the hills there, in the woods. But now my mother has them visiting the garden. They sit on her spade as she digs. Their song is the same though.' Ahmed whistles a few squeaky notes and creeps a little closer.

The bird on its wooden perch jumps about a bit, puffing out its fuzzy little chest and tilting its head to one side, letting out a few high trills of its own song.

'He's checking you out,' I laugh. A real one this time. Not a stutter.

'Yeah, he likes me.' Ahmed stands straight, satisfied that he's close enough. He holds his empty palms out towards it. 'Sorry, buddy, no worms.'

A few more notes of song. The robin raises its tail, leans forward.

'Apparently they sing for territory. They don't like other people stepping on their patch.' The robin bounces up and down a few more times. Ahmed turns back to me, 'Maybe he thinks I'm trying to steal something from him.'

Ahmed's movement is too quick, too sudden for the small bird. It pitches forward and flies low over our heads to a nearby hedge. I flinch involuntarily as it passes just a foot or so above me.

Ahmed is smiling as he climbs back over the rail. 'They were my father's favourites.'

'Yeah, mine too.' I hesitate for a second, then say it. 'Do you fancy a walk? I want to show you something.'

FIFTY SEVEN

I don't know why I decide to bring Ahmed here, now. A part of me is screaming that it's not the right time. Every step we took was more difficult, Ahmed finding it amusing that I wouldn't tell him where we were going. Me trying to smile back.

And now we're standing in front of Dad's tree.

Even though the evenings are supposed to be getting longer, there's not much light left in the sky now. I see Ahmed notice the 'Woodland Burial Ground' sign as we walk in. He says nothing as we pick our way across some slightly soggy ground, up a slight incline, and stop at the frail-looking rack of branches.

'Dad, Ahmed. Ahmed, Dad.'

'Hello Mr Milton.'

Ahmed smiles. I smile back. I don't know if he's playing along, or if we both are. He turns around, looking back down the slope.

'It's a beautiful spot.'

I turn and do the same. Ahmed's right. The small lights of town are glowing beneath us, and you can see beyond them to some low hills. The sun going down behind them lights the horizon a deep orange. I've never looked this way before.

'And it's a sycamore tree, yes?'

I nod, remembering the name as he says it. Something in me opens with the naming of it.

'We have a similar tree back home. It is known for its long life and the shade it gives. It's a good choice ... for a...'

'Thanks.'

'Look, it's budding.'

He takes hold of a thin branch. At the end, a tiny, dark green spear-tip has pushed up through the bark.

'Do you know how he died?' I ask him.

'Yes. Jamie told me. But I think you'd rather tell me about how he lived.'

And I do. I tell him about Christmases, about his taste in music, about when he used to watch me play football, about the cats and how they'd sit on his shoulders at meal times and how Mum would get angry, about the holiday we went on the year before he died: America, the drives, the huge beaches, the size of the forests. I talk for about twenty minutes without stopping. Then we stand in silence. It's the most comfortable silence I've shared with anyone in years.

An understanding silence.

Ahmed speaks first. 'My father would have liked it here, I think. We don't do this at home. Maybe we should. We weren't really "practising" Muslims, my family. We rarely went to mosque, just at Eid. And we haven't been to a mosque since we arrived here. I guess we're Muslim in the same way most British people are Christian.'

I smile, nod.

Ahmed casts his eyes around again, takes in the other trees of various sizes, their branches swaying almost imperceptibly in a light breeze. The sun has dipped below the horizon. There's a last streak of crimson on the bottom of the furthest clouds. 'But I like this idea. It's a beautiful place. We didn't get to bury him, my father. We never will. We left home before we even knew for sure that he was dead. We still don't, not for certain. So every day it feels like we're burying him again. Digging him up in the mornings and burying him each night. Sometimes it's the other way around.'

'Nothing to bury, nothing to mourn.' I murmur the words.

'What was that?'

'Nothing. Something a friend said. Do you dream about him?' I ask.

'My father? Never. Well, not yet. You?'

'No. Not yet. Do you know who ... did it?' It feels invasive, asking this.

'It isn't a person, or people. There isn't really a *Who*, I think. Just a *What*. It was the same *What* that killed your dad, I think. Just ... hatred. Nothing but a deep, ugly hate that takes away what other people have. What other people love. People attach reasons to it, try to make sense of it, but there is no sense. I can see why people get angry.'

Ahmed pauses. He bends down and brushes a hand against the grass. Satisfied it's not too damp, he sits, facing out over the town, the sky almost dark now. 'Being in the UK is hard. I don't expect you to understand how. In the big cities it can feel better, I guess. Maybe we're more invisible in a big crowd of people, easier to ignore. But here? How do you put it? In the arse end of nowhere? We stick out like sore thumbs. Everyone looks at us. And those that don't look directly at you have this way of not looking at you that almost says "I'm not looking at you because if I look at you it will show that I've noticed you".'

'Why would they want to not notice you?'

'I don't know. Maybe, with things as they are, the way it's always in the papers, we're impossible to not notice. So maybe people are trying to be kind and not draw attention to it when they see me. But I feel them fizzing with it when they walk past me. Like they're electricity. Like it takes so much energy not to notice.'

'And because everyone notices you, it makes you feel completely alone.' I think back to all the times I walked into a room and brought silence with me. The eyes of everyone in a room flicking over me, checking where I was, checking that I was on my own. And I remember the eyes that stayed averted, made a show of ignoring me, or pretending not to notice.

307

'Yes, you feel completely excluded. You understand this?'

'After Dad died, when I came back to school, it was like everyone was looking at me, but no one would meet my eye. They'd see me coming down the corridor and deliberately not look at me, even if there was no one else around. I'd never felt so completely on my own.' I sit down next to Ahmed, the orange glow of the town's lights reflected in his eyes.

The thing that we carried here together, the weight I felt less than an hour ago; it's gone. It's gone completely and I feel lighter than I've felt for a long time, so I want to really *mean* the thing I say next. I've never meant anything so much in my life. 'I'm sorry about how I was. That first time we met. And about everything—'

'I can see why you…' Ahmed cuts me off, but his eloquence quickly reaches the obstacle of my recent past.

'Why I what? Has Jamie said anything?'

'No. Jamie's said nothing. Look, what I was doing earlier, on the computer. I'm part of a group, a network, OK?' He laughs, 'It's not as CIA as it sounds, it's mostly just talking about fantasy football leagues. But we also report on anti-Muslim behaviour, and we share our data with the police. Apparently, it gets shared with the government too, for policies and things. But I'm not sure about that. It's mostly about keeping safe, letting others know what to look out for.' Ahmed fiddles with his shoelaces as he talks. 'I got a message a few weeks ago from a guy, and I was using the school computers to check up on something.'

'What, like hacking?'

Ahmed smiles, 'Well, maybe. Like I said, it's not as James Bond as that, but there's VPNs and proxy servers and I could go on at you about the number of backend issues this school has got. But you'd get bored, I think. Don't worry, it won't get traced back to me.'

'Who will it get traced back to then?'

'No one. Or… No, no one.'

I know Ahmed's not telling the whole truth here, but I've never been good with technical stuff, so I let it go. 'And …?'

'And, this network I'm in, we all track those groups like the one Alan's brother is running. Those deep, ugly hate groups? And…'

Shame washes over me like an ugly, slick wave. 'You found me.'

'I found your email address. Your school one. And that link. Not that I needed it; I could have got to that page of videos anyway. Like I said, it's handy being good with computers.'

'I'm…'

'With all the running I've done, Josh. All the people who've chased me, spat at me and my mother. All the people who have smashed our windows or painted words on our garage, I know what being scared is like.

Our journey to the UK was easier than some, but it still wasn't easy. I know what fear looks like. So I know that look you have. I know you're not one of them.' Ahmed's words can't lift this new weight that's pushing down on my chest, however kind and honest they are. 'In first school, I remember being pinned down by older kids and forced to swear allegiances to their beliefs, to the right "sort" of people. Playground stuff, really.'

A pause.

'Then, in the camps, there were groups of people who would be looking for … for soldiers, I guess. I was young, and my mother kept me close, but I wasn't too young for them to notice me. What they could make me into. I know the tactics they use to get you to feel that ugly, the switches they press to make you feel like there's no alternative. Like you're making a good choice. And this,' he points at Dad's tree, 'this is a pretty good lever to pull.'

I ask the question before I've thought of it. 'So, what's the answer?'

'To their way of thinking? I guess it's just your basic humanity.'

'My what?'

'Look. It might be that each argument they make seems justified on its own. And you may even find yourself nodding along at the start. So what, there's a few more people using the schools or the doctors or whatever, but they turn that into some huge threat, like things are being overrun. And some money has to be given to house asylum seekers at first, because they're not allowed to work. But my mum's been working for years now, and her taxes have easily paid back what we owed. But they turn that into words like handouts and scroungers and fraud, and labels like refugees, asylum seekers. Whatever, once there's a label, people are never seen as more than that, you know? You don't see people in the news described as 'potential IT Consultant' do you? They're just 'immigrant'. Then you get hate, then you get violence. But the comeback to all of it is just realising we're all people. We're all trying to be alive in this world, you know? It's about getting to know people for who they are, not what you think they represent. Basically, it's just being human.'

The poem from Mrs Burgoyne's class comes back to me. How stupid I was. I knew I was doing it at the time, ignoring the whole point of it, enjoying the role that Alan and Vince had cast me in, seeing the world in the most simple terms – ally, enemy. It had felt easy at the time, being a soldier, and I'd equated *easy* with *right*. But, recalling it now, a new wash of shame goes through me. 'Yes,' I manage to choke.

'And you're human, Josh. Like me, right? You know about compassion, and kindness, and love. He taught you that.'

He's pointing to the tree, and I nod. The tears in my eyes feel cool, oddly cleansing, natural. I don't brush them away like I would if I were talking to anyone else. I wonder if Ahmed would understand about the bucket I've felt has been coming up through my body these last few weeks. Is that what's inside it, shame? These tears feel cleaner than that. Perhaps it's shame that's been trying to pull it back down, keep it in the murky dark.

'But listen, Josh. I think I've found out something over the last few weeks. Since before the holidays, there's been much less traffic on that site. Much less activity. Now that could mean one of two things. One, everyone's packed up over Christmas and hasn't gone back to work yet. Who knows, maybe the Ghost of Christmas Present has visited them and they've all decided on an ordinary life full of Dickensian charm.'

I can't help laughing as Ahmed does a near-perfect impression of Mrs Burgoyne in full flow.

'Or,' he continues, his voice darkening a little. 'There's another option. The traffic has moved elsewhere. Which means something is happening that they don't want anyone to know about. Or the police.'

'The police?'

'What, you think that these sites can just go on preaching hate and violence without being watched? Come on, you're smarter than that. The police know it's there. They know about all of them. Like I said, this group I'm in, we share things with a national police network. They might not do anything about most of them, but they certainly know about them. And they've got a pretty good idea of who visits them.'

I think of the interview at the station, the smashed laptop at the bottom of the well.

'Look, Josh. Ninety-five per cent of the traffic to these sites is just curiosity. Kids messing around, looking for something shocking. They like a few Pepe the Frog memes on social media and take one click too far, then U-turn pretty quick. You won't get anyone knocking at your door any day soon. Unless…'

'Unless what?' Even I can hear the desperation in my voice.

'Unless you know something? But, if you do know something, perhaps you should be thinking about knocking on *their* door.'

'Yeah,' I reply. 'Maybe I should.'

FIFTY EIGHT

The next day, I'm walking between lessons along the science corridor. There's a commotion up ahead. I can see Vince's head – freshly shaved again – above the sea of bodies. I think about taking a longer route, but I'm too late; he's spotted me.

'Where's Dana?' he shouts, elbowing his way towards me through the throng.

A wall of students forms behind me – I'm blocking the flow and there's no way out. But I haven't seen Dana all day and I say so.

'Where the fuck is she then?' Vince comes very, very close to me, his nose just an inch from my own. When he presses his forehead against mine, his extra six inches in height mean it feels like he's trying to drive me into the floor.

'Vince, back down. He doesn't know.' Alan comes up behind him, tries to pull him by the arm.

Vince shrugs him off. 'What if he's lying? What if he's lying like that bitch is lying?' On either side of us, throngs of other students start pushing, shoving. A whisper goes through the crowd that there's going to be a fight. Some students are jumping on the backs of others for a better view and the noise is getting deafening.

Mr Walters suddenly appears from his classroom. He bellows, 'What on earth is going on here?' Seeing Vince and me squaring off, he wades through the throng, pulling bodies out of the way by their rucksacks, and plants himself between Vince and me. He locks eyes with the snarling youth. 'What are you doing, Vince?'

'He's not doing anything, Sir, just asking our mate Josh if he's seen someone.' Alan's attempt at carefree gives away his own tension. I bristle at being called his mate, reminded of how recently I'd considered it to be true.

Mr Walters retorts, 'And from what I heard, he hasn't. So perhaps you'd better ask elsewhere. Or, even better, get to your lessons.' He says the last part not just to Vince and Alan's retreating backs, but loudly to the gathered mob around us.

Students start to move along again, disappointed that nothing really happened. The two rivers of school uniforms flow around Mr Walters and I, still stood in the middle of the corridor. Mr Walters watches them go by for a few seconds, his angry-teacher-face fixed. Then he turns to me. 'Alright, Josh?'

I nod.

'Actually, there's a bit of an investigation going on into Dana's whereabouts since this morning. We've all been asked to keep a look out for her, stealthily mind.' He winks. 'So, you really haven't seen her?'

'No. Definitely not.'

'Good, good. On your way then. But if you hear from her, you let me know, OK? Or any other member of staff, of course.'

And he disappears back into his classroom, shutting the door.

The corridor is empty again. Except for me.

When I knock on the garden door after school, Dana opens it almost immediately. She fidgets with her hands and has made one of her nails bleed slightly. She sucks it as we speak.

'It's got to be soon, Dana. Now, maybe.'

'Tomorrow.' Dana is firm, despite her clear nervousness.

'We can't put this off anymore.'

'I'm not putting it off, but there's something arriving at Carl's tomorrow that he has to keep hold of for a few days before passing it on.'

'What's arriving?'

'I don't know, exactly. But I know it's the kind of thing you're not supposed to have without a permit or something. It's definitely something he doesn't want to get caught with.'

'OK then, tomorrow. We'll go in the morning. First thing?'

Dana is hesitant, nervous. 'I can't go back there, Josh. To my house, I mean. I can't do it. Not anymore.' Dana seems to root herself into the soil. I know I can't argue with her, and I don't want to anyway.

'Why not?'

'I can't go anywhere he'll find me. If he gets hold of me, he'll kill me. I'm not supposed to be here. I was supposed to stay with him. He—'

'Slow down,' I say, placing a hand on each of her shoulders. 'Look at me. Breathe. Slow down.'

She takes a few gulps of air. Her hands stop worrying at each other.

'Dana, what's going on?'

Her words come with difficulty. 'Last week, when he said about this thing arriving, he said he wants me with him all the time now. He wasn't going to let me go to school but I persuaded him that'd look bad. Made up some crap about my attendance being so low that if there was anything unexplained, they might send someone to look for me.'

'Yeah. Mr Walters was asking after you today, too.'

She seems a little surprised at this. 'Right, yeah. So, Carl said he'd pick me up every day straight after school at the front gates, and that Alan would be keeping an eye on me, and I wasn't to leave his sight. And I haven't, and it's been… But…'

'But you've slipped away. And you've come here.'

'I snuck out before break this morning. I've been here all day, waiting for you, hoping you'd come.'

'And you need somewhere to stay.'

'I was going to camp here. I've done it before, in the summer. But it's supposed to rain tonight, and…' She is desperately fragile. Standing in the protection of her garden, her own walls – walls which she's been dismantling for weeks – are crumbling to dust.

Now I'm the one who needs to be strong. 'You can stay at mine. Mum's off to her parents' this afternoon. Can you wait here another hour or so, then I'll come and get you?'

FIFTY NINE

Unexpectedly, Mum's home when I get there. She wants to make sure I'm going to be OK on my own – it's the first weekend this year that I've not been with her. I explain that, so far this year, there haven't really been that many weekends.

She smiles. 'I'll be back late again on Sunday.'

'You and Walters starting things up again?'

'I wish you'd stop calling him that. He's got a first name you know.'

'It feels weird. He's my teacher.'

'I know, love. But he's…'

'Yeah, you said. He's "good for you". I get it.'

What with the following mum-fussing, and being told exactly what's in the fridge, freezer, cupboards and shed, it's almost two hours before I can get back to the garden.

The door is ajar when I arrive. Dana is leaning against a wall, shivering, her coat zipped and buttoned up to the throat, her hands deep inside her sleeves. It's a tense walk, darting along pavements, turning at every engine we hear. On top of this, there's a cold stiffness to her that doesn't thaw out until we get to my house and I place a cup of tea between her palms. She keeps her coat on, huddled over the curls of steam.

'Do you want a bath?'

Dana's flashes me an accusatory look. 'What do you mean?'

'To warm up. Did you think I—'

'I don't like baths.' She cuts me off. 'Why would I want to float around in my own dirt?'

'Just thought it'd warm you up. Sorry.'

I go and fuss around in the kitchen, pull a couple of pizzas out of the freezer and rummage through the fridge for the bag of salad Mum had described in detail. Twice.

A few minutes later, Dana comes in. There's a bit more pink in her cheeks, and her lips have lost their blue tinge. She taps her fingernails against her empty tea cup.

'Want another one?'

'No, thanks. Can I have a shower, please? You're right. It'll warm me up.'

I get fresh towels from the airing cupboard and show her where the power cord for the hot water is, then go back downstairs to turn the oven on and put the pizzas in. As I pass the door to the lounge, a sweep of headlights arcs through the front window as a car pulls into the driveway. I hear a door open and close, but the engine is still running. I recognise the deep, throaty grumble it makes.

Then comes the knock at the door.

I can't pretend I'm not home; there's lights on all

over the house, and probably steam rising from the bathroom window that faces onto the front garden.

'Josh, I can see you by the stairs!' Alan's voice confirms that I can't hide.

When I open the door, Alan is struggling to conceal his worry.

'Is she here?'

'Who?'

'Dana. Fuck, Josh, who else would I be running around town for on a Friday night?' He's trying to make jokes, but he keeps twitching his head back over his shoulder to the car.

'No. Why would she be here?'

'I don't know. Maybe because we've tried everywhere else. And Carl has this strange feeling that you know something.'

As if on cue, the driver's door opens. Carl is a silhouette behind the glare of his headlights, but no less terrifying for it. 'Is she here?'

'No,' Alan and I say in unison.

'Fucking liar. Who's upstairs?'

'My mum, in the shower.'

'Where's her car then?'

'At the garage. Something about a part not arriving until tomorrow. Brakes I think.' I'm amazed at how quickly I'm thinking. I feel fierce. Protective.

'You're lying. You're trying to cover for her aren't you, you little shit? Alan, bring him here.'

Alan, leaning in the doorway, shrugs slightly, flashes me a weak smile, then grabs me by the scruff of my jumper and pulls me outside. I almost trip over the doorstep, and stumble clumsily into the bonnet of the car. Alan brings a firm hand down on the back of my head and the vibrations of the engine make my jaw rattle as I'm held against the warm metal.

'If she's in there, and you're lying, then I won't just stop at that immigrant friend of yours. I'll do you too. The same way. And her as well. Now, tell me. Is Dana in there?'

'No, it's my mum. I promise.'

'And what if I checked?'

I shake my head free enough of Alan's grip to get the words out. 'Then you'd see my mum in the shower, and if you're trying to keep a low profile at the moment, you don't want the police called, do you?'

'Fuck do you mean?' Carl deflates, but only slightly. I'm amazed at my own confidence, and when I feel Alan's grip ease slightly, I yank myself free, stand up and continue

'You can't walk in on a middle-aged woman in the shower and expect her not to scream, right? Or call the police? Or do you want to blow our cover and ruin this plan we've all been working towards? Remember, that's why we're doing this. The immigrant's not my friend. I'm doing my job.' The words stab as I say them. I try to summon up the old fire, the one that coursed through my veins like battery acid at the end of last year. But all I can find is the surface of it. It will have to be enough just to act it. 'Why aren't you out there doing yours?'

Carl is momentarily speechless. He didn't expect this reaction. I press my advantage, however flimsy it may be.

'What Dana knows and doesn't know about what's going on isn't my problem, it's yours. If you've told her too much, you need to deal with it. Any idiot can see she's unstable. Always has been. She can't be trusted. You're supposed to be some kind of leader, right? So why can't you control some little girl who's half your age and stop fucking around making it my problem?' I try, as much as I can, to sound like his superior officer.

'Careful,' Carl's voice is low, quiet. I think I may have gone too far. 'Be very careful.'

There are a tense few seconds when things could go either way. I hold Carl's stare through the headlights' insistence.

It's working. Carl looks away first. 'Fine, it's your mum upstairs. But if you see her, you know what to do.'

I nod. I'm nearly there. 'Of course I do.'

'And if I find out you've been lying, I mean it, after this business is done, I'm coming for you. And your mum if I need too.'

'Fine, now get the fuck off my driveway. My neighbours' curtains are twitching. I'm sure Martin wouldn't want this whole thing brought crashing down because of your useless slut of a girlfriend.'

Carl stares at me for a few seconds – a cold, hard look. I am unflinching, unwavering, unmoving. Despite how much that hurt, I don't move.

Nor do I move when he gets back into the car and guns the engine. The bumper quivers against my legs, but still I do not move. As the car leaps backwards, out onto the street, and the revs rise and fall away towards the main road, still I do not move.

The sound of the shower upstairs stops a full minute later. This brings me to my senses and I rush back through the front door, slamming it behind me. As I lean against it, my whole body begins to shake.

I take several deep breaths until I'm calm enough to support my own weight again, and with a hand against each wall for support, I make my way down the hallway to the kitchen and sit heavily in a chair.

When Dana comes in, a towel curled around her head, she finds me in the same pose. 'I hope you don't mind but I borrowed some of your clothes.' She looks idly at the bag of salad on the sideboard, tosses it to one side, then sniffs the air.

'Is something burning?'

SIXTY

We spend the evening eating lightly charred pizza in front of the TV, not speaking much. I try not to, but my eyes keep drifting across to her, stretched out on the couch in a pair of my old joggers and a hoodie. Her hair has dried curlier than it usually is, and in the soft light of the TV and the glow from the fire (she was amazed we had a working fireplace and insisted on using it) it shines a deep amber around her face.

She smiles at me from time to time, but her attention is on the screen: an old film about some people who keep meeting on a long journey – I'm not really paying attention. She laughs at the jokes in it, and when she does, her eyes light up in a way I haven't seen before. I'm used to angry Dana, or anxious Dana, and I know the determined, fulfilled Dana from the garden, but I've never seen this Dana before. I think she's relaxed. Maybe even happy.

When the film ends, she throws the remote at me, 'Next!'

We move on to the second half of some comedy quiz show. I go and get ice cream.

When I come back, she pulls her legs up and makes space on the sofa, then pushes her bare feet underneath me. The clinking of our spoons and the audience's laughter fills the room.

While I fill the dishwasher and tidy up, Dana goes upstairs. When I walk into my room, she's stepped out of the joggers and is taking off my hoodie.

'Oi! Get out, perv!'

I back out quickly and shut the door. 'I… I thought you were in the bathroom. Sorry.'

'You can come in now,' she says, a few seconds later.

She's wearing a pair of my boxers and an old T-shirt. It looks very different on her than it does on me.

'What do you think?' She turns around and strikes a pose. 'Hope you don't mind.'

'Er… nope. No. That's fine.' I try and fail miserably to look anywhere in the room but at her.

She notices. 'Josh. You're sweet. But not now. I—'

'Oh. God. No. Of course not. I didn't—'

'Have you got a blanket? I'll sleep on the sofa.'

'No, you stay in here, I'll go downstairs.'

'Are you sure?'

'Yeah. Yes. Yup.' The sleeve of my jumper is caught on the door handle. I yank it free. 'I'll be fine.'

'Thanks for tonight, Josh. We'll go to the station tomorrow. First thing.'

I look blankly at her for a moment.

'The police?'

'Oh, yeah. Yes. Of course.'

'Good night, Josh.'

'Yes.' I don't move.

'Goodnight hug?' She holds her arms out, takes a step towards me.

'Er... OK. Yeah.'

I stand awkwardly in the doorway as she approaches and winds her arms around my waist. I put mine over her shoulders and try to apply the lightest of squeezes.

She looks at me, her hands still on my waist. 'So, good night then.'

There's a ringing in my ears as she stands on her tiptoes and brushes her lips against mine, then I'm standing on the landing looking at the closed door.

SIXTY ONE

I wake early, still dressed in last night's clothes. I watch some TV for a bit and make myself breakfast.

Dana comes down in my dressing gown after about half an hour and puts some bread in the toaster.

'Sleep well?' I ask.

'Brilliant, thanks.'

I put another round in for myself and we sit and munch toast for a few minutes.

'Do you mind if I grab some clothes from my room?' I ask.

'Of course. You stink.'

The curtains are still closed and the bed unmade, still heavy with sleep. There's a light, delicate smell, a bit like shampoo. I get some jeans and a T-shirt from my drawers and change quickly, aware that I'm trespassing in some way. Which feels ridiculous; I'm in my own room.

As I'm pulling the T-shirt over my head, Dana's head appears around the door.

'Oh, too late.' She smiles. 'You saw me, thought I'd try and perv on you.'

Then it disappears again.

She calls from the landing, 'Can I borrow some of

your mum's clothes, do you think? I've only got my school uniform. And I'm not wearing your stuff out of the house.'

I've not been into my parents' room for a long time. Mum's room, I mean. It's neater than I'd imagined it to be. There are a few things flung on a chair in the corner, a few pairs of shoes by the wardrobe, but the bed is made, and there's just one book on Mum's bedside table.

Dad's bedside table hasn't changed. There's his alarm clock, the clay dish bought on holiday when I was six where he keeps – kept – his change, and the little stand for his watch that I made him years ago in DT; two pieces of wood with a pretty awful mortise and tenon joint, all gloopily coated in varnish, but he'd used it every night.

I must have been standing in the doorway for a while. Dana shoves me in the back. 'Something plain, yeah? I don't want to look like an old woman.'

I find a black pair of jeans that look OK, a T-shirt and a thin, yellow jumper. Mum doesn't really dress 'young' but I guess this stuff is fairly neutral. I hand it all to Dana, who takes it into the bathroom. 'Not falling for that trick twice. I want a lock this time.' She winks through the gap in the door as she closes it.

Just like my old joggers, when Dana puts the clothes on, they're transformed. She gives me another twirl on the landing. 'OK?'

'Yeah. Fine… Yeah.'

'I hope you're not getting into me in these clothes, Josh. That'd be weird.'

I smile back at her. I think we both know we're buying time; trying to keep everything normal for as long as we can. Just the two of us.

Until we know we have to go. Back out into the not-normal world.

And try to save it.

SIXTY TWO

There's a back way to get to the police station, and we agree that the extra half an hour it will take is worth it. I haven't told Dana about Carl turning up last night, but she knows he's looking for her and that there are probably others on the lookout too; the types of characters we really don't want to run into.

As soon as we step outside, the mood between us is suddenly different. Dana walks fast, her chin deep inside her coat collar. Getting somewhere quickly without being seen is probably something she's used to doing. I have to jog every third step or so to keep up.

'We could go past the garden, if you like?'

'Not now. After, maybe. When it's done. Then back to yours if that's alright.'

'Sure.' Mum has already confirmed she'll be away a second night.

After forty minutes or so of walking in silence, of speeding single-file down footpaths and alleyways between houses in quiet streets, of hot-footing it along stone tracks that wind eventually down towards the centre of town, all the while seeing no one, we get to the much more public bit that we can't avoid. Luckily, this Saturday is market day, and a whole group of pet-food stalls, bakers' stalls and others will line most of the route to the police station on the other side of the town centre.

As we round the corner onto the normally quieter end of the high street, we join a throng of people. I feel relieved that we can blend in with the crowd and achieve a kind of anonymity. But Dana tenses. Her arm, which she has had slipped through mine for the last five minutes, is plunged back into her pocket. She puts her head down and charges forward through the sea of people. Following in the wake of angry heads and occasional 'oi's behind her, I know that we'll be spotted soon if we carry on like this.

I grab her arm and pull her into a side alley, behind a pair of large bins. 'Hey, what's wrong?'

'Let's just get there, alright?'

'OK. But you need to slow down a bit. You're drawing a lot of attention to yourself.'

'For God's sake stop *looking* at me, Josh. It's your problem. No one else's.'

The glare she gives me could nail me to the brick wall we're standing next to. I stare back at her, trying not to show how much it hurt.

'Sorry.' She softens a little. 'I'm just nervous. I lash out sometimes.'

'I'd noticed,' I smile, trying to diffuse the atmosphere. 'I'm nervous too. But we'll get there. We've got another five minutes, and there'll be crowds all the way. And then it'll be done.'

'Yeah, OK.' We head back towards the street. 'Josh?'

'Yes?'

'I do like it, you know?'

'Like what?'

We're standing at the end of the alley when she grabs my hand. 'When you look at me.'

She doesn't let go, and we slip back into the flow of people.

As casually as possible, we pass between the rows of market stalls with their blue-striped awnings and tables full of products; cellophane bags done up with red tape, gloves and hats in baskets, crates of light bulbs, ten-packs of tights. I've never been so alert to the sights and smells as my head darts this way and that. I bridle a few times as a shaved head emerges from the crowd, and I try to match them with the images of the other men I saw just a few months ago in the upstairs room of the Crown – the men who loom at me in my dreams. But these men don't match those pictures: they are men pushing prams, walking with their wives or girlfriends, or escorting their mothers around the stalls.

I stop in my tracks as one man, who's angry look I think is aimed at me, turns to the small girl who is holding his hand, 'The toilets are this way, love. Can you hold on a minute?' And just like that, his anger melts into concern. I need to relax.

'Josh?'

I don't recognise the voice. Not at first.

It belongs to a man with a kind face, standing behind a market stall of bagged-up pet food. But there's a kind of reaching look in his eyes.

'It is Josh, isn't it? How've you been, Kid?'

He's wearing a blue jumper. It's the same unravelling blue jumper he wore when we first met. It's Dan. I flashback to what Carl said about him not running away. The nightmare visions. But Dan looks … fine.

'Erm, I'm OK thanks. You?' As soon as I heard my name called, I felt Dana's hand slip from mine. Now she's nowhere to be seen. Maybe that's for the best. If Dan sees us together, who knows what will happen next.

'Can't complain, mate. Can't complain. John, you OK if I have a quick break, mate?'

John is a short, black guy in a denim jacket. He gives Dan a nod, then goes back to selling bird feed to a woman next to me. Dan shuffles around the stall, wincing a bit, and it's then that I notice the large white cast that runs from his left foot all the way up to his thigh. It's even bigger than Jamie's was.

'Is that what Carl—'

His eyes look panicked. There is the slightest shake of his head. 'It's a bit sore today. It doesn't like the cold I don't think.' He raises his voice a little, makes sure John can hear him. 'Bloody foolish of me, falling down those stairs like that.'

Catching on to his meaning, I join in. 'Oh. That's awful. Er… Sorry to hear it.'

John looks away from the growing queue at his stall, looks at Dan. 'Two minutes?'

'Thanks, Boss.' Then, to me, 'Mind if we sit down, Kid?' Dan picks up a crutch from behind the stall and gestures with it towards a nearby bench. 'I can't lean on this thing for too long.'

'Sure, yeah. Fine.' I think I see the back of Dana's head. She's fifty yards or so down the high street. It's OK. I know where she's going.

'Look, Josh,' Dan begins, placing himself heavily on the bench. I perch on the other end. He leans in and his voice drops. 'If you happen to see him, Carl I mean, can you tell him I'm alright?'

'Yeah, sure.'

'It's just, John offered me this job, and it's alright actually. Doesn't change how I feel about … you know … things. But I don't want him thinking badly of me.'

I've never heard a less convincing statement, but I let it go. Other things to worry about. 'Is that why Carl … your leg?'

'Don't know. That and some other stuff. I asked a few times about this whole plan. Maybe I did a bit too much asking. Just all seems a bit … much. I mean it's just a kid, isn't it? He's what, your age? Not that I don't agree that *something* has to be—'

'Yeah, of course, Dan. I'll pass that on.' I can't stand the hollowness of his voice. Is that what I sound like?

'And I suppose I should apologise to you, too. For not … you know, with your dad and everything…'

'Oh.' I'm struggling for words. Should I let on? His loyalty to Carl, despite everything, suggests I shouldn't. 'Well … it's OK. I guess. Don't worry about it.'

'Thanks, Josh. You're a proper hero.' Dan goes back to sounding jocular, friendly. 'So what's he got you running around with today then? Suppose you can't say much about it really, can you?'

'No, not really.' My discomfort must be pretty clear by now. One knee won't keep still.

'I won't keep you, Josh. Good to see you though. Maybe see you about sometime, back at the Crown maybe?'

'Yeah, maybe.' I stand to leave.

Dan heaves himself back onto his one good leg. He's wrapped the handle of his crutch in cloth bandages, like Jamie did, but I can see his left hand's all sore where it's been rubbing.

'Vaseline,' I say, pointing to it.

'What's that?'

'For the hand. Happened to a friend of mine recently. He said if you put Vaseline on your hand it doesn't rub so much. Have to keep changing the wrapping on the handle though. Otherwise it gets all manky.'

'Oh, right. Thanks. I'll give it a try. Nice to see you, Josh.'

I watch Dan go, lumbering back to John's stall, giving his boss a friendly wave.

Turning back down the high street, I move quickly past the shoppers. There's something about Dan's loneliness that's upset me. I guess it upset me that first time, at the Crown. But I was too busy then with feeling like a man, like I was being accepted. Like I was standing in a kind of spotlight. And then with feeling like a caught rabbit when I realised it was actually the headlights of a truck coming straight for me. Dan is a man who'll grab at the first human contact he can find. Funny that the people he did find were people who have no interest in human contact at all. The opposite, in fact.

I'm in a kind of reverie when I feel a hand on my arm. I almost jump in the air. But it's Dana. Just Dana, who'd been waiting for me in another alleyway between buildings. And she smiles at me.

'Well done for getting rid of him. Come on.'

A few moments later, and we're standing at the wide entrance to the police station, its rotating door quietly turning.

'Ready?' she asks.

'Ready.'

Inside, it's darker than the street and instantly feels strange, despite how recently I was here. I suppose it's the kind of building that shrugs off familiarity and always manages to look inhospitable. A female officer is sitting behind the glass screen. She looks up as we come in.

I try to sound cheerful. 'Hi, I'd like to—'

'Hang on. Start again.' The officer flicks a switch and there's a tinny squeak as the microphone on my side turns on.

'Hello, I'd like to change a statement I made last month, please.' I hear the echo of my amplified voice, coming back at me through her microphone to the speakers on my side. It's like having a conversation with someone on the other side of the world.

'What statement? Do you have a case number?'

'No, it was an accident involving a cyclist. I was involved.'

'Right, that doesn't really help. Were you the cyclist?'

'No, but they thought I might have caused it. The accident.'

'And you don't have the case number?'

'No. I don't know if there was a case number. I don't know if …' I can see where this is going. My plan to talk to a familiar face – to make this easier – might not work after all.

'Do you know the name of the officer involved?'

'No, sorry. She was about your height, maybe a bit taller? Dark hair?'

'PC Reynolds?'

'Yes. I think so.'

'She's not on today. Can you come back in the week?'

'Not really, it's…'

Dana pushes past me, her hands clutching the edge of the desk, her mouth close to the microphone. 'We have some information about an attack someone's planning against someone in town. Against a group of people I mean.'

'Could you stand back please, Miss, and wait your turn.'

'Oh, we're together,' I add.

'So it's not about the incident with the cyclist?' The officer crosses her arms.

'No, but I thought PC Reynolds might—'

'So what's this attack?' There's a squeak of feedback from the microphone, and the last word rings around the waiting room like a siren.

Dana rejoins, speaking quickly, 'There're a group of people who are going to hurt someone – some people – soon. We're part of that group but we want you to stop them. They're looking for us – for me – fuck – so can you hurry up?'

The officer gestures towards a large notice above her head about how abuse or bad language will not be tolerated.

I place a hand on Dana's back, steer her gently to one side. 'I'm sorry, but she's right. We really need to talk to someone quickly. The … situation. It's quite … advanced?' I know that I'm failing to sound as if I know what I'm talking about. 'And they're looking for Dana. I think they'll hurt her if they find her.'

The officer appraises us slowly, her eyes moving from me to Dana and back again. Despite the seriousness of the situation, I try smiling at her to be as disarming as I can. Dana's technique is the opposite. She shrugs off my hand and is just about to throw herself at the microphone again when there is a noise from the door. A man is shoved into the foyer, his hands handcuffed in front of him. Behind him, holding him by the collar, is the officer who sat in my living room.

She speaks to the woman behind the glass. 'Graham's been doling out fake tenners again. I'm going to book him and stick him in number five if it's free.'

'Really? Again, Graham?' The microphone seems to working fine now.

The man hangs his head.

'Yeah, fine.' The officer behind the desk presses a button, there's a loud noise – somewhere between a grinding of cogs and a foghorn – and our police officer pulls open the door to the right of the window.

'PC Reynolds!' I shout. The officer, still man-handling the fraudster, stops and looks at me a moment.

'Do I know you?'

'That's not PC Reynolds,' comes the voice from behind the glass. 'That's Sargant Prangle. I think these kids are after you, Sarge. Something about an attack and some people being after them.'

The Sargant looks at me, quizzically. 'You were the kid from the bike crash, end of last year, right?'

340

'Yes, that's me. I gave a statement.'

'Wait there.'

And the door clicks shut.

The tinny voice behind the glass squeaks again. 'You should have said Sargant Prangle if you meant Sargant Prangle. She looks nothing like PC Reynolds. Take a seat. She'll probably be a while.'

Before I can reply, I hear a squeak as the microphone is switched off.

SIXTY THREE

'I don't like this, Josh. We need to be on *that* side of the door.'

I shrug. 'They're not going to come looking for us here, are they?'

'They will if they think that's where we're going.'

'Would Carl think that? What if Dan says something.'

'I don't think Carl's taking Dan's calls at the moment. That thing with his leg. That was Carl.'

Dana sits down heavily in one of the three plastic chairs in the foyer. I take the one next to her.

We leaf through the out-of-date magazines on the table. Dana wastes some time on her phone. Every now and then, I catch the eye of the officer behind the glass screen. At one point, there's a brief exchange between her and a middle-aged man who comes in to complain about a parking ticket. He doesn't seem to understand that it's the council, not the police, who issue parking tickets, and that he needs to take his complaint there. He then asks if he can submit a criminal charge against the parking attendant, at which point the microphone clicks off.

Several times the buzzer goes off and officers go in

or out through the door, but it's a slow half hour before Sargant Prangle comes into the foyer and ushers us through. Though it's a relief to be back here at last, getting closer to the moment of telling our story is anything but.

We follow her past the rows of desks in the middle of the station, most piled high with files and paper. We go along a couple of corridors, their various posters peeling slowly in the half-light of more fluorescent tubes. The paint on the walls is doing the same. We follow the Sargant into a small interview room towards the back of the building.

She waits until Dana and I are sitting down before she starts. 'I had a feeling I might be seeing you again. How's your friend's leg?'

I realise after a second she's talking about Jamie, not Dan. I tell her he's been out of plaster for a while now, and is showing everyone at school the thick, black hair that's grown where the cast was. He should be able to start football training again after Easter.

'Good. But this isn't about the accident with the cyclist, is it?'

'No,' I say, a little surprised.

'Josh, the people that you have been … associating with have been on our radar for some time. And you,' she checks some paperwork, then turns to Dana. 'It's Dana, isn't it?'

Dana shuffles uncomfortably.

'You look familiar, Dana. Have met before?'

'So you know about Carl? The meetings? The Lions? All of it?' Dana's voice is tense and she's gripping the edge of the table. She wants to change the subject.

Sargant Prangle looks at her for a few seconds, then leans back in her chair. 'Maybe not all of it. Why don't you tell me what you know, and I'll see where it fits with what we *do* have. The events that we know about. We know, for example, there are regular meetings at the Crown, and there have been some other... *instances* of other members' activities.'

I think back to the meeting, Carl's talk about *agitations*, the big guy called Barney laughing at what he'd done.

Dana speaks again, quieter this time. 'Did you know I was... involved?'

'I'll have to check. But if you're not on our records, probably not. Is there a reason you'd be on our records?'

Dana is silent, staring at the table. I see a pulse in her jaw.

Sargant Prangle turns back to me. 'OK, look. Carl and his Lions are in our sights, and he's gone quiet recently. I'd like to think it's because the momentum has gone out of his campaign – or whatever he calls it. But from talking to other forces around the country that's unfortunately not always the case. Which means he might be planning something.'

'That's why we're here.' I am more than a little

relieved that the hard part of this whole thing – explaining the group and about Carl – has already been done. Dana is picking at the chipped table-top with her thumb nail.

'We've been clocking the meetings for the last eight months, I'd say. Not long after they started. Of course, we were informed when Carl moved back here, his previous offences. But he was quiet to begin with, kept himself out of mischief.'

Dana tightens in her chair. I hear her breathing change, like her throat's closing up.

Sargant Prangle notices too, her eyes locking on Dana as she continues. 'Until that stunt at the mosque last year when he was chucking rocks from right underneath his own banner. We've seen the videos on that private section of his website and—'

Dana speaks again. Her voice is thin. 'So why haven't you done anything? Why have you let him get away with it?'

Sargant Prangle leans forward. One hand edges across the table, towards Dana. 'It's … complicated, Dana. The videos won't stand up in court. It's not clear enough who's who, and we can't identify the gentleman that gets attacked. He's never reported it. So we don't really know who's doing what. Except…' She looks back at me. 'You're lucky no one was hurt at that charity shop, Josh.'

My breath stops in my throat. I can't speak.

Sargant Prangle continues. 'I had a hunch it was you. They didn't show your face, but I thought I recognised your coat, the way you were walking. I was going to come knocking on your door for the full story, but something told me you might come looking for me, so I waited.'

Dana stands up suddenly, her chair falling backwards and clattering against the wall. 'You're *playing* with us! You could have stepped in at any time. Stopped it. Arrested him, Carl, all of us, so I didn't have to … So he wouldn't have …'

It all pours out of Dana then, all the hurt she's been carrying. I thought I was doing an OK job of helping her but, as she lets out a deep groan that quickly takes flight as a scream, it's obvious I haven't been. The anger at her father, her mother, at Carl. All the 'what ifs' form on her face in the second it takes Sargant Prangle to get round to our side of the table. She grabs Dana's fists, holding her by the wrists as they flail towards her. Dana only has a few good attempts in her before she's weeping into the Sargant's chest, arms flopping in the Sargant's tight grip, and then hanging limply at her sides.

Sargant Prangle speaks into the walkie-talkie on her shoulder, and soon there's a knock at the door. A woman enters with her hair cut into a soft bob. She looks kind. She leads Dana away. When the door shuts, it's just the two of us.

Sargant Prangle lets the silence stew for a while. 'So, what are you here for, Josh?'

346

My voice is barely above a whisper. 'Something bad's going to happen. People are in danger.'

More silence, then she speaks the words I've been dreading.

'Josh, we need to call your mum.'

SIXTY FOUR

It takes a few hours for Mum to arrive. I have to wait in one of the juvenile cells. There's a mattress, covered in green vinyl, on the narrow bed, and a door between the toilet and the main area, which is about three metres square. Apart from that, it's just bare, white tiles on the floor and the ceiling. And silent.

After the first hour, I ask if I can see Dana. I'm told she's sleeping in a cell on the same corridor. I go back to sitting on the bunk, counting the tiles, figuring out how I'm going to explain all of this.

After a lot more waiting and counting tiles (I keep losing count after about two hundred and thirty, and counting the same tiles twice) I finally hear a key in the door. It swings open to reveal Mum. She's standing next to Sargant Prangle. She's like the sun; I can't look directly at her. I'd go blind and melt if I even tried. I don't know if she's more relieved or furious.

'You ... silly bugger,' are the first and only words she says to me as we make our way back to the interview room.

She sits quietly as I tell Sargant Prangle – and the tape recorder – what I know. I start from the beginning, with Alan's link to the website. About going to the meeting at the Crown. About how they're doing it all for me. Because of me. About the SIM card that I stuck inside my drawer which I've brought with me. It goes straight into a little plastic bag marked 'evidence'. I tell them about how the plan is to kidnap Ahmed after school on a particular day, use him as bait to draw his mother out, then kidnap her as well, film what Carl and his machete will do to them and put it on the internet with a list of demands. For every day the demands are not met, a target will be bombed by the White Lions. I don't know what the targets are, but I explain to the tape machine what Dana has explained to me, about the chemicals that Carl's been stockpiling, where he's keeping them. The words, what they signify, feel like bile in my throat. The thought of Carl's plan has coiled itself around my every waking thought for months, but the hard fact of speaking the words aloud feels like releasing a thousand serpents into the room. Then Ahmed's words come back to me, about decency, compassion, humanity. I explain my role, what I was supposed to be doing. It gets hard to talk towards the end. I tell them about Vince and Alan and Carl taking me to the charity shop, about what they made me do, how I injured my hand.

When I finish, Mum is crying.

Sargant Prangle goes to press stop on the tape recorder, but hesitates a moment, then leaves it running. 'That's a very brave thing you just did, Josh. Thank you.

I want to tell you that this is not your fault. These people have been preying on you for a long time. What they're doing is not because of you, or for you. You are not the centre of this. I want you to think about something for me for a minute. Before Alan and Vince and the meetings, has anyone else ever talked to you about these kinds of things? Used that kind of hate speech? Consistently brought up the topic or asked you about it?'

I think very hard, but nothing comes. It's almost like the life I had before that first meeting belongs to someone else now. 'No. Nothing I can think of,' I say.

'OK. Just one final question. Do you think you were followed here today?'

'No.' I'm certain of this.

She speaks the time into the recorder, then presses stop, leans back and sighs, rubs her eyes with the palms of her hands before speaking again. 'We're going to act on this immediately.' Despite the hardness in her voice, there's a sense of uncertainty about her. 'I'm going to make some calls, get the boys in who specialise in this. We're only a rural station.' She looks a little guilty at this point. 'Now, if no one suspects you're here today, as you've said, the boys'll probably prefer a dawn raid – gives us time to verify a few of these allegations. We can't send an officer home with you, but we'll make sure a local patrol passes your house more often if that would make you feel safer?'

Mum shakes her head. Perhaps she's had enough of police officers at our house. Or perhaps she didn't hear. Too busy thinking about what I've done.

'OK. We'll be in touch. Tomorrow probably.'

'What about Dana? She can't go to her house.'

'We know. We can't get hold of her mother. We'll … make arrangements.'

'Can't she come with us? Mum?'

Mum jerks her head, as if just waking up at hearing me call her. 'What's that?'

'Can Dana stay with us? Until we hear from the police?'

'Fine with me.' Her voice is barely above a whisper.

There're some forms to sign, and Mum double-takes when she sees Dana in her clothes. Dana quickly wraps her coat tighter around herself.

'Hello again, Mrs Milton.'

'Hello, Dana. I'll get the car and meet you both out the front. Five minutes.'

'There's a back door, Mrs Milton. Best to use that, I think. It's on Pond Street. I'll get someone to wait there and they'll radio me when you arrive.'

We spend an awkward ten minutes with Sargant Prangle at her desk as she types away on her computer. There's an indiscernible crackle from her radio, and she stands. Leading us even deeper into the bowels of the station, she speaks over her shoulder to me. 'Anything suspicious, you call us, here at the station. OK? Your mum's got my direct number, Josh, but if you can't get through, dial 999 if it's urgent. Stay out of the way. Stay home. We'll be in touch tomorrow.'

The blue, steel door opens onto a thin road and some dumpsters. Mum sits rigid in the driving seat of the car. I'm not sure what I was expecting, but now we've emerged back into daylight the world looks no different at all.

SIXTY FIVE

I open the front passenger door for Dana and get into the back. We're halfway home before anyone speaks. It's Mum who breaks the silence.

'Don't think that you two will be sharing a bed.'

The heat in my cheeks is immediate. 'Mum, no. It's not like that.'

'Oh. Well. OK then. It's not like I know anything about your life at the moment, Josh, so how would I know? It's not as if you tell me anything anymore, is it?'

'I'm sorry, Mrs Milton.'

'Don't worry, Dana, it's just very difficult when your son is something of a stranger to you. When he's the kind of boy who smashes shop windows with hammers and wants to kidnap the son of one your colleagues and blow up the whole world.'

'Mum, I—'

'Don't, Josh. Not now.' I can see her knuckles whiten on the steering wheel.

'He didn't want to, Mrs Milton. The guy who's in charge, Carl, he's horrible. He makes you do things you don't want to.'

'I'm sure you're right, Dana. But I raised a son – your father raised a son, Josh – who didn't get involved with those sorts of people. A son who spoke to us about things that worried him or that he didn't understand.'

'What don't I understand, Mum? I told you about the website – those websites I'd been going to – about how it felt like it was helping. About how it felt good to be angry. What is it that I still don't understand?'

'Your father would not have tolerated—'

'But he's not here, Mum, is he?' I'm shouting now, my anger filling the car. 'He's not here and he's not been here for a long time now. And nor have you. So what am I supposed to do while you're off with Mr fucking Walters?'

'I don't know, Josh!' Mum is shouting too now. A long blare from a car horn sounds behind us as we speed through a red light. 'I don't fucking know, OK? I don't have an answer. Any answers. And don't think that I'm not fucking angry too!'

And as quickly as it came, the anger goes again. It's as if someone opened the window and sucked all the rage out into the growing twilight.

'I'm sorry,' I say again.

'Me too, love. Me too. And I'm sorry to you, Dana.'

'What for?'

'For having nothing suitable for you in my wardrobe. I've not been shopping in years. Maybe we could go together one day.' She offers us both a watery smile as we pull into the driveway. 'Maybe if I can't get to know my son, I can get to know his girlfriend.'

I'm about to protest again about the 'girlfriend' label before Dana has to, but I'm interrupted.

'Thanks, Mrs Milton, I'd like that very much.'

'And I keep telling you he's got a name you know, Mr Walters. Could you please just call him Martin from now on?'

And my stomach hits the floor.

His first name's Peter. PMW are the initials on the timetable. But he's known by his middle name. Martin. It takes Mum more than a little convincing from both me and Dana to turn the car around and head back to the police station.

While we're on the way, everything settles in my head. It all starts to make sense. All those comments about my dad after I'd asked him to stop. Him reading the newspaper while I was in the room. What was it Ahmed had said? *A pretty good lever to pull*. He'd been pulling on it subtly since I'd first gone back to school.

And that first Thursday session, the conversation we'd had – *they'd* had – in front of me. How it had all sounded so natural at the time. But it had been planned. Of course it had. And it explained why Alan and Vince treated him differently from any other teacher.

And the fact that he'd been in my house, had sat at our table. My skin won't stop crawling. We're stuck in traffic – shoppers coming home – and I keep re-seeing Mum touching him on the arm. Where else had she touched him? I can't think about it.

'Did you know?' I ask Dana outside the station as we wait for Mum to park the car.

'No idea. But it makes sense, doesn't it? Alan and Vince—'

'Alan and Vince? They know. Definitely. The way they are with him.'

I think about it. The language they use, the way Carl commanded that room at the Crown. 'Yeah, you're right.'

The woman behind the glass screen is surprised to see us again, but buzzes us straight through. We find Sargant Prangle at her desk. She unfixes her eyes from her computer screen and blinks a few times before realising we're standing in front of her.

'We need to tell you something else,' I say.

Mum did tell him about the websites, she admits when we're back in the room with Sargant Prangle and the tape recorder again. Or she didn't tell him so much as ask advice 'for a friend' and he'd worked it out. But of course he'd already known. And before that, he knew about how I'd got the bruise on my face.

I feel a little uncomfortable listening as Mum recounts the details of their meetings. The first few times they'd bumped into each other at the supermarket, the flirtatious coffees and text messages. Like earlier, I try to turn my mind off, to focus on other things.

He'd waited for a catalyst, struck me while I was most vulnerable. Maybe he and Carl had even planned the punch at the party. It seems like years ago now. Hard to believe it's not even been six months. Then he, 'Martin', had set himself up as some kind of confidante, had invaded my home, pretended to offer some kind of support when all along he'd been calling the shots. It was probably him who'd told Alan where I lived, had given him the textbook to drop off. Him who wanted to know about where Dana was yesterday. And it was him who had ordered me to smash that shop window.

Perhaps Mum is picking up on my thoughts. She grows more and more incandescent with rage as she talks more and more about the interest Martin had shown in me, how he'd always ask after me and who I was seeing. He seemed, she says, far more interested in me than in her.

'This can, of course, only be taken as speculation,' the Sargant says when Mum's finished. 'We'll follow it up, of course. But all we have is a first name to go on here. That's the only common factor.'

But it was him. It *is* him behind this plan, this savage and inhuman plan. And the way that Carl spoke at that meeting, the way he controlled the room. He could only have learnt that from Mr Walters; it had his stamp all over it.

Back on the road home again, Mum is still furious.

At herself, mostly. 'I can't believe I could have been so stupid. What was I thinking?'

Dana does a good job of calming her. She knows about men, about what they're capable of saying, of doing. Mum talks to her as if there isn't a gap of thirty years between them.

That evening, we put the fire on, order take away and wrap ourselves in blankets in front of the TV, trying to make the world no bigger than our living room. We flick between re-runs of old TV shows and a couple of films to avoid the advert breaks. At one point, the old show that Mum and I used to watch together is on, and we switch across just in time to hear 'it is what it is.' I look at Mum, she looks at me, and despite the day it's been and all it's held, we start laughing.

'What's funny?' Dana smiles.

'Nothing,' I say. 'I'll explain another time.'

There's warmth in this little nest we've created – our own, unbreachable corner of the universe – that I know won't last. Can't last. We're all nervous; we laugh too loudly, or jump on the back of each other's comments too quickly. We're trying to pretend we're not, but we are. Even so, I feel a lightness this evening that I haven't felt for years. Or maybe I've never felt it, not even before Dad died. The only way I can describe it is that it's like after you've been swimming in a cold sea on a hot day; as if your skin has been scrubbed clean, or has re-grown, brand new. And in that moment when the sun hits your skin and you can feel your body just drinking the warmth in, and as your foot hovers above the dry sand at the tideline, and you know you're about to get its grains all over your foot and your legs and everywhere else, you feel a moment of being ... I don't know ... clean, maybe. Perfectly clean.

'Right kids, I'll leave you to it,' says Mum at about half past nine, reluctantly unwrapping herself from the blankets and picking up the tottering pile of plates and foil cartons. 'Goodnight.'

''Night,' we reply.

We listen as she bustles around in the kitchen, and to her footfall on the stairs.

'So you *are* my girlfriend, then?'

'If you like. You don't have to ask me or anything. People don't really do that anymore.'

'No.' I'm trying to sound informed, well-versed in the ways of the modern relationship.

'Are you going to kiss me then?'

And I do. I lean over and I do. Her lips taste sweet, somehow metallic and a little sharp. It's like putting a battery on your tongue. We do it again and again.

SIXTY SIX

That night, while I'm lying on the sofa, covered in blankets, while Dana is asleep upstairs, I dream of Dad's tree again. The ants have gone, and so has the little plastic sheath, and the whole tree is green. Not just the leaves, but the bark as well. Grandad told me years ago how to check if something is still alive in the middle of winter; you scratch a little bark off with your thumb, and if there's green underneath, it's good and healthy. I don't remember much else when I wake up except this luminous, totally green tree.

I hear footsteps on the stairs and assume it's Mum. Then I hear the catch on the front door.

I run into the hall to find Dana putting on her shoes in the open doorway.

'What are you doing? The police said to—'

'I know. But I plugged my phone in. It went flat last night. And Carl's been calling, and messaging me. He says the police were at his house last night but he got away. He was bragging at first. Then he started getting angry that he couldn't find me. Then he worked it out. He knows it was me that told them. And then he sent this really late last night.'

She thrusts her phone at me. There's a picture of a

woman sitting on a sofa. Vince is on one side of her, Carl is on the other. Each holds a knife their hand.

'I have to go, Josh. I can't leave my mum like that. Whatever she might be, she's still my mum.'

'I'm calling the police.'

'No. Don't. He said if the police come he'll do it. He'll do to her what he was going to do to Ahmed.'

'Then I'm coming with you.'

'Fine, but hurry up.'

I hurtle upstairs and scramble into some clothes. Mum appears at her bedroom door as I'm pulling my coat on.

'What are you doing?'

'Dana's mum. He's got her. She's—'

'Wait, Josh. You're supposed to stay here. That's what you were told. If you know where this Carl person is, you should tell the—'

'We can't. He'll kill her.'

'Stop! You don't just throw yourself into the mouth of these things. That man is…'

But we've already closed the door.

We run until we have to stop running, our legs heavy and lungs burning. Mum's right, this thing is a mouth. I thought – last night – that I was out of it, but it's still got us in its jaws, chewing on us. Above the houses, the first smear of dirty pink light is hitting the undersides of the clouds.

From down the street, we see Carl's car parked

outside Dana's. We edge closer and soon make out the shape of a body in the driver's seat. It's Alan. Asleep.

'This way.' Dana pulls me down a side alley that leads behind the row of terraced houses.

At her back gate, I help her onto the top of a wheely bin and she peers carefully above the wall.

'I can't see anyone. There's no lights on either. There's a security light on the back wall, but it only comes on if the kitchen light's on.' She whispers.

As delicately as I can, I lift the latch on the back gate and ease it open. There's a creak and a groan from the rusting hinges, and we slip through into the garden.

About twenty yards from the back door, a yellowish glow starts flickering through the kitchen window like an eyelid fluttering. Half a second later, the whole garden fills with a flood of dazzling white light. There's slight movement inside, and in a second, beneath the glare, the back door opens. Vince stands there, looking like he's just woken up, bare toes poking through holes in his socks. It doesn't take him long to regain his senses though.

'Carl! It's them!'

Vince is after us as we spin round and sprint for the gate and back into the alleyway. I'm following Dana, who pulls the half-full bin sideways as she passes. I just slip through as it tumbles, but there's a huge crash as Vince collides with it. It barely seems to break his stride and he's just a few feet behind us when he stops, suddenly, swearing. I chance the quickest look back and see him hopping on one bare foot, pulling something out of the bottom of the other.

Back on the road, neither of us turn when we hear the shouts, or the engine start up, or the squeal of tyres on tarmac. Dana darts across the road, running wildly, me following, and we sprint down another alleyway which links one street to the next. It has bollards at both ends. A screech of brakes, then the engine guns again as Carl seeks another way around.

When she hears this, Dana pulls up. I run into the back of her and we fall. I manage to get an arm around Dana as we go down, roll her on top of me so I land first. I hit the pavement hard.

'Other way, now,' Dana gasps. 'Back past my house. There's a path to the main road. Quick, before he works it out.' Of course, she knows exactly what she's doing. And I thought I was rescuing her.

We get to our feet and run back the way we came, clinging to each other. The front door of Dana's house hangs open. Dana sprints through it. I stop next to the still form of Alan, lying face down on the pavement outside, against the fence. He groans, trying to raise himself. There's blood coming from one side of his head and a smear of it on the concrete fencepost he's reaching for to pull himself up. Carl must have dragged him out of the car and thrown him pretty hard.

Groggily, he notices me. He's not going to put up

363

much of a fight, but when his hand emerges from his pocket with his phone, I pluck it from him without difficulty. I put it in my pocket.

I'm about to follow Dana inside when I hear the sirens. Faint, some way off, but growing louder. But even closer, the sound of Carl's engine, growing louder again. I crouch by Alan's ear.

'Are you OK?'

He nods, feebly.

'And Dana's mum?'

'Inside. She's fine,' he croaks.

Dana is running back outside now, shouting. 'She's OK. Fuck's sake, Josh, Come on!'

As the note from Carl's engine rises and falls again, getting steadily louder, we run for the path that leads to the main road. I can't stay with Alan – poor, clueless Alan, whose first crime was loving his brother and seeing him as a god. Carl must be only seconds away as we emerge from the footpath onto the main road. Crossing it, in the growing light of the morning, the building site stands silhouetted against the sky. We run towards it.

Above the sirens – and much, much closer – we hear the furious engine of Carl's car at our backs. We run. He must have worked out what we'd do. As Carl rounds the road's sweeping curve, the noise is almost deafening. He revs even harder as he mounts the pavement behind us.

We throw ourselves through a gap in the building site's metal fencing a second before Carl's car would have hit us. Getting to our feet as quickly as possible, we set off across the churned ground. Carl is outside the car now, which has slid to a halt about fifty yards past the gap we came through, and he's shouting at us. The sirens are almost on top of him, and as I look over my shoulder I see two police cars stop either side of him as he starts to climb the fence. He's over before they get to him, and I give my full attention back to following Dana around the deep tracks and deeper puddles.

The sirens continue. And there's a new sound; the low thud of rotor blades. A flash of the helicopter's searchlight reflects in the dirty water at my feet.

In through the gaping front door of one of the new houses, into the darkness of its shell-like rooms, and out through the back into more mud we run. I force myself to get ahead of Dana and start to lead her towards a rack of scaffolding that looks familiar. I don't need to look back to know that Carl is gaining on us, each shout and insult louder than his last. As we squeeze down what looks like an impossible gap between two houses, a gap that I'm certain has narrowed since last time I was here, clogged up with bits of brick and roof tile underfoot, we emerge into the space I was hoping to find, the wooden hoarding rising tall in front of us.

'It's a dead end,' Dana gasps, trying to catch a breath.

'No it's not. Wait.'

I grab at the wooden boards and try to prize them open, but they're not shifting. The gap I crawled through a few months ago has been nailed shut. There's a short length of iron rod poking out of a small pile of rubble. I grab it and start working away at the corner of the hoarding. Dana gets the idea, and she takes the rod while I get my hands behind the wood again and start to heave against the nails. With a sharp pop, the wood is free, and there's the hole again, just big enough to get through.

Carl's shouts are getting even closer. He's inside the gap between the houses.

Dana goes first as I hold the wood back. I throw the iron rod through after her and wedge myself under the panel. But the angles are all wrong. Every time I move forward I pull the wooden boards closed on myself, and Dana can't get enough weight behind it from her side to keep it open. My shoulders and most of my torso are through, but my waist is stuck. I roll onto my back, pounding away at the wooden board as it pins me down, stuck against the waistband of my jeans.

Squirming against the slick mud, I manage to get one leg out. I put all of my strength into it, pushing against the wood which moans but won't release me. Then I feel strong hands on my other leg, pulling me back. Carl's voice seething, incoherent, like a slavering dog.

Panic rising in me, I push again as hard as I can and

with a splintering groan the wood suddenly splits and the corner of the board snaps off. My leg, behind the board, carries on and connects with a part of Carl, knocking him backwards. He lets go.

I scramble to my feet inside the walls of the garden, ready to follow Dana towards the door she's already gone through. My hand is on the lock when the iron rod smashes against the wall next to me, ricocheting back against my face. I fall to the ground, a searing pain across my forehead and down one cheek. Carl's boot connects with my stomach, then he bends to pick up the iron rod again. I have a sudden sensation of floating. And then the pain comes.

Scrambling along the wall, I raise my arm against the iron rod as Carl thrashes down with it. His first blow I manage to block, my forearm against his wrist, but the second strike catches me on the elbow and the world explodes into showers of sparks and white flashes.

'Stop!'

It's Dana's voice. She didn't go through the door after all. She's standing against the wooden hoarding. Carl must have gone straight past her, chasing me.

Slowly, Carl rounds on her, the iron rod grasped in his fist.

'You.' His voice is animal, wild.

'Leave him alone.' Dana edges along the wall towards the big, red bush. The bush with the well behind it. I pull myself to my feet.

'You fucking bitch! You traitor slut!' He re-balances the iron rod, bouncing it his palm. Overhead, the roar of rotor blades. Someone shouts through a loudhailer.

Dana is almost in front of the well when Carl launches at her. She runs back on herself, wrong-footing Carl for the split second that I need. With all my strength, I hurl my body against Carl's side, driving into him just below his shoulder. He takes two, three steps sideways and I keep pushing, my vision split and pulsing from the pain in my arm. Through the snowdrops, leaving smears of mud on their bowed heads, into the red-leafed bush he goes, trying to get a foothold. I stop, falling to my knees, my body beginning to shut down.

To steady himself, Carl takes one more step backwards, into the bush. Watching me fall at his feet, his eyes narrow again, and he raises the rod ready to finish me off.

There's a wet crunch. The boards on top of the old well must have crumbled like dust.

Then, three things happen at once.

Two policemen appear on top of the wall and drop heavily into the garden.

Dana throws her arms around my neck and we fall, panting, to the wet grass.

Carl's eyes widen, then, along with the rest of him, disappear into the ground.

The bush leaves resettle themselves above where

Carl stood. A hollow clang echoes up a second later as the iron rod hits the bottom of the well.

Even against the blast of the rotor blades, for a second or two I hear only my own heartbeat fast in my ears. Then there's a shout from the bush.

Their tasers raised as they peel back the foliage, the policemen discover that Carl hasn't fallen completely down the well; he's wedged in the top, his arm crooked over the brickwork. One policeman, kneeling down, holds Carl under the shoulder. He screams.

'He's popped his shoulder. Maybe his collarbone too. We'll need help here,' says the policeman to his colleague, who radios to the helicopter overhead. It pitches to one side and flies off.

The first policeman, returning his attention to Carl, tells him it's going to be a bit of a wait. Carl screams again as the policeman's grip tightens. 'Get comfy,' is the policeman's stoic reply.

The second policeman turns to us, gingerly lifting my arm to check my elbow. The sparks and white lights come back each time he touches it, bringing my arm delicately across my chest. He tells me to hold it there and, taking off his jacket, gets Dana to help him slip it underneath me.

'You OK, Miss? Not hurt all?'

Dana shakes her head, then turns to me, 'It's over. It'll be OK, Josh. I promise. It's over.'

I smile, or try to.

Dana's smiling too. 'Look.'

I turn my head. Beneath the wall, beyond the remains of the crocuses scuffed and scattered by the policemen's heavy boots, a broken row of short, green spears are poking up out of the ground. At the top of each is a swell of papery skin and, from one or two, a waxy, yellow flower is emerging with a brilliant gold trumpet at the centre. They haven't all come up – I probably put some of the bulbs in too deep, or too shallow – but in a weak ray of sunshine that's coming through the gap in the wooden hoarding, the daffodils that I planted are dancing.

SIXTY SEVEN

There's explaining to do, after my arm is X-rayed and examined and put into a plaster cast. Sargant Prangle sits awkwardly in a plastic chair next to my hospital bed, her notepad on her knee, and asks question after question about the chase, about Carl hitting me, about how he fell down the well. Those are the words she uses again and again – 'he fell down the well', never 'you pushed him.'

Mum sits on the other side, holding my good hand, stroking and squeezing it. She only speaks to agree with Sargant Prangle about how we should have stayed home and called the police. It was Mum who did that, in the first few seconds after Dana and I left. And she was right.

'Thanks, Mum.'

She smiles a little, but won't meet my eye.

Dana is quiet as well, leaning against the opposite wall of the hospital room. When she arrived in A&E, Mum had hugged her first, patting her shoulders and down her arms as if to check she wasn't broken. Then she had thanked the two paramedics who had brought us in, then she looked to me strapped to the gurney.

She had looked sad, exhausted and drained. Her

grey face is only just now starting to regain some colour as I try to reassure her, again, that I'm fine.

I suppose it'll be a while before she believes me.

The next day, what happened is on the news. It's not the headline, but after a couple of more urgent stories the reporter turns to our sleepy town, and there's a police photo of Carl, then shots of Mr Walters being led from his house in handcuffs and manhandled into the back of a police car. He's ranting about freedom of speech and is cut off by the reporter's voice again and a helicopter view of the garden – our garden – from above. They've put a square, white tent over the well. Dana gasps when she sees that they've pulled the bush up to get to it; its branches and red leaves are lying on their side against the wrong wall. Then there's Sargant Prangle talking in front of a bunch of flashing bulbs and microphones. She says that a violent and divisive hate crime has been avoided. Dana and I aren't mentioned – Sargant Prangle's idea.

Going back to school is a bit strange, especially how I explain my arm. Alan and Vince vanish overnight. Apparently, they found a bunch of alt-right and racist content on their school accounts. I didn't think they were that stupid, but I have some idea of who might have put it there. And when the substitute Biology teacher is still there after the Easter holidays, it feels like she always has been, and that Mr Walters never really existed. Besides, we've got exams to focus on.

I have sessions with a counsellor in a nearby town. I can't get out of them, but after the strangeness of the first one I quite enjoy going. They're a mixture of talking about Dad, about how I remember him, and about letting go of blame, of pain, of guilt. It's weird to say it, but after each one I feel like I'm getting better, like things are starting to happen inside me again, like something is growing. I'm not sure what it will grow into, but it's exciting.

I'm crossing the car park with Mum on the way to one session, and I think I see Vince coming out of the main entrance. I don't really recognise him, his hair's a little longer, and before I can get close enough he's gone the other way around the building. I'd like to think it's him, and that he too is getting a little better, one day at a time.

Jamie keeps nagging at me, talking about how he's nearly done with the physio on his leg, and how we made a great team, so once my arm comes out of the cast I start playing football again in the spring. Ahmed does too, and gets a few games starting in goal. We talk a bit, but not much. Almost as if the weight of what we could say to each other is too heavy for the first words to make their way out. Like they're something stuck at the bottom of a well, maybe.

And then, in the late spring, Mum asks how I'd feel about moving away. Somewhere nearer Nanna and Grandad's house, she says. She thinks that, if they're closer, she won't need to lean on them as much. And it'd be a fresh start. New pastures. I get it, and I agree.

But it means moving away from Dana.

We've been together every day since it happened. Once the investigation finished, the garden returned to being just another ignored corner of land on the edge of the building site, which moves slowly closer to being a new housing estate. We go back as often as we can, and Dana shows me the new plants as they come up, or the old ones as they bud and come into leaf all over again. We try replanting the bush over the well, which was filled in properly when the police finished – no sign of my laptop though, Sargant Prangle had said. The replanting seems to work, and we watch the scarlet shoots slowly growing every day. And so we try, with what time we have between all the exam revision, to put things back to normal. But it doesn't feel like her place anymore, Dana says. And that's OK, she says. She doesn't feel like she needs it as much. Not anymore.

Dana's back at her mum's house. There's a social worker who she doesn't talk about much, and she's been going to school every day, and going to every lesson.

And she's doing pretty well, considering. Even Miss Amber has told her so. If she gets her English and Maths, which she will because she's brilliant, she's going to go to the sixth-form college in a different town. Which is one town closer to where I'll be. I've got the brochure for the college at home. Alongside A Levels in biology, they do courses in horticulture, and plant sciences. So who knows, maybe we'll keep on growing together after all.

As spring moves towards summer, just before the exams start, with butterflies starting to gather around the huge cones of purple flowers on the buddleia bush, we close the door on the garden for the last time. We spent one last, long, sunny evening lying on the grass, looking up, the shouts of men from the building site drifting across the top of the walls from behind the repaired wooden hoarding. Now the roofs are all finished, you can actually see their ridgeline if you sit with your back on the opposite wall. Soon, they'll probably pull down the wooden hoarding and replace it with a proper fence. People will be able to see in. I hope they like it.

There's a heavy quiet over us both as the lock, which Dana fitted, clicks shut for the last time. Taking the key from her keyring, Dana pulls one of her shoelaces out of her shoe and threads the key onto it. She ties the key to a low branch of the bush we stand beneath, and we watch it for a while, swinging under the premature twilight of the canopy. Someone will find it, perhaps, one day.

Or maybe they won't.

We weave between the nettles on the way back to the main road, stepping clear of the undergrowth as the streetlights shimmer into life, a faint shadow drawing itself beneath the brambles, thistles and shrubs at the roadside, and a few early and heavy-headed poppies loll and nod to each other. The headlights from passing cars start to turn on as we cross the road.

Looking back, you can barely see the gap we've come through. A single, green frond has fallen away from the rest, and hangs across the path. We watch its dip and rise, buffeted in the wake of the passing traffic.

ACKNOWLEDGEMENTS

This book began its long journey into being in 2015, as a series of conversations with students about race, immigration, Brexit and the movement of peoples. I'd like to thank you, first and foremost, for your honesty, candidness and for always pushing me to know more, to think more and to expect more of the world we are all living in, together. I hope this is the impression you left with, too.

Secondly, to my family, my brilliant wife and daughters, my mum and dad, without whom this book would never have gotten finished, for spurring me on, and for leaving me in the shed for hours on end when I needed to be left.

To my colleagues, Katherine for a vital and perceptive early read, and to Will, who never shied away from a difficult conversation when I was stepping deeper into this book, for occupying that space, even when it felt uncomfortable, and for your integrity throughout.

To Jane, my agent, for believing in Josh from the start, even when I didn't, for finding no reason to turn this manuscript away and for all your support since.

To Penny and all the team at Firefly Press for taking this raw material and turning it into an actual book that takes up space in the world, that I can hold in my hand and marvel at – you guys work magic.

To Dereen, and readers from Inclusive Minds and

HOPE not Hate, for your honest feedback and advice along the road that this story has taken, without which this book would be less than it is.

To those who work tirelessly and hopefully towards a better society, one in which the hatred in these pages is a thing of the past, who have educated and continue to educate me in so, so many ways, who shouldn't need to keep fighting and pushing for all of us to be better human beings but who do, because the alternative is unthinkable.

And, finally, to Josh, who has lived in my head for so many years now, and will no doubt reside there in perpetuity. May you continue, always, to grow.

To all of you, my deepest and most heartfelt thanks.

For a downloadable resource pack on Grow,
please go to www.fireflypress.co.uk

CLIMATE EMERGENCY

At Firefly we care very much about the environment and our responsibility to it. Many of our stories, such as this one, involve the natural world, our place in it and what we can all do to help it, and us, survive the challenges of the climate emergency. Go to our website www.fireflypress.co.uk to find more of our great stories that focus on the environment, like *The Territory, Aubrey and the Terrible Ladybirds* and *My Name is River*.

As a Wales-based publisher we are also very proud of the beautiful natural places, plants and animals in our country on the western side of Great Britain.

We are always looking at reducing our impact on the environment, including our carbon footprint and the materials we use, and are taking part in UK-wide publishing initiatives to improve this wherever we can.